# THE REFORMER

# THE REFORMER

# S.M. STIRLING
# DAVID DRAKE

THE REFORMER

This is a work of fiction. All the characters and events portrayed in this book are fictional, and any resemblance to real people or incidents is purely coincidental.

A Baen Books Original

Baen Publishing Enterprises
P.O. Box 1403
Riverdale, NY 10471

ISBN: 0-671-57804-9

Cover art by Gary Ruddell
Interior maps by Preston Wilson

First printing, April 1999

Library of Congress Cataloging-in-Publication Data

Stirling, S. M.
    The reformer / S.M. Stirling, David Drake.
        p.    cm.
    ISBN 0-671-57804-9 (hardcover)
    I.  Drake, David.  II. Title.
PS3569.T543R4      1999                           99-17126
813'.54—dc21                                       CIP


Distributed by Simon & Schuster
1230 Avenue of the Americas
New York, NY 10020


Typeset by Windhaven Press, Auburn, NH
Printed in the United States of America

To Marjorie Stirling

# ONE

The High City of Solinga had been the core of the ancient town once; first a warlord's castle, then the seat of the city council. Three centuries ago, when Solinga was capital of the Emerald League, several million arnkets of the League's treasury had mysteriously found their way into a building program to turn it into a shrine to the city's gods—to the Gray-Eyed Lady of the Stars, first and foremost.

*Money well stolen and spent,* Adrian Gellert thought, as the procession mounted the broad flight of marble stairs that led to the plateau. Right hand tucked into the snowy folds of his robe, left hand holding the gold-capped scroll that marked him as a Scholar of the Grove, he kept to the slow hieratic pace suitable for a religious occasion. About him gulls swooped and shrieked; before him stood the cream-white marble pillars, the golden roofs, the great forty-foot statue of the Maiden holding Her bronze-tipped spear aloft to guide the mariners home. Behind him was the tarry workaday reality of Solinga smelling of fish and offal and sea salt, narrow crooked streets and whitewashed

1

walls peeling to show the mud brick, tile roofs and only
occasionally the walls and colonnades and courtyard
gardens of the rich. But here, amid the scent of incense
and the light silvery tones of hand bells, was the ideal
the reality served.

*We may have fallen from our forefathers' power, but
this at least we can say—that we alone gave godlike
things to the gods,* he thought with a melancholy pride
that edged out the anxiety and grief of his father's
funeral.

The procession halted as a priest confronted them,
a blue-edged fold of his blanketlike mantle over his
head like a hood. "Why do you come to this holy
place?"

"To render homage to the Goddess, in such seemly
wise as is allowed to mortal men," Adrian's uncle said,
speaking as the eldest adult male of the Gellert clan.
Besides, he was paying for the ceremony. "In memory
of Ektar Gellert, a free citizen of this city, that the
Maiden may judge him kindly; and in the name of his
sons, Esmond and Adrian Gellert, that She may watch
over them in the trials of life."

"Come, then, and do worship."

The procession resumed; Adrian, his brother Esmond,
uncles, cousins, grandfathers, hangers-on, with hired
musicians following behind playing double-pipes and
lyres. Pilgrims and priests and citizens making sacrifice
parted before them. Their sandals scuffed across the
pavement, slabs of white-veined green marble edged
with gold. They passed the Plinth of Victories, a huge
column set with the beaks of captured warships; past
the black-basalt fane of Wodep the War God, the pink
and gold marble of Etat the All-Father, and at last to
the great raised rectangle of the Maiden's fane. It was
a simple affair of giant white columns, each ending in
a riot of golden acanthus leaves. The roof was copper-
green tiles, and all around from pediment to architrave

ran mosaic panels done in gold glass, lapis, amber and semiprecious stones. Some showed the Goddess giving Her gifts to men—fire, the plow, the olive, ships, the art of writing. Others were scenes from the Five Year Festival, the city's knights on their velipads, the Year Maidens bringing the great embroidered shawl, the athletes naked in their iron pride.

"Follow, then," the priest said.

Hot charcoal fires burned in a pair of tall tripods of fretted bronze. Gravely, Esmond and Adrian strode up the steps. Each took a silver bowl from the acolytes, pouring a stream of translucent grains into the white-glowing bed. Fragrant smoke rose, bitter and spicy.

The others drew up a fold of their mantles to cover their heads as the priest raised his hands; the Goddess' moon was visible over the horns of the roof, the other two moons being below the horizon at this hour. Adrian's uncle led the sacrifice forward, a white-feathered greatbeast with four gilded horns and a myrtle wreath around each. It came to the altar willingly enough—*drugged,* he thought: no sense in courting a bad omen—and collapsed almost soundlessly as the broadaxe flashed home with a wet, heavy thud on its neck.

Slowly, the tall ebony and silver doors of the temple slid open, rolling soundlessly on bronze bearings. Adrian's mind reflexively murmured three citations and an epic poem on the building of the Maiden's Temple; all of them described the effect, and all of them inaccurately as far as he knew. The cult image came forth on brass rails set into the marble of the pronacs floor, gliding with oil-bath smoothness. It was hidden in a tall cedarwood and silver shrine, emblazoned with the full moon on all sides. At a touch the sides sank down to reveal a rock. Black, slagged and metallic-looking in spots with a trace of rust, a metorite and very ancient.

Adrian Gellert had long since been trained in the precepts of the Grove; that God was Number and Form, and all the lesser images merely avatars or imaginings of men unable to conceive of the One. God did not need to Do, only to Be—but he still felt a trace of numinous awe as he extended his hand. And of course a gentleman showed respect for the ancient cults.

"Scholar of the Grove—"

Adrian held up the scroll in his left hand.

"Scholar of the Blade—"

His brother Esmond raised his sheathed sword.

"Receive the blessing of the Goddess, your patron."

Adrian closed his eyes and let the hand rest on the sacred rock. It was cool, cooler than it should have been, and—

*Where am I? Where am I?*

He thought he screamed the words, but he had no lungs. No eyes, for surely even the darkest night at the bottom of the silver mines of Flowerhill was brighter than this. He was nothing but Fear, adrift in a world of midnight. Stroke. Heart attack.

*Compose yourself,* he thought sharply. *Remember that anything that can happen, can happen to* you. *All men are initiates of the mysteries of death.*

That was the comfort of philosophy, but a little hard to remember when one was only twenty-one.

Light. He blinked . . . and saw a room around him. Furnished in an alien style, strange padded furniture, a fire burning in an enclosed brick space in one wall, tables and chairs of subtly foreign make. And a man standing there, a dark man with bowl-cut black hair. Odd clothes, something like those worn in the Western Isles, or even among the Southern barbarians; trousers, those marks of the savage, a curious tailored coat of blue with tails dangling behind. A curved sword and a holster with something rather like a carpenter's tool were lying on one table.

*Either I have gone mad, or something very strange has happened,* Adrian thought. He was conscious of his own terror, but it was distant, muted. He looked down at himself, and he was there again—not in the snowy draped robe of ceremony, but in an everyday tunic, with inkhorn and pen case slung from his belt.

"Adrian Gellert," the oddly-dressed man said; he spoke good Emerald, with a hint of a soft accent. "What is it that you desire?"

It was the manner of the Academy to teach with questions. He closed his lips on his own enquiries, on the fleeting ephemeral desires of every day, on the anxieties of his father's untimely death. That question had asked for *truth*. Perhaps there was truth in the old stories of Divine intervention in the lives of men.

"I want to *know*," he blurted.

The dark man nodded.

"An excellent dinner. Many thanks, Samul," Esmond said, from his couch across the table.

Adrian nodded and murmured something. His brother-in-law Samul Mcson had been a catch for his sister Alzabeta. A catch of sorts; the Mcson family was important in the dye trade and had a fish-sauce works whose products were sold by name as far away as Vanbert, the Confederacy capital. He'd never liked the man, and the sneer on the heavy fleshy features showed the feeling was returned. Also there was honey-glaze sauce on the front of his robe, which was rose-colored silk from the Western Isles. *Probably brought back on one of Father's ships,* he thought, smiling and nodding at his surly relative by marriage.

The servants—Mcson retainers as well, since the Gellert retainers were dispersed—cleared away the fruits and pastries and cheeses; the dinner had been the traditional seven courses, from nuts to apples. Restrained, at least by Confederacy standards; the simple tastes of the antique Emeralds only survived in Cadet training and the Academy's dining halls. The broken meats and scraps would be distributed at the door to the city's poor, who gathered whenever the garlanded head of a greatbeast was hung over a door to mark a household that had made sacrifice.

Adrian dipped water into his wine and poured a small libation on the mats set out on the tile floor. He suppressed a stab of unphilosophic anger at his father for dying at such an inopportune time; the business had been going well enough, but the capital was all in goodwill, contacts and ongoing trade, and neither of the Gellert sons were inclined to take up the shipping business to the Western Isles. Their father wouldn't have heard of it, anyway; what had all his ignoble labor been for, if not to buy his sons the leisure to be scholars and athletes, gentlemen of Solinga, greatest of the Emerald cities? But he'd died too early. By themselves the physical assets were barely enough to cover the debts, dower their youngest sister and provide a modest but decent living for their mother. The younger Gellerts would have to cut short their education and find their own way in the world.

He looked around the room; two dozen guests reclining on the couches, some of them rented for the occasion. It was the men's summer dining room, open to the garden on one side, with old-fashioned murals of game and fish and fruit on the walls. Scents of rose and jasmine blew in from the darkness of the courtyard, and the sweet tinkle of water in a fountain. Most of the guests were older men, friends or business acquaintances of his father. Esmond lay on one elbow across from him, his mantle falling back, exposing the hard muscle of his chest and arm, tanned to the color of old beechwood. It made the corn-gold of his hair more vivid as it spilled down his back; a rare color for an Emerald, and the only thing besides blue eyes he and his brother had in common physically.

*I'm weedy, in fact,* Adrian thought. Short, at least, and only middling competent in the athletic part of the two-year course of Cadet training every well-born Solingian youth had to take when he turned eighteen. Once it had been preparation for military service, but that had ceased to be important long ago, in his great-grandfather's time, when the Confederacy's armies had conquered the Emerald lands.

The servants brought in another two jugs of wine, yard-high things with double looping handles and pointed bottoms. They splashed into the great bulbous mixer; light from the oil lamps flickered on the cheerful feasting scene painted across its ruddy pottery. Not much like tonight's memorial dinner; no flute-girls or dancers or acrobats here, since it wouldn't be seemly. His father hadn't hired such for most of his parties. *These things are for men with no conversation.* He smiled slightly, remembering the deep gravel voice and the face weathered by twenty years of sea weather and spray.

"Excuse me," he murmured. Three parts wine to one of water now, and the talk grew louder.

The garden was warm and still, starlight and two of the moons showing the brick pathways between beds of herbs and flowers. Not very large, only fifty paces on a side, but tall cypress trees stood around the perimeter wall, throwing pools of stygian blackness. The pool and fountain shone silver; he could see the mouths and tentacles of the ornamental swimmers breaking the surface, hoping for a few crumbs of bread as he passed. Down towards the end of the garden was a little pergola, an archway of withes covered in a flowering vine, with a stone seat beneath and a mask of the Goddess in Her aspect as patron of wisdom set in the wall behind.

*The most private place in the house.* Outside the womens' rooms, and from the noise coming from those, the female side of the party was getting more lively than the mens'. He'd often come to this bench to read, meditate and think.

"If you wish to speak—if you are more than the imaginings of my mind—then speak," he murmured.

**it is not necessary to vocalize your thoughts,** the cold, relentless voice in his head replied. It felt . . . heavy, as if it were packing more meaning into the forms than the words could properly carry. **merely articulate them internally.**

He did so, not an easy task . . . but then, he'd trained himself to read without speaking, or even moving his lips, an uncommon skill even among scholars.

*Who are you?*

**We,** the other voice replied, the voice of the strange dark man. ***I am Raj Whitehall, and my . . . companion is Center. I'm . . . I was a man, on another world. Center is a computer.***

Despite the utter strangeness, Adrian's dark brows drew together at the last word. *Computer.* It wasn't one he was familiar with, but in the Scrolls of the Lady's Prophet there was a remote cognate . . .

*A daemonic spirit?* he thought. *Interesting. I thought those superstition. And you are a ghost, you say?*

A mental sigh. **Not exactly. Let me start at the beginning. Human beings are not native to this world . . .**

An hour later he was sweating. "I . . . understand, I think," he muttered, and looked up at the starry sky.

*Other worlds, whole* worlds *attendant on the stars! The stars are suns!* It was more radical than even the speculations of the ancient Wisdom Lovers, the ones who'd spent their time trying to measure the sun or the shape of the earth, before modern philosophy turned to questions of language and virtue. The scale of time involved staggered him; the vision of men coming to this world of Hafardine in great ships of the aether, falling out among themselves, tumbling down into savagery after wars fought with weapons that had eerie parallels to the most ancient legends.

"Why?" he went on. "Why me?"

*Because, lad, you're a man who wants to find out the truth of things,* Raj's voice said. *This world has gotten itself on a wrong road, and we need a man to set it right. So that, in due time, Hafardine may take its place within the Federation of Man.*

Adrian gave a shaky laugh. "Me, a world-bestrider like Nethan the Great?" he said. "You should have picked my brother Esmond; he's the warrior in our family, the one who burns to bring back the days of the Emerald League."

**not a conqueror,** the slow, heavy voice of the . . . machine? continued: **a teacher. although elements of collective violence may well be necessary to disturb the established order on this world.**

"What's wrong with the established order?" he said, curiously. "Apart from those vulgarian bumpkins from the south ruling the Emerald lands, that is."

**observe:**

The world vanished, as it had in the High City by the temple of the Maiden. Again he saw Hafardine as it had been just after the fall of the Federation's machine civilization. Little villages of farmers scattered through the valleys and plains of the figure-eight-shaped main continent and along the coasts of the islands; bands of hunters in the vast forests of the mountains and the southlands. Some of the villages grew. He gasped as he recognized the great cities of the Emeralds in their earliest days, their rise to greatness, the long struggle with the Lords of the Isles and the founding of the Emerald League. His heart beat faster as he saw

Solinga in the days of her glory, as the deathless beauty
of the High City rose from the dreams and hands of
men. Then the long, terrible civil wars, city against city,
the League against the Alliance. Solinga's defeat that
solved nothing, and then the Confederation's armies
moving in from the south.

**observe. the world as it now exists.**

A view from above, first. The Confederacy's wall
across the narrow waist of the continent, separating the
barbarian southlands from the land of cities and law
to the north. The estates of the Confederacy's nobles
expanding across valley and plain; Vanbert growing from
a straggling shepherd's camp to a city far vaster than
any in the Emerald lands. He could sense years passing.

**the maximum-probability result of a continuation
of present trends.**

Images . . .

    . . . armies clashed, both sides in the armor and
equipment of the Confederacy. Behind them a city
burned . . .

    . . . a view down a street. It was the buzzing heat
of noon, and nothing moved; a fine broad paved street,
arrow-straight, obviously in the Confederacy's heartlands.
A body lay in one gutter, the exposed skin purple and
swollen. Flies buzzed around it. A handcart came slowly
down the pavement, drawn by men with cloth masks
around their faces and more of the swollen bodies piled
high behind them.

"Bring out your dead!" one of the men called. "Bring
out your dead!"

    . . . men in shabby tunics and women in drab gowns
gathering as a proclamation was read from a plinth in
some anonymous farm town. The plump official droned
on, and on, some sort of edict setting prices and wages:
*"And the price of leather harness for a carriage velipad
shall be no more than one hundred twenty-five New
Arnkets, of which one in four shall be paid to meet the*

*needs of the State, in cash or kind. Sandals shall be no more than . . ."*

. . . slaves worked on a hillside, dragging boxes of earth on ropes looped over their shoulders; he could see the cheap sleazy fabric of their tunics, hear them grunt as they tipped the earth into a deep gully that slashed across a sloping wheatfield. It began to rain, and muddy water torrented down the cut in the field, washing away the earth a hundred times faster than the slaves could hope to haul it back.

. . . Vanbert itself, capital of the Confederacy and the known world. But it was on fire, greasy black smoke rising to hide the outlines of temple and palace and tenement block. Down one street a noblewoman ran, the silks of her gown trailing behind her. Behind her rode a Southron, a barbarian in greasy furs, his long yellow braids swaying with the gallop of his velipad. He leaned sideways in the saddle, one arm out to scoop the fleeing woman up and a gap-toothed grin on his face. A priestess' necklace of amber and gold bounced on his bare, painted chest.

. . . Vanbert again, but it took a moment for his eyes to recognize it. Trees covered the ruins, *old* trees. A few small fields stood, among log longhouses. A woman scattered grain to chickens, and a lean bristly pig rooted along the outskirts of a fly-buzzing midden.

Adrian gasped as the vision released him. Raj's voice spoke in his mind: **Your world is trapped in a cycle of war, empire, decline and war,** he said. **It could repeat itself indefinitely, the only difference that each cycle falls further and climbs less as the land itself becomes less fertile.**

**this is what you must prevent,** Center's passionless tones went on. **we have waited seven hundred years for a man such as you.**

"*Me?*" Adrian squeaked. "Why not my brother Esmond?"

**this world does not require a warrior,** Center said. **it needs . . . wisdom.**

"Philosophy?" Adrian asked, bewildered. "Rhetoric? Yes, they're the arts of civilization, but our thinkers and speakers are the finest that have ever lived. How can I—"

Raj cut him off. ***I'll explain; the concept wasn't very easy for me, either, back on Bellevue—back on the world where I was born,*** he said. ***It's called "technological progress."***

Adrian felt a familiar excitement; it was like the first time he grasped that this syllogism thing the lecturer was talking about *meant* something, or understood just *why* the angles of a right-angled triangle had to add up in a certain way—the feeling of real knowledge, like a conduit to the mind of God.

"Tell me," he whispered.

"Way!" the soldier's voice rang harsh and loud. "Make way!"

Adrian and Esmond reined their velipads to the side of the highway. It was a Confederation road, built a century ago to nail down the Confederacy's control of the coastal river valleys to the north. Twenty paces broad, ditched, and paved with hexagonal blocks of volcanic rock, built to last for the ages—Adrian had seen one undercut by a flash flood once, and it was five feet thick. A layer of fist-sized stones in lime mortar, a layer of sand, another of mortar with smaller rocks, then a layer of mortar and gravel, and then the paving blocks . . .

Hobnailed sandals crashed down in unison as the battalion came down the center of the roadway in a column of fours, legs moving like a single centipede. *There goes the thing that ended the glory of the Emerald cities,* Adrian thought. Out of the corner of his eye Adrian could see Esmond's hands tightening on the reins, then relaxing with an effort of will, one going forward to stroke the feathery bronze-colored scales of his mount's neck. Their ancestors had fought in dense-packed squares, each man locking shields with his neighbor and thrusting with the long spear. The Confederates . . . Adrian focused on one soldier, conscious of a very slight feeling of pressure behind his eyes, more mental than physical. Raj was taking an interest.

The trooper was a typical Confederate peasant of the central territories, a little stockier and thicker-built than the average Emerald, a little lighter in complexion, his face a beak-nosed harshness closed in with the long effort of the march and wet with sweat. He wore a short-sleeved tunic of mail that hung to his knees, with doubling patches on the shoulders; beneath it was another tunic of scarlet wool. On his left shoulder hung a big curved oval shield with an iron boss; on the march it was covered by a canvas sheath, with the bearer's name and unit neatly stenciled on it. Clipped to the interior of the shield were three short thick javelins with barbed points, each weighted behind the point by a small lead ball. On his feet were thick-soled sandals studded on the bottoms by iron nails, and strapped up the calves over wool leggings. On his head was a round helmet with a shelflike projection over the eyes, hinged cheekguards and a lobster-tail flare at the rear protecting his neck.

A pack and rolled blanket were on his back, but beneath them rested the weapon that had cut the proud spearmen of the Emerald cities to so much bleeding meat. Ready to draw over the right shoulder jutted a three-foot length of hardwood, topped with a lead ball. In the sheath hidden by the pack was the business end, a broad two-foot blade that tapered to a razor point; in battle the man would throw his darts in volley with his companions, then pull the assegai free and close, shield up, blade poised for the underarm gutting stroke.

The column gave off a peculiar smell, of sweat and leather and the olive oil rubbed on armor and weapons, a rank masculine odor.

The battalion's commander rode at the column's head beside the standard-bearer, on a high-stepping velipad. *He* wore a version of classic Emerald war gear, bronze breastplate cinched with a scarlet sash, long single-edged sword, bronze helmet with a flaunting scarlet plume running fore-and-aft like a cock's comb, kilt of leather strips. He rode easily, one hand on his hip, hawk-nosed face disdainful; beside him the standard swayed, an upright hand with gold wreaths below it to mark the unit's victories. The standard-bearer himself wore an antique hauberk of brass scales, and his face was hidden by the tanned head of a direbeast, eternally snarling defiance and hunger at the world.

"Useless bastard," Esmond muttered. "It's the noncoms make the Confederacy army what it is." He grinned suddenly; neither of the brothers had seen three years past twenty. "*Useful* bastards, those are."

Adrian nodded in agreement, looking at the weathered faces beneath the transverse helmet crests, marching along in ranks with the others.

***Several centuries of collective experience there,*** Raj murmured at the back of his mind, scanning the veterans' faces. ***A lot of stored knowledge.***

"Reinforcements for the Ropen forts," Esmond said judiciously. "Islander raids out that way, I heard."

The last rank of soldiers tramped by, followed by a few plowbeast carts and pack-velipads; most of those were probably carrying the commander's dunnage. Merchants, travellers, pilgrims and peasants surged back into the roadway, the brothers with them; the travellers on foot mostly made way for the brothers, given their gentlemen's cloaks and the loaded pack-velipad behind them. They made way in their turn, for a courier, a noble lady in her palanquin borne by picked slaves who could trot longer than a velipad . . . although the armed outriders helped, there. They could smell the towns coming a fair distance before the road arrowed through them. Not from the sewage; Confederates were lavish builders of sewers and water systems.

"Another token," Esmond said, wrinkling his nose and glancing up.

The pole stood leaning slightly in a barren patch of sand by the side of the road, the unevenness giving it a weird demihuman quality. The man hanging on it was suspended twenty feet in the air; the short crosspiece ran through the elbows of his bound hands so that his body slewed forward, twisting at the spike that nailed his feet to the wood. A leather-winged flyer landed, hooking onto the naked body with the small claws on its wings and the longer ones on its legs. The long snaky neck bent and twisted as the toothed jaws poised consideringly. When they lanced home and began to worry loose a titbit the man awoke and began to scream weakly, unable to thrash hard enough to disturb the feasting scavenger. His cousins had taken much of the meat off the bones of the next half-dozen.

"Savages," Esmond muttered. "Why not an axe across the neck, if a man needs killing?"

Adrian nodded, breathing through his mouth. "Probably to keep the rest in order," he said.

Most of the bodies had lead plates nailed beneath, inscribed with their crimes. RUNAWAY SLAVE was the most common, next to INCENDIARY. There were slaves everywhere, of course, but in the heartlands of the Confederacy they outnumbered the free men, sometimes by a considerable margin, the fruits of centuries of conquest.

The velipads were sniffing with interest, opening both pairs of eyes and pulling the rubbery lips back off the stubby ivory daggers of their omnivore teeth.

"Let's keep going," Adrian said. He glanced up; the sun was about a handsbreadth from the mountains on the west, turning their snowpeaks to blood-red. "We can stop with father's guest-friend in Kirsford."

"Better than fighting bedbugs in an inn," Esmond agreed.

For a moment Adrian let himself envy his brother. *Now,* there's *the picture of a hero from the age of greatness,* he thought. Chiseled straight-nosed, square-jawed features, six feet tall, broad shoulders tapering to a flat stomach and narrow waist, long legs, every muscle moving beneath the tanned skin like living bronze. *And he's not even stupid.* Not a Scholar of the Grove, but he'd read the chronicles of Themston on the Pelos War, and Epmon's work on the Art of Battle. Sunny-natured, too; and the gods had stinted him nothing, making him brave as well.

Soon Esmond was whistling through his teeth, a jaunty marching song popular among the Cadets of Solinga; their father's guest-friend proved to set a good table, and they set off early the next morning. The land rolled away before them, sloping to the great central basin that held Vanbert, the largest of all the valleys in the center of the northern lobe. Tall forests of broadspike and oak mantled the mountains and foothills; then came the lush level lands. It was more orderly than an Emerald countryside, lanced through with the straight tree-lined expanses of the Confederacy's military highways and gravelled secondary roads, every town laid out on a grid. Canals looped more gracefully, carrying water from dams in the mountain valleys and spreading it into irrigation channels. The fields were almost painfully green, where great blocks of fruit trees were not flowering; Adrian looked with interest at cherries and apples, rare on the subtropical northern coast.

*No olives or citrus,* he thought. *Must be too cold in the winter.*

Here and there a peasant cottage stood, often abandoned and falling down; on hills some distance back from the highway he could make out the groves and gardens of a gentleman's mansion. Four-horned great-beasts grazed quietly in the meadows, or pulled plows turning the rich reddish earth; herds of baaing fleecers went clumped with shepherds and dogs guarding their brainless vulnerability. Once they passed a field of maize that must have been a hundred acres in a single stretch, with fifty or sixty leg-hobbled slaves weeding in long rows.

Esmond looked and made a *tsk* sound between his teeth. "I'll say this, when these Confederate magnates are *rich*, they're *rich*. How much did it take to get into the highest voting class in Solinga, back in the old days?"

"Four hundred bushels a year, or equivalent," Adrian said, reaching up and snatching a spray of blossom, putting it to his nose for a second before tucking it behind one ear.

"Four hundred lousy bushels," Esmond said, shaking his head. "By the way, you'd better not do that when we get to Vanbert."

"Why not?"

"Because only pansies wear flowers in their hair, among the Confeds," Esmond grinned. "Pansies and girls. So unless you want to attract the attention of some rich old Councillor—other than as a teacher of rhetoric, I mean—"

Adrian laughed and punched his brother on the arm; it was like striking a tree. "You're the pretty one in the family," he said.

They passed the field, and rode under the arches of an aqueduct that ran over the road as it dipped into a shallow valley. Esmond's mouth tightened again as they glanced back along the length of it, where it disappeared into the heat-haze.

"Arrogant bastards," he muttered.

"And you'd better learn to control your tongue, or

you may lose it, in Vanbert," Adrian said. "They don't
take kindly to Emeralds who don't keep their place."

Traffic grew steadily thicker; by the time they were
within a day's travel of Vanbert itself, they rarely managed more than a trot. *Everything comes to Vanbert,*
Adrian quoted to himself. Most of it prosaic: long wagon
trains of grain and jerked meat, herds on the hoof stopping traffic—one memorable half-day spent behind a
flock of waddling geese ten thousand strong—salt fish,
smoked sausage, vegetables, cheeses and butter and giant
tuns of wine. Once a fast two-wheeled carriage, with
*snow* packed inside its sawdust-insulated box chassis,
passed in a clatter and clangor and cracking of whips.
More whips over the shuffling coffles of slaves, walking
chained neck and neck with hard-eyed mounted guards,
most of those barbarians from the Southron territories.
Wagons and pack trains and wheelbarrows and porters,
salt and iron and copper, gold and reed-paper and spices,
and more races and tongues than he'd thought existed.
Once he even saw a man whose skin was *black*, striding along in an ankle-length robe of cotton, ignoring
pointing and whispering and daring small boys who
darted in to touch his skin to see if it was real.

"I keep expecting to see the city over the next rise,"
Esmond said, on the fifth week of their journey.

Adrian grinned. "We're *in* the city," he said. "Have
been for hours."

Esmond gaped, then looked around. The truck-
gardens of yesterday had given way to elegant suburban
estates; most of the road was lined with high walls of
brick and concrete, usually whitewashed, broken here
and there by an elaborate gate of wrought iron and
brass. Each gate had at least two direbeasts on chains
guarding it, their heads all mouth and the great overlapping pairs of canines often tipped with bronze or
steel. The human guardians in the gatehouses were
sometimes chained to the walls by their ankles as well;

it made the slogans set in tiles by the entrances—
WELCOME or HAIL HOSPITALITY—seem a little hollow.

*Of course, that means hospitality for their own kind,*
Adrian thought.

"What can you expect," he said, "from a people who
have a word in their language that means 'kill every
tenth person'? And who think their first ancestors were
nursed by a direbeast."

There was no edge to Vanbert of the type they were
familiar with, no wall marking the place where city gave
way to country. Not even the fringe of grave-memorials
that ringed an Emerald city, since Confederates burned
their dead and kept the ashes with the living in little
pots under their wax masks—something he'd always
considered rather gruesome, but then as Bestmun said,
"Custom was king in every land." The suburbs grew
thicker, the traffic denser, and above them rose the
famous eight hills; and *those* were only higher places
among the buildings that carpeted the land for more
than a day's journey in every direction. Virtually the only
breaks in the spread of buildings were the small groves
that surrounded temples—usually round with pointed
roofs here, or domes on some of the more recent—
or the courtyards of the very wealthy; even the drained
swamplands that had once helped feed an earlier
Vanbert were built over.

"Dull, though," Esmond said critically, as they led
their velipads aside to let a wagon loaded with column
drums pass. "Brick, little shops—nothing really magnificent."

"We just haven't seen that part yet," Adrian said.

The street they were on didn't look like much in truth.
It was five-story, brick-and-concrete apartments, remarkable only for their size; between the arches on their
ground floors were shops. Bakers' shops, or so he thought
until he saw the lead chits the ragged-looking patrons
exchanged for big round loaves. *Bread dole,* he thought

sourly. *Our taxes at work.* Others were taverns, or little restaurants with soup kettles sunk into the stone of the counters, or tailors' shops, or cubicles where shoemakers fitted their customers and then worked with awl and waxed thread and tapping hammer while they waited. Or others selling sharp-smelling cheese, or hanging birds and rabbits, or anonymous lumps of flesh. The crowds might just as well have been from an Emerald city, save that their tunics covered both shoulders and that women wore less and walked more boldly.

And the size of the crowds. "A million people in Vanbert, they say," Adrian muttered. A thought struck him. "How in the name of the Lame Craftsman are we going to find this Redvers fellow?"

Esmond's face paled as he looked around. That wasn't a problem in Solinga—even if you didn't know the city, you could just take your bearings from the High City temple roofs or the docks. Nowhere was more than a half-hour walk from anywhere else within the walls, after all. Vanbert didn't even have the right-angled network of streets of the newer Confed towns, it was too ancient, and its roadways had been laid out as greatbeast tracks.

**here is a map,** Center said helpfully. **take the following turnings.**

"How did you suddenly become an expert on the streets of Vanbert?" Esmond asked an hour later.

Adrian grinned. "The Gods of Wisdom whisper in my ear," he said, looking up at the high blank wall of the mansion; only slits on the upper stories and an iron-strapped borkwood door faced the street, with a surly-looking ex-games fighter lounging by it, tapping his brass-bound club against the pavement to discourage loiterers.

They dismounted and walked towards the gate. "Let's go find our fortunes," Esmond said.

*And change the world,* Raj whispered.

❖    ❖    ❖

"Yer'll hafta keep that higher, m'lady," the trainer said, the point of his spear touching lightly at the base of his pupil's throat.

Helga Demansk nodded curtly and raised the small round shield as they backed and circled. The sword in her hand was an old Emerald model, forged for her of Solinga steel, single-edged except for a handspan on the reverse back from the point, and about as long as her leg from mid-thigh to toes. The hilt was sawfish hide, good for a grip, even with the fingerless chamois leather gloves her father insisted she wear—if she was to have a personal trainer at all. A bell-shaped guard of pierced bronze protected her hand; that and the shield were her only burden save for a short tunic. The trainer wore a leather corselet and brass helmet with a faceguard; his spear was tipped with a mock head of hide, but Helga's sword was sharpened to a knife edge.

That didn't worry him. He'd been a games fighter for fifteen years, and lived to see retirement before he slowed down too much. The full-busted, auburn-haired good looks of the young woman across from him were more of a distraction than her sword, although she really wasn't bad. The looks could kill him just as dead as a blade, if he forgot himself—she *was* Justiciar Demansk's daughter, after all. You didn't survive the games that long without learning self-control, though, and he had a couple of very nice little servant girls attending to his needs. This post was a retired fighter's dream, and he wasn't about to risk it for a pair of titties, no matter how nice they looked heaving away there with the thin cotton sticking to them.

Both fighters moved, bare feet scuffing the packed sandy dirt of the training shed. The sun was hot outside, coming in shafts of white-gold light through the gaps between the timbers that upheld the roof. He feinted with a one-two, felt the shiver as the spear shaft was

turned aside, beat the point of the sword out of line
with his own weapon.

"That's right, missie!" he cried. "Keep 'em moving
*together*."

Really not bad at all. If she weren't a nobleman's
daughter, she might actually do for the games—matching
female pairs against each other was a staple sidelight of
the more elaborate games these days, despite how some
of the magistrates huffed and puffed about it. And she
kept at it, too, the better part of a year now, back in
Vanbert and on this country estate in the westlands.

"Faster—keep it smooth. Push at me, get inside the
spear's point!"

It was the screams that alerted him. Far too many
of them, long and high; and underneath, something else,
a harsh guttural shouting. He froze, and if Helga hadn't
pulled the blow the sword might have laid open his
right arm. "What is it?" she said, stepping back and
breathing hard.

"Pirates," he said shortly, tossing aside the practice
weapon. There were real spears racked by the door;
he took one in his shield hand, and a couple of javelins.

"How—"

"I know Islander." He'd known men who spoke it,
in the games—slaves, mostly, and freedmen who'd done
well. That was an Islander war cry, and they *were* within
a day's march of the coast—closer, if you counted rivers,
and an Islander galley could run far up into the
shallows. "Let's *go*, woman!"

She quieted; he opened the door a crack and peered
out. They were a couple of hundred yards or so from
the main building, a big open house with tall windows
sparkling with an extravagance of glass, colonnades that
looked out to the gardens rather than inward to a
courtyard like a townhouse. He could hear more
screams now, and men's laughter, and see figures
moving about . . . sparkles in the sun. Light from blade

edges, and from the metal studs of light Islander-style armor, much like what he was wearing himself. A man with a tall fountain of plumes on his helmet seemed to be directing things as they dragged out armloads of loot from the house. Others were shepherding the house slaves into a clump, and some raiders were bringing out animals and carts from the business part of the plantation, down past a clump of cypress trees.

"This way," he hissed, the smell of his own sweat harsh in his nostrils.

They dodged out, climbed the fence of a disused corral, crossed it and ran across a meadow, heading for the shelter of an orange grove. *Damn,* the trainer thought. *I'll be set for life—rescue the Justiciar's daughter—*

The thud of velipad paws brought his head around. Four men riding fast after them; the pirates must have looted mounts near their landing and dashed inland, hoping to catch rich unguarded targets like this by surprise. One of them was raising a bow, the short horn-backed type the Islanders used, but he couldn't hit anything from velipadback.

"Keep running!" he screamed, and tossed one of the javelins up, caught it, let fly. "You stupid bitch!" he yelled in frustration, as he saw her taking up stance beside him, waving the sword and shouting some family battle cry.

The javelin caught a velipad between neck and shoulder. It went down, and the man on it rolled and tumbled, losing his bow. He was up at once, drawing the short curved sword at his belt; a stringy active-looking youth with a brown face and a gold ring in his hooked nose, black hair in a queue at his back. The trainer took a chance and ignored him for the moment it took to throw his second javelin; that slammed into a mounted man's shoulder with an audible thud. He twisted desperately to face the youth on foot, only to see him falling backward with a foot of Helga's sword coming out of his neck.

*Not bad at all.*

"*Will* you run, you dumb twat!" he yelled, backing up himself. "Thank the *gods*," he added in a snarl, as she finally obeyed.

The Islanders had gotten themselves untangled from their mounts, which were going berserk at the scent of so much blood, torn between appetite and fear. One promptly set on the pirate who'd stolen it, leaving the trainer facing two men; the third unwrapped a sling from around his head and reached for a pouch on his belt. The trainer charged, ducked under the swing of a sword and threw himself to the left, cracking the shaft of his spear on the man's knee, and then stabbing him hard through the spot where the latches of his leather corselet fastened into the side of his gut. There was a stink of shit as the point came out, infinitely familiar, and the pirate shrieked in quick shocked agony.

*Move, move, move!* the trainer screamed to himself. The armor was squeezing his ribs; he wasn't in shape for this sort of thing any more. *Go, go.* He got himself turned around just in time to knock a sword cut aside with his shieldboss, springing back to give himself distance to use the spear.

*Crack.*

The slung stone hit him over the breastbone. The edges of his world went gray, and the shield and spear dropped as his arms lost strength. The swordsman hacked at him twice, into the collarbone and then up into the side of his thigh from below. He fell to the ground, feeling himself yawning in reflex. There was time enough to see Helga dragged back, one leg limp from the stunning impact of a slingstone.

A pirate turned him over on his back with a foot. *What a complete fuckup,* he thought, watching the spearpoint rise over his face. *Guess I didn't make it out of the games alive after all.*

An impact, then blackness.

"I've got to admit, the Confederates outdo us in this, at least," Adrian said, lying back in the cool water.

Public baths in an Emerald city were usually small and utilitarian. This was a palace, and not a small one either. The main pool lay under a high dome, the tiles that coated its interior silvered to reflect light from the round windows that ran completely around the base. The walls below them were rose-pink and snow-white marble, with a ten-foot band of bas-relief murals below *that*, and the floors had fifteen different types of colored stone. Water arched from the mouths of fabulous bronze beasts into the pool; in halls leading off on three sides were steam rooms, hot tubs for soaking, rooms for scraping down and massage, exercise and workout rooms, small libraries . . .

It *was* rather noisy; someone was making the air hideous with song as he stood under a stream of water and rubbed himself with a sponge. He could hear the slap of hands on flesh from a massage table, the click of dice from a friendly game in a corner, the grunting of would-be athletes as they swung lead weights, the tremendous splash as someone did a belly flopper in another corner of the pool, the cries of a vendor with a tray of sausages and pickled artichokes.

"When you've got the whole world to loot, you can afford the best," Esmond said. "Shameless degenerates," he added.

Adrian smiled. Public baths in the Emerald lands didn't mix the sexes . . . and the women here weren't all whores, either. It certainly added to the scenery, he mused, watching a statuesque redhead go by in nothing but the towel draped over her shoulder.

"Come on, we'll get weak as girls if we just lie about like this," Esmond said.

His brother attracted more than his share of looks as they walked over to the steam room—mostly from women. The hot chamber was empty, the time being a little early—the baths really filled up after three o'clock in the afternoon, when free men knocked off work and came to meet their friends and spend a pleasant few hours before dinner. They said you could meet anyone from a Priestess of the Hearthfire to the Lord of the Western Isles in the Vanbert baths, and hear what the Council was going to do before the Councillors knew themselves.

"Don't sneer too much at Confederate wealth," Adrian said. "Since you're going to get your hands on some of it yourself . . . Three hundred arnkets a year, plus your keep, a room and a servant! You can easily save two hundred of that. With three thousand, you could open your own *salle d'armes* back in Solinga, or buy an olive grove or shares in ships."

Esmond made a restless gesture and tossed a dipperful of water on the hot rocks in the corner of the room. A smell of hot cedarwood went up from the chips mixed with the glowing stones, and the heat struck like a padded club.

"Here," the older brother said, tossing Adrian a blunted, curved bronze knife from a rack. "Do my back."

Adrian began scraping the smooth, rippling muscle. "It only costs a copper *dimeh* to get a slave to do it," he teased.

"They never get it right . . . harder."

"What's really bothering you, brother?"

The broad shoulders shrugged. "I don't know why in the Gods' names Wilder wants a trainer. He's middle-aged, fat, and sluggish."

"Maybe he wants a weapons trainer *because* he's

middle-aged, fat and sluggish?" Adrian suggested. "He's certainly paying enough."

"To him, three hundred arnkets is like you or me buying a spiced bun in the street," Esmond said, and then shrugged. "I'm to get a bonus for working as a bodyguard, though—protecting him and his wife when they go out, and so forth. It's work with a sword at your belt, at least."

"Don't they usually hire old games fighters for that?" Adrian said, curious.

"I'm better than any of those broken-down masses of scar tissue," Esmond said scornfully.

"And a lot more decorative," Adrian grinned. "There— your turn now."

"*Decorative!*" Esmond said, in mock indignation. "Here—I'll show you how they scrape loudmouths down at the wrestling ground for the Five Year Games!"

He whirled and came at Adrian with his arms out, the wrestler's pose. Adrian fell into the same stance, and they circled on the hot planks. It ended as it always did, with the younger man facedown on the boards and slapping his free hand down on the floor in sign of surrender.

"Peace! Peace!"

"Peace is a suitable theme for a teacher of rhetoric," Esmond laughed, letting him up. "A rinsedown and a cold plunge, and then we'll have to get back—move our things out of the rooms and into the Redvers house. I managed to get you permission to use the library, by the way."

"Thank you, brother; I'll take advantage of that. But I won't be teaching cauliflower-eared ex-generals how to give speeches, nor their pimply sons."

Esmond paused. "You won't?"

"No, I'm going to go to work in the law courts."

"Clerking?" Esmond looked shocked. "That's slaves' work."

Adrian shook his head. "Pleading cases."

"But . . ." A puzzled frown. "That's illegal, only Confederate citizens can appear before the Vanbert courts."

Adrian tapped a finger along his nose and winked. "In theory. In fact, if you're formally reading the speech of some Citizen advocate, it's allowed."

"You won't get far in front of a Confederate jury," Esmond warned, shaking his head. "And think, brother. I don't doubt you're an expert on Solingian law, but this is Vanbert."

"Oh, I don't know, I've picked up a good deal," Adrian said. He shifted into the Confederacy's tongue: "And I'm fairly fluent, aren't I?"

The blue eyes went wide. "No accent at all!" he exclaimed. "How did you do *that* in four months?"

"Divine intervention," Adrian laughed, slapping him on the shoulder. "Let's go take that plunge."

# TWO

The Redvers family had an extensive library in their townhouse; Adrian bowed a greeting to the Emerald slave who ran it. The man was wrinkled, bald, stooped, and dressed in a long robe uncomfortably like that of a Scholar of the Grove. His grandfather might well have *been* a Scholar, enslaved in one of the endless wars.

"Greetings, learned Salman," Adrian said.

His reply was a sniff and a quick shooing motion of the hand. Adrian walked past the simple slab desk where Salman worked, repairing and recopying and keeping every one of the six thousand or so scrolls in its proper niche. The library beyond was nearly as large as the Academy's, and far more sumptously fitted. The ten-foot-high racks were Southland curly maple, clasped and edged with gilded bronze, each bolt end wrought in the shape of a woodspirit's face. The scrolls lay in the familiar manner, each one in the hollow of a honeycomb in the rack, the same way that wine bottles were kept. These were mostly fine goatskin vellum, though, not the cheap reed paper. The twin winding rods were gordolna ivory, and the little listing tags that

29

hung down on cords from each were ivory and gold, bearing the title of the scroll in elegant cursive silver inlay. The walls on either side were clear glass, large panes fully a foot on each edge in metal frames, and there were comfortable padded couches and marble-topped tables at intervals for the use of readers. There was a pleasant smell of well-cured vellum, ink, and furniture wax.

*So much, so good,* Adrian thought critically; suitable for a man of immense wealth and some pretension to culture. The statuary along the walls, one in each window bay, was far too much—just to begin with, most of it was loot from the Emerald cities, and from *temples* at that.

*Only a Confederate Councillor would* boast *of having loot from temples in his study.* The piece of Gellerix, the Goddess of Passion, was a case in point. Fine enough in one of Her temples, but a life-size marble depiction of the act of generation was scarcely conducive to philosophic calm in a place of learning.

Adrian shrugged, sighed, and walked around the statue to the row of legal case-scrolls he knew resided there. Then he stopped, turned on his heel and came again, coughing and clearing his throat.

Lady Tinia Redvers was composed and cool when he appeared for the second time, her long clinging silk gown—itself a violation of every sumptuary law the Confederacy Council had ever passed—draped as decorously as anything that sheer could be. She was a woman of about thirty-five, with a figure that would be plainly fat in another decade but was now on the ample side of superb, and a mass of black ringlets piled high on her head; she had the good taste to avoid more than a gold armring in the shape of a snake and ruby eardrops. The full-lipped features were amused as he bowed.

"Ah, the little Emerald . . . my bodyguard's brother, aren't you?"

"I have that honor, most excellent lady," Adrian said, straightening.

Esmond was standing by the couch now, at a creditable parade rest; he was dressed in a studded belt of black leather, a breechclout of the same, high-strapped sandals and a sword and dagger; the hilts were rich with gold and sapphires, but the edges were functional enough. His long blond hair was tousled, and there was a red mark at the base of his neck. Adrian lifted a brow a fractional inch, enough for a grin between the brothers. He lifted it a bit more at Esmond's look of well-hidden throttled fury.

"With you guarding us in the courts, and Esmondi's sword, my husband and I are *quite* safe," she said, and snapped her fingers.

Two maids in long plain gowns—plain Western Isle cotton that would have bought two good riding velipads—came from somewhere they'd been discreetly waiting. Lady Redvers swept away in a waft of lilac scent.

Adrian calmly walked along the row of scrolls and found *Smanton's Commentaries on Early Popular Assembly Edicts and Precedents Thereunto*, sat on the couch and began reading, scrolling left to right.

"Bit distracting, all that perfume," he said after a moment. "And are there foundation garments under that sheer silk? I find it hard to believe they stay up like that naturally."

He looked up sharply at his brother's growl. "Something's wrong," he said, a statement rather than a question.

"Of course something's wrong," Esmond growled, flushing and rubbing at his neck. "I didn't come here to be a he-whore, for one thing."

"No, you came to be a weapons trainer," Adrian said. "Maybe you can teach our esteemed patron to use his double chin to throttle his opponents."

"Wilder Redvers would fall down with an apoplexy if he ran three times around a training track, much less fought a bout in armor," Esmond said bitterly. "It's the *fashion* to have an Emerald weapons trainer, a victor of the Five Year Games. Next year it'll be philosophers, or dancing dogs. And his *wife*—"

Adrian grinned. "Come now, it's not as if she was eighty—and *bodyguard* is a perfectly respectable job here." Insofar as being anything but a wealthy Confederate citizen was respectable. "And Wilder Redvers would fall down dead if he had to do *that*, as well."

His smile died as Esmond looked around, making a careful sweep of the nearby parts of the library. "Brother, that isn't why I asked you to meet me here—*she* just happened in, damn it. You've got to listen to me. This is serious."

"*What* is serious?" Adrian said. "Beyond our patron's imminent bankruptcy, conviction for extortion and malfeasance in office, and cordial invitation from the Conciliary Court to open his veins in the bath? And *that's* the talk of the law courts, let me tell you."

"Because Redvers isn't going to sit and wait for the man with the dagger," Esmond said bluntly. "Listen." His voice dropped to a whisper. "This morning . . ."

"Admit the Emerald," a voice said from beyond the doorway.

The guards weren't Redvers family slaves, Esmond saw. They were Confed Army veterans, grizzled stocky men with legs and arms like knotted trees. Not the smooth athlete's muscle Esmond wore, but perfectly servicable . . . and the assegais that glittered in their hands had seen plenty of use.

"Sort of a tall, tow-haired one, looks like a pansy with a sword, sir?" one of the veterans said, grinning and leaning on his shield. "Give us a kiss, pretty boy."

"Admit him, I said, you oaf!"

"Shall we take his sword, sir?"

"Admit him!"

The veterans straightened to a braced attention. "Sir, yessir!" the other barked. They slapped the blades of their assegais across the bosses of their shields. "Pass, Emerald!"

Esmond straightened his shoulders and walked through the fretted-bronze doors. He'd never been in to Redvers private apartments; they were less gaudy than he'd expected . . . although that was probably his wife's taste. High coffered ceilings, decent murals—by an Emerald artist, of course—and geometric-pattern floors. Pillars gave out onto balconies overlooking a courtyard of rosebushes and palms, with fountains in the shape of seagods. A dozen silk-cushioned couches of silver-inlaid bronze surrounded a table with cherries, figs, and ewers of wine; a dozen Confederate nobles lounged at their ease. The only thing missing was the bodyslaves who should have been hovering behind the couches, ready to fill cups or fan away a fly or run an errand.

The Emerald brought a fist to his chest and bowed. "Lord," he said, suddenly conscious of his native accent. "You summoned me?"

His eyes flicked across the assembled nobility. A good ten or twelve million arnkets around the low table . . . but at least twice that in debts. Young Mark Silva, who'd managed to assemble the slowest stable of racing velipads in Vanbert, and bet the family estates on them. Johun Audsley, a famous general and famously bitter former associate of Ark Marcomann, an even more famous general who'd died in retirement and not left a thing to his right-hand man. Tows Annersun, who'd run for every elective office and managed to offend so many highly-placed people that he'd won none of them, despite a fortune in bribes and games and free wine . . . and his esteemed patron Wilder Redvers himself, ex-governor of Solinga Province for the Confederacy, extortionist and thug. A fleshy balding man just on the wrong side of fifty; muscled like a bull greatbeast when he was young, and now with a great sagging belly and wobbly undersides to his arms.

*But not entirely a fool,* Esmond reminded himself. He'd even been a competent general once, in the western wars a decade back.

He'd also spent every penny he'd wrung out of his province on trying to be elected Speaker of the Popular Assembly, one of the two magistrates who ruled the Confederacy, as much as anyone did. Virtually every well-established noble family in and around the city must have thrown their influence and clientage against him, for him to have lost after spending *that* kind of money.

And without the opportunities of a Speaker, he was doomed. If his creditors didn't get him, the lawsuits of the provincials would—they'd be able to attract more than enough patrons in the capital, anxious to bring Redvers down and feed on the estates that would go on the block.

"Do sit down, over there, Esmondi," Redvers said. "Pour me some wine, and yourself, my boy."

*Little Esmond, the little Emerald,* Esmond thought, grinding his teeth as he smiled and obeyed.

"We've brought you here to discuss a little matter of politics," the Confederate noble said.

Esmond managed not to choke on the wine. Politics were for Confederate citizens—*rich* Confederate citizens, if you went beyond the level of the dole-feeders selling their Popular Assembly votes. Vision took on the clarity of desperation, the same bright hopping focus he'd had before the Five Year Games. One or two . . . no, three of the guests weren't what they appeared. Purple-edged tunics and robes, yes, but those hard furtive eyes didn't have the lordly arrogance of the nobles beside them. *Gang bosses,* he thought. The type who could deliver a ward for a patron, or see that the other side's canvasers hurt bad or just disappeared. Some of them were as powerful as many Justiciars or generals . . .

The others murmured among themselves, nibbling on little pastries rich with nuts and creamed bananas, sipping at their wine. *And looking at* me, *Goddess be my shield.*

"My lord honors me beyond my worth," he said smoothly. *I may not be a rhetorician, but I've been listening to Adrian all my life.* "If my lord will open his mind to me, I will assuredly do my poor best to aid him."

Redvers nodded. "As you may know," he began, "I was recently cheated—foully cheated—of my legitimate election as Speaker of the Popular Assembly. By corruption! Unprecedented, extra-constitutional corruption! Interference from the Council!"

Esmond darted a quick look at Audsley. Audsley's mentor Marcomann had been the one who ended the last round of civil wars, and he'd restored the powers of the Council and restricted those of the Popular Assemblies . . . Audsley smiled and nodded.

"To cleanse the State, a fire is needed. Drastic measures! Only thus can justice, peace and good order be restored!"

Grave nods, glittering eyes.

"My lord, may the gods *themselves* aid your enterprise." Esmond shot to his feet, then went to one knee, drawing and offering his sword. "I see that a new age is about to dawn for the Confederacy!"

"Well, well, that's very handsome of you, Esmondi," Redvers said. "Each one of us has a part to play, you see. Councillor Audsley is collecting a sufficient force among Marcomann's veterans—many of them living in poverty, despite their many services to the State."

*Having blown their loot and land grants on whores, dice and wine,* Esmond thought. They'd come back from the Western provinces staggering under the gold . . . or rather the innumerable slaves they'd taken had staggered. Marcomann had used them to climb to the highest office. Usually the Confederacy had two Speakers, one for the Popular Assembly and one for the Council; Marcomann had been Sole Speaker from the day his troops marched in and the proscriptions began to the utterly unexpected day of his retirement. He'd died in bed, too, which was a strong argument for the belief that the gods did intervene in human affairs.

"These other gentlemen will rise in arms on the appointed day. Some will seize the public buildings; others will start fires and riots to distract the City Companies. And you, my dear Esmondi . . ." Redvers smiled. "It struck me just now . . . there are so *many* foreigners in Vanbert these days. Emeralds especially; why, there are twenty or thirty Emeralds in *my* household, aren't there? And you're what passes for a great and famous man among them, aren't you?"

"I have some small influence, yes, my lord," Esmond said. A Five Year victor *did* have a fair number who knew his name. That wasn't exactly what Redvers was looking for, but Esmond had no intention of lessening his value. He'd already heard far too much to live if they suspected for an instant he wasn't with them or wasn't useful.

"And you'll be rewarded for it," Redvers nodded. "Why, even Confederate citizenship . . . perhaps the narrow stripe and a modest estate in the provinces." He beamed, the furrows beside his fleshy beak nose deepening. "All you must do is call on the Emeralds and whatnot to rise and kill the leading corruptionists on the appointed day. Won't *that* cause confusion!"

"My lord, it's brilliant," Esmond said, his voice hushed

and sincere. "But please . . . pardon my ignorance . . . what will Councillor Ion Jeschonyk be doing? I've never seen the Speaker of the Council abroad in the streets without two dozen of his retainers, many of them army veterans or games fighters. And if *any* of the magistrates should escape and reach loyal garrisons . . . loyal to them, I mean . . ."

"Clever, these Emeralds," one of the men drawled.

"Well, my boy, all these things have been considered," Redvers said indulgently. "Indeed, mine is the hand— along with a few of my friends here—who will strike down the tyrant Jeschonyk. We'll call on him at home, you see, in the third hour of the morning, before his clients arrive to pay their respects. We'll stab him as he comes to greet us, and with him dead nobody will dare lift a hand against so many Fathers of the State. And Justiciar Demansk has twenty thousand men under arms not far from the capital, the levy for the coming Island campaign."

"Justiciar Demansk is of your party, my lord?" Esmond strove to put worshipful admiration in his tone. *Don't overdo it,* he warned himself. But then, dealing with these people it was nearly *impossible* to overdo it . . . on the other hand, the gang bosses were less likely to be taken in. If Demansk was with them, they actually had a chance to bring this off.

"Justiciar Demansk . . ." Redvers smiled, "is a man of ambition, shall we say, who has been . . . approached. So. What do you say, Esmondi my lad?"

Esmond stood and gave Redvers a salute, fist to chest. "Command me, lord, and success is ordained as if the gods themselves had spoken."

"Are you *serious*?" Adrian blurted, as his brother finished his tale, running his hands through his long curling hair.

"Deadly. Most probably simply *dead*," Esmond said.

Adrian stared at him, appalled. "Oh, Maiden of the Stars," he whispered. "They're all going to die."

"That doesn't bother me," Esmond said grimly. "You're right, incidentally. The only reason they haven't gone up the post—" in fact, most of them were of high enough social standing that they'd be offered the knife "—is that the Council and the Speakers are nearly as much a bunch of amateur buffoons as they are."

The tall form of his brother sank to a bench. "How in the name of the gods did we ever end up being subject to these people?"

"They had a better army," Adrian said absently, the eyes of his mind fixed inward. "And in those days they didn't fight among themselves as much as we did. You know the saying: two Emeralds—"

"—three factions and a civil war," Esmond said gloomily. "And the hell of it is, we're involved in this . . . this abortion. I wouldn't give them one chance in twenty. The Confederacy may be ruled from Vanbert, but it isn't a city-state or a monarchy. You can't just seize one man or a couple of buildings and rule, or parade a little bodyguard the way . . . what was his name, somebody the Tyrant, the one who came into town with a big girl dressed up as the Goddess, way back?"

"Petor Strattis," Adrian said. Strattis had been Boss of Solinga for twenty-three years back four centuries ago, and his reforms had laid the basis for the later democracy and the Emerald League. "Wait—let me think."

**esmond gellert's appraisal is remarkably accurate,** Center said, a slight tinge of surprise in the machine voice. **stochastic analysis indicates that the probability of a successful coup is in the range of 8% ±3.**

Raj's gray eyes opened inside Adrian's head. *Remarkable young man, your brother,* he said appraisingly.

*I'd have been very glad indeed to have him as a junior officer; he's got natural talent, and I think men would follow him. Hmm . . . that's something to consider. Center?*

**correct. we must reevaluate long-term plans . . . however, esmond gellert's fundamental belief-structure offers impediments to his usefulness as a tool.**

*My brother isn't a tool!* Adrian thought hotly. *He's a human being!*

**Human beings can be the tools of mankind,** Raj thought gently. **There's no higher honor. Better to serve mankind than some politician's greed or a myth that turns to ashes full of dead children.**

*Sorry,* Adrian thought. *What can we do?*

**Well, Redvers and his friends have one great merit,** Raj mused. **Two, actually. First, they're corrupt, amoral, shortsighted and utterly selfish. Responsible nobles wouldn't listen to you if you told them about earth-shaking innovations—they'd look beyond immediate advantage and realize that they could destabilize the system, and those of them who're loyal to anything besides themselves are loyal to the system here. Second, they're desperate. They'll grasp at straws, because it's a tubful of very bloody water for them if they lose.**

Adrian raised his head. "Did they give you any idea of the time of this . . . uprising?"

"Not immediately. They want to get Demansk on their side if they possibly can. Beyond that, at least a couple of months—I doubt if they know precisely themselves. Why? Do you think we can make it to the Western Isles before then?"

"No, I think I have an idea," Adrian said slowly. "But I need some time for it to work."

One of Lady Redvers' maids came back into the alcove where the brothers sat. "Oh, Esmond, I was so frightened—" she began, speaking a pure upper-class Emerald.

Then she saw Adrian, and froze. Esmond went defiantly to her side and took her hand. "Brother, this is Nanya. Formerly of a citizen family of Penburg."

Adrian bowed gravely; Penburg had been sacked after a revolt six years ago, while Wilder Redvers had been governor of Solinga Province. Every adult male sent to the pole, the rest sold into slavery. His eyebrow lifted: *Do you know the risks you're taking?* it signaled. If Lady Redvers found out . . . being flogged to death was the best Nanya could expect. Killing a free resident of Solinga like Esmond wouldn't be legal . . . but that wouldn't stop the lady, and she'd get away with it, too.

"And, when the gods allow, my wife," Esmond went on.

Nanya looked up at him with adoration, her large brown eyes going soft. Adrian closed his eyes. *Give me strength.*

**We will, son,** Raj's voice spoke silently.

Vanbert's law courts had grown with the city. The highest of them—the Assembly Courts of Appeal—were housed in a new marble complex not far from the Temple of the Dual God, on the Spring Hill. The building was in an exaggerated form of the classic Emerald style, adapted to the needs of Confederate legal institutions. Two square blocks on either side held long halls where advocates, clients and hangers-on could walk and speak and deal; they were plain as Emerald temples, surrounded by giant columns supporting a Confederate invention, a barrel-vaulted roof. That was coffered and gilded, and tall windows ran around the eaves just below it. Even on a cloudy winter's day like this the light diffused off the hammered gold leaf in a shadowless glow, lighting the pale marble of walls and column and floor.

Joining the two halls to make a square C-shape was a connecting bar, with a covered amphitheater in its center. Juries in Confederate cases were huge—in theory any citizen could sit, although the requirement for a purifying sacrifice excluded the poor—and they sat below the advocates and judges, like spectators at a games fight. Adrian had often thought that the comparison had merit on more levels than one; though more subtle, the clash of wit and quotation below was just as savage as sword and spear, or tusk and fang. The expressions on the jurors were similar too. Except that nobody was paid to attend the games, while jurors received a stipend, not counting bribes of money or patronage.

An important case could be almost as expensive as a municipal election.

Adrian gathered his plain white mantle around him and strode towards the low symbolic metal fence that surrounded the sun disk inlaid in mosaic on the floor of the court. The acoustics were wonderful; he could hear whispered conversations on the top benches, and even sleepy belches from the inevitable seedy hangers-on taking a nap.

A man with a ceremonial whip and axe stopped him at the entrance. "If you come to speak, proclaim your citizenship," he said in a bored voice; his equipment was meant to indicate the magistrates' power to punish and kill, but it had been a long time since they were used on the spot.

"I come not to speak, but to speak the words of another," Adrian said, pitching his voice in the way Center had trained him to do. The computer had also eliminated the last trace of the soft Emerald accent; now his voice had the slow, crisp vowels of a native Confederate—the upper-class city dialect, at that.

"Pass, then," the usher said.

Adrian advanced, his soft kidskin sandals noiseless,

and made a deep bow before the panel of judges. They were all older men today, he saw, seamed hard faces with tufts of chinbeard and disapproving eyes.

"This seems to be in order," the senior magistrate said, examining the scroll which deputized Adrian to speak for a citizen advocate. "I suppose we have to let the little Emerald speak. I don't know what Vanbert is coming to. A girl costs more than a sword, a pretty boy more than a tract of land, a jug of imported fish sauce more than a good plow team, and they let foreigners speak in the courts of law where Confederate gentlemen once showed their mettle. They'll be allowing them into the army next. Go on, Emerald, go on."

His voice rolled heavy with disapproval. Adrian bowed again.

"We are faced," he began, "with a case which runs on all fours with the notable—"

He spoke easily, his voice conversational at first. That itself was daring—the usual mode was Oratorical, one hand outstretched, the other gripping the front fold of your mantle, right foot advanced, voice booming. He was using a rather daringly avant-garde style, at least for the introduction.

Center's prompting flowed through his mind. Precedent, allegory, snippets of verse, or the doggerel that passed for poetry in this land. He could feel the coldness of the jury turning, men leaning forward in interest.

"A pretty tissue of words to hide the plain truth," the other side's advocate said at last. "Yet *Dessin and Chrosis* clearly establishes that provincial corporate bodies have no standing for a petition *for and through* in this esteemed court. Citizens! Such appeals are *your* prerogative!"

*An appeal to Confederate pride rarely fails,* Adrian noted. He'd expected that.

"Citizens!" he replied. "Citizens . . . what pride, what glory, what power resides in that simple word. Citizens of the Confederacy of Vanbert! Yours is the power to bind and loose; yours the hand that wields the assegai of justice. It is beyond dispute. The esteemed advocate for the Smellton Tax Farmer's Syndicate is entirely correct. A mere assembly of provincials—without standing in this court—*cannot* assume the right to present a petition 'for and through' in strict form."

"Eh?" The chief magistrate's mouth moved, as if he was chewing toothlessly. "Are you conceding the case, Emerald? Is that what your 'principal'—" the scorn was back, this time for the legal fiction "—has set you to read?"

"By no means, excellent magistrates, do I concede. For indeed—" he moved into Formal Mode "—even as my humble self is but a mouthpiece for my principal, who *is* a citizen of the noble Confederacy, so this petition is launched in the name of the following indisputable citizens, their names on the ten-yearly roll: I speak of Jusin Sambert, Augin Melton—"

He rolled on, his voice booming up to the eaves. Faces along the rows of jurors' benches began to nod; heads leant together with murmurs of agreement.

"Justice! That strict Goddess with axe and flail in hand, terrible in aspect, unbending in righteousness, watches us even now!"

Adrian launched himself into the conclusion of his speech. When he halted, head bowed, hands out-stretched, the jurors rose to their feet and applauded, the noise ringing back from the dome overhead. The mantled heads of the magistrates huddled together, mouths working beneath the sound.

"Petition accepted for examination," the senior said, looking down on Adrian from the high seat. "Jurors and panel of magistrates in accordance." Which virtually guaranteed that the petition would be reviewed favorably . . . which meant that the Smellton Tax Farmer's Syndicate would face a swingeing fine. "Dismissed."

Adrian left slowly, despite an overwhelming impulse to bolt for the hall and get a glass of lemonade, or watered wine; you needed a throat of brass and a bladder the size of a wine jug to work the courts. Instead he strolled, smiling and bowing and exchanging a few deferential words with some of the long-established advocates and their clients.

*You can see how surprised they are,* he thought ironically. *How does an Emerald do so well in a place where* real *men are supposed to shine?*

If ever the Confederacy was destroyed, he suspected it was going to be because somebody simply couldn't refuse the temptation to smash a lead-weighted fist into the face of that bland, complacent assumption of superiority. You could only swallow the sour bile at the back of your throat for so long.

"Ah, young Adrian," a voice said.

He felt the cold clutch of fear, the sort that makes the stomach clench and the scrotum try to draw itself up into the abdomen. *This is* exactly *what I had planned,* he told himself.

"My lord," he said, turning and bowing. Wilder Redvers in the life, his ample form looking impressive in the wrapped mantle of a Councillor, with the broad purple stripe along the edge.

"I heard the summation of your speech. Most impressive, most impressive—a Confederate advocate couldn't have done it any better. I can see that giving you the run of my library was a sound decision, yes, sound."

"My gratitude is eternal, my lord," Adrian said. He glanced around. "If I might beg a minute of your time?"

"Well . . . I suppose."

"Alone, my lord. It's a very sensitive matter."

The plump beak-nosed features changed. ***He***

**suspects you know something,** Raj cautioned. **He's
remembering that you're Esmond's brother.**

In the privacy of his mind Adrian nodded. *And I'd
be dead inside the hour if he confirms his suspicion,*
he thought. *Or even if he doesn't. Now to show myself
useful.*

"As you may know, my lord, I've been putting together
some notes for a history," he said. Redvers' face relaxed
slightly; that was a traditional hobby for lawyers. "And
I've come across some information in the most ancient
chronicles that may be of importance to the State. Naturally, I didn't presume to judge such matters myself, but
thought first of you—my patron, a citizen of standing
and influence, one competent to judge such matters."

"My boy, I'm glad you show such wisdom and matu-
rity," Redvers said softly. "To others may be given the
art of speaking, of shaping marble so that it seems to
live—but to the Confederacy alone is given the mandate
of the Gods to rule, to spare the humble and subdue the
proud," he said.

*That would be more impressive if I didn't know you
were quoting,* Adrian thought, the words dry under the
hammer of his pulse. They reached one of the inset
niches along the walls, this one holding a small chrysel-
ephantine statue of the God of War, flourishing an
archaic spear, heroically nude, with his foot on a dead
Southron barbarian.

"I have found a series of formulae known to a select
few among the ancients," Adrian began. "Knowledge
long since lost."

Redvers nodded; it was well-known to educated men
that before the Age of Iron had been an Age of Gold,
whose glories were forgotten.

"With devices based on these formulae, an army
would be invincible—it could sweep aside forces many
times its size. And the formulae are quite simple; within
three months—" *Six months, but let's not get too*

*realistic* "—given the resources and artificers needed, a force could be so equipped as to sweep the Western Isles, or the Southron barbarians . . . a great boon to the State, and of course undying fame and glory to the commander."

Redvers stood stock-still, his eyes hooded. "And you've come to your patron with this knowledge. Very proper, my boy; very proper."

**He's going to buy it,** Raj said, his mental voice almost as dispassionate as Center's.

**probability of agreement 92% ±5,** Center added.

"What on earth is the Emerald babbling about?" one of the nobles said pettishly. "Invincible weapons . . . what does he mean? A better catapult, something of that nature?"

The Redvers family was wealthy enough that their townhouse gardens had a secluded nook like this out of sight and most hearing from the main house. Adrian would much rather have conducted the trial somewhere outside the city . . . but Center had decided that Redvers was becoming quite dangerously impatient.

The stretch of lawn ahead of them held an oak tree and a circle of scarecrowlike dummies, each hung with the mail tunic and helmet of a Confed soldier. In front of them rested a simple jar, stoppered with a clay disk that was pierced for a wick of cotton that Adrian had soaked in the solution that Center showed him . . .

He shuddered at the vision, one from Raj's memories. A vision of what the explosion of a *shell* or *bomb* could do to men's bodies.

"The jar contains my mixture, my lords," Adrian said. "Surrounding it—"

"Get on with it, Emerald! We're not apothecaries, you know."

"Yes, my lord. If my lords will step behind this barricade . . ."

Adrian walked towards the jar, blinking at the bright sunlight, a lighted oil lamp in his hand. He held it by the loop at one end and touched the flame to the wick with the other. It started to sputter and fume with evil-smelling blue smoke, and he turned and walked—it was an effort not to run, but the nobles must be *impressed*—towards the thick pine logs of the barricade.

"See here," one said as he ducked gratefully behind the thick wood. "How are we supposed to see whatever-it-is if we're huddling behind here?"

He started to rise. Adrian clamped a hand on his shoulder and pulled him down again; sheer surprise helped him, since the Confederation nobleman couldn't *imagine* that an Emerald would lay hands on him.

"You—"

*BWAAAAMMP.*

The sound was louder than thunder, louder than anything Adrian had ever heard, loud enough to stab pain into his ears. He'd been expecting it. The other men there had not. Esmond's sword flashed out in a movement too fast to see except as a blur. One or two of the Confederate nobles threw themselves down with their hands over their ears; another turned and ran for the villa, tripping on a chair leg and lying sobbing and beating his hands against the ground. Most of them simply stood and stared at each other. Audsley, the ex-general, gathered himself, shook back his shoulders to settle his mantle, and walked around the edge of the barricade.

He stopped, staring at the forward part of the logs. Holes had been gouged into them; he ran his little finger into one, and pulled it back with a jerk.

"That's hot," he said. "What is it?"

"A ball of lead, like a sling-bullet, my lord," Adrian said. "Hurled by the daemonic force of the ancient formula's mixture. And that is a hundred feet from the bursting. If a man was closer . . ."

He smiled and spread his hands. Audsley and the others moved towards the place where the jar had rested. A knee-deep hole had been gouged in the soft black dirt, and bits of sod flung all over this corner of the garden. The front of the oak tree gleamed cream-white, the bark scarred and blasted away. Bits and pieces of the armor on the scarecrow stakes were scattered about; one helmet was embedded in the tree itself, three inches of the plume holder driven into the living wood. Audsley examined a mail shirt, putting a gingerly finger through a hole in the iron links.

"Well . . ." he said.

"Consider, my lord, catapults throwing dozens of such vessels into a tight formation of infantry," Adrian urged. "Still more into cavalry."

"Yes, I do see," Audsley said. A grin stole across his lined, weathered face. "Redvers, I thought you were wasting our time, but you weren't. Brilliant, man—brilliant!"

The nobles gathered around Wilder Redvers, slapping him on the back and laughing like men reprieved from death . . . which might well be what they were. Adrian turned, feeling the pressure of eyes on his back. Esmond was standing by the barricade, looking at the havoc the bomb had wrought and then at the sword still clenched in his hand.

"What exactly am I supposed to be doing out here?" Esmond asked, looking back over his shoulder. "You've got your infernal machines to tinker with, but I should be back in the city."

"Don't worry," Adrian said. "She's a lot safer with you *gone* than she is with you there."

Esmond nodded gloomily. "The question remains."

They were two days travel out of Vanbert's outskirts, and an hour's travel down a gravelled road that turned off the military highway west of the city. They'd been travelling on Redvers land that whole hour; past slave villages, wine presses, an alum mine, past fields where the yellow grain was mostly reaped and stooked, past pastures and orchards where green fruit swelled . . . and now they were turning into the paved laneway that led up to the villa of Wilder Redvers, one of many he owned. It was a handsome building, a simple rectangular block with a portico of pillars in front and the usual formal gardens behind; to the front was a stretch of close-cropped pasture dotted with trees, and the cypress-lined driveway.

"Two things," Adrian said. "First, most of the higher-level staff here are probably Emeralds. I need you to deal with them."

"Why? You're just as much an Emerald as me."

"But I'm not a victor of the Five Year Games, and I don't look like Nethan the Great returned," he said. "By the Goddess, brother, I think you're blushing."

That brought an unwilling crooked grin. "Besides that," Adrian went on, "somebody's going to have to command the unit that actually uses this stuff . . . and the guards that make sure nobody spears us while we're doing it."

Esmond glanced over at him. "Nonsense. Redvers will never let a bunch of foreigners get their hands on something like this."

"Redvers will," Adrian said. "When he sees what *they* make of it."

He nodded to the left of the manor house. The pasture there had probably been for the master's riding velipads; right now it was covered with leather tents in neat rows, each just the right size for a squad of eight men.

"Marcomann's veterans, joining Audsley," Esmond said. "Must be about three battalions there . . . say, fifteen hundred men."

"And there isn't one single one of them who's going

to admit that he has *anything* to learn about fighting from a foreigner," Adrian said. "Trust me."

*And my unseen advisors,* he added. *Never forget them.*

"This little thing is supposed to *kill* somebody?" the soldier guffawed.

The hilt of his assegai jerked as his thick shoulders moved; he was in full fig: mailcoat, dagger, stabbing-spear, shield across his back, helmet with transverse plume. There was a fair bit of gray in the stubble on his square chin and in the thick hair on his scarred forearms, but he moved easily under all that weight of iron and wood and leather. This was one of Audsley's elite, a hundred-commander in Marcomann's wars; there wasn't enough equipment to kit out all the volunteers gathering on the Redvers estate.

"Yes, sir," Adrian nodded. "You light this"—he pointed at the fuse where it came out of the little wine jar—"throw it, and drop flat. Believe me, it's dangerous."

The hamlike hand tossed the bomb up and down. "If words were blades, you Emeralds would rule the world," he laughed. "I've defeated plenty of Emeralds in my time, from the North Range to the sea—talking less, and hitting harder." He shrugged. "Oh, well, the general says we've got to try this stuff, so by the cleft of Gellerix we will. Hand me that striker."

A little way off a baker's dozen of soldiers stood, leaning casually on their shields; Adrian saw one of them reach down into the calf-high grass and pull a stem to chew.

Adrian smiled and handed over the flint-and-steel, taking a few steps backward. The soldier grinned at that, and worked the scissorslike action. Sparks shot out, and on the third try the fuse caught in a sputter of blue smoke.

"Funny smelling," the soldier said with mild interest, holding it up.

"Please throw it now, sir," Adrian said calmly, backing off another few steps. "Right out there in the pasture, towards the crabapple tree, if it please you."

"Maybe it doesn't," the veteran said. "Don't get your loincloth in a twist, Emerald."

The thick-muscled arm arched back and whipped forward and the jar soared out, trailing smoke. Adrian's movements had put him behind a low swelling in the ground; he went down on his belly with prudent speed. Dew soaked into the front of his tunic, chill on his skin. As he'd expected, the veteran remained upright. He did bring his shield around, peering curiously over the rim.

*Crack*. The sound of the grenade exploding was a malignant snap; he knew what it would look like, too— a red snapping spark and puff of grayish-black smoke. This time he was far too close for that, and his face was pressed firmly into the grass and clover. Something hit the ground with a heavy thump; he looked up to see the soldier on his back, hands clapped to his face and blood leaking out between them. Then he went limp, with a final drum of heels on the turf. Over by the spectators, another was shrieking endlessly, louder than a wounded velipad.

Adrian moved over to the dead man. He'd felt like smiling, until he saw what was left of his face.

"Idiot! I ought to have you poled right now. Do you have any idea of how valuable four trained soldiers are?"

Adrian and Esmond bowed low, their heads level with General Audsley's foot where it rested in the steel loop of the stirrup. The big hairy saucer feet of his velipad moved on the grass before them, each with its seven blunt claws. The cinnamon-and-musk scent of the animal was strong in their nostrils, and the naked tail with its tuft of fur swung angrily as the beast sensed its rider's mood.

"Most excellent lord," Adrian said softly. "I fully realize it, and my apologies are most abject. Using these devices is more a matter of the mechanic arts than real soldiering. Could I—once more—humbly beg that men more suitable for such lowly occupations be assigned to them? Freedmen, even slaves, would be more suitable."

"Arm *slaves*?" Audsley said, quick anger in his voice. It had been only two generations since the Great Revolt; Audsley's father had been a young officer when Justiciar Carlos poled six thousand of the rebel survivors of the last battle along the road from Vanbert to Capeson.

"*Freed* slaves," Adrian said. "And perhaps . . . there are foreigners among the slingers recruited by the great Confed Army as light troops, are there not? Some of those would be most suitable. If I might consult with my lord Redvers . . ."

Audsley scowled; Redvers was providing far too much of the money to be offended lightly. "See to it, then. And keep them out of the way of real soldiers!"

He wrenched the velipad's mouth around, bringing a blubber of protest and a waving of the big round ears. Esmond stood silently until he was out of earshot.

"For every insult, for every slight, I'll see a Confed liver," he said at last.

Adrian nodded. "We've actually got some prospect of that, now," he said. "As long as we can get what I need."

"I don't know whether it was the Gods or the daemons who told you where to find the formula for this stuff," Esmond said roughly. "But *by* the Gods, you'll get what you need."

"It's quite simple," Esmond said to his audience of four. "This is our chance."

"Our chance for *what*?" the assistant steward of the estate said.

He was an Emerald freedman; his nominal superior was a one-legged Confed veteran who hadn't been sober past breakfast for ten years. They were meeting in his office, a pleasant room with plastered walls carrying scrolls and dozens of the wax-covered tablets of folding wood used for taking temporary notes; a latticework window opened onto the kitchen gardens. His fingers played with an abacus on the desk as he leaned forward and spoke, twitching nervously. A slave girl came in with a tray of cups and jugs of wine and water. The steward motioned her away impatiently and poured himself.

Esmond rose and stood facing them. He was wearing Emerald light-infantry armor, a tunic of three-ply greatbeast hide boiled in wax and vinegar and fastened with bronze studs, armguards of the same and high-strapped sandals.

"There's going to be another civil war among the Confeds," he said.

The steward blanched. So did the head stockman, the superintendant of field workers, and the woman who directed the household staff proper.

"We can't stop it; we can't stay out of it," Esmond went on. "You all know what my brother has brought here."

"Death," the stockman muttered.

"We're *all* initiates of the mysteries of death," Esmond said. "But in this case, an awful lot of Confeds are going to die."

"So? There have been civil wars before—Penburg rose during one of them. The wars end, and then the Confeds stamp on anyone who rebelled like a boot on ants."

Esmond nodded. "That might have happened without my brother," he said easily. "Why do you think we're helping with this idiot coup?"

"Because your patron told you to," the steward said.

"Velipad shit. We could have lifted a few thousand arnkets and headed for the Isles—our father traded there, and we have contacts in Chalice. This madness of Redvers would have been over in a few months, and all his properties would have been forfeit to the State."

He watched them shudder at that. Sale at auction, families split up . . . and freedmen were always suspect when a man was put on trial for treason. Their testimony was taken from the rack, or with burning splinters put under their nails.

"With my brother to even things out, the war will go on for a long time," Esmond continued. "Many things could happen. For example, one side or the other could get so desperate that they offer concessions to the Emerald cities . . . they might even withdraw, leaving at least nominal independence like the Roper League has. Or they might weaken each other so much that the provinces can revolt and *win*. Or at least if Redvers and Audsley win, we personally stand to be rewarded."

The steward looked at his subordinates. "Well, it's worth a hearing, at least . . ." he muttered. "Tell us more. What exactly does your brother need? We've all heard the explosions and heard the rumors."

Adrian held the handkerchief to his nose. It was soaked in vinegar, but even so the stink from the bottom of the manure pile was overwhelming; there was a row of piles in back of the barns for the master's racing velipeds. He didn't envy the field slaves who were set to the task, even if they were shambling dull-eyed brutes.

**A few years in that underground prison they keep them in would do that to most men,** Raj pointed out.

*Sorry,* Adrian thought.

"Don't you ever put the manure out on the fields?" he asked the chief stockman.

The stockman was from the Isles, a short brown-skinned man, wrinkled but still agile. There was a strong gutteral accent to his Confed. "Not very much of it," he said. "Place is too big to make it worthwhile, too much trouble to haul it out to the distant fields. Sometimes if it gets in the way we dump it in the river."

"Stop!" Adrian said.

He walked over to the base of the pile. "Here," he said, pointing.

Gray crystals like granulated sugar carpeted the ground. "That's what we want, those crystals—the saltpeter. Scrape it up and put it in the barrels."

"Here, now, sir, you're a gentleman—you can't do that!"

The carpenter's voice was shocked and reproving.

Adrian smiled. "I'm afraid I have to," he said sympathetically.

The tub was an old wine vat, big enough to hold several hundred gallons. They'd set it up at a shed half a mile from the house, in case of accidents. Slaves were rigging a simple machine over it: a pivot on the beam above, with a hanging pole inside the barrel turning paddles. The power was furnished by ten more slaves, each pushing on a long sweep set into the pole at its top, near where it turned on the iron bolt set into the roof beam.

Adrian pulled his head back and dusted his hands; there were blisters on them, and a few splinters. He was surprised by how little that bothered him, as he pulled one free with his teeth. Not the pain; any Scholar of the Grove was expected to master the body's needs. It was the *disgrace*, the manual labor.

"My father captained his own ship, when he got started," he said by way of explanation.

*Although he did it so that his sons* wouldn't *have to do it*, he thought. Only leisure could give a man the freedom to cultivate his mind, or shape his body as an athlete . . . and there was no slavemaster like an empty belly. That was why all the best philosophers were agreed that manual labor and its necessities were essentially degrading. Bestmun had held that labor should be delegated to those whose natures fitted them for slavery . . . of course, in his day Emeralds had rarely been enslaved.

"Now here's how you do it," he went on. "You take *three* of those barrels—" he pointed to the ones that held the saltpeter, boiled and dried and reground "—and two of those—" the finely powdered sulfur; there was a hot spring on this estate "—and *one* of those with the charcoal dust, and you put them in. Three and two and one, three and two and one, until the big tun is two-thirds full. And all the time you're doing that, the paddles have to be kept going."

He turned and put his face close to the carpenter's. "And I'll be coming back now and then to *check* that you're doing it right, and the master will be *very, very angry* if I tell him that you're not. Understand?"

The carpenter nodded; he was as jumpy as a cat around a diretooth. Most of the estate slaves were, these days, with all the soldiers on hand. None of the troopers cared much about preserving Wilder Redvers' propery.

"And they *still* don't do things properly unless you stand over them," Adrian said in frustration.

*Why should they?* Raj replied.

A vision flashed into Adrian's head; a steam engine, that's what it's called . . . on Raj's native Bellevue. A mass of metal tubes and wheels and parts, wrecked and fused. A man with a whip was beating another man, nearly naked and with an iron collar around his neck.

*A slave has a positive incentive to damage things,*

*unless he's a coward or unusually well-managed.*
*And simple carelessness is bad enough.*

The velipad was an estate animal, and knew the
laneways better than his rider. Any landholding of this
size had its artisans; Redvers had his in a series of
workshops not far from the cottages that housed the
home-farm segment of the plantation's workforce.
Adrian pulled up and tapped his toes on the elbows
of his velipad; the animal crouched to the ground, and
the young man stepped off. The smell of hot metal
came from within the bronzesmith's forge. Experiment
had shown that bombs launched from a catapult tended
to disintegrate if they were housed in clay pots of
practicable thickness. Redvers had grumbled at the
expense of sheet bronze, until they showed him a few
survivors of the effects of a finely-divided mist of
gunpowder meeting open flame.

The problem was, the bronzesmith had trouble
grasping the concept of turning out large numbers of
uniform containers without ornamentation or excess
effort.

*Why not?* Raj said again. *This man turns out fine*
*work because it gives him pleasure. He's not*
*particularly concerned with Redvers' political*
*ambitions, or with anyone else's convenience. Why*
*should he churn out things that don't give him*
*satisfaction? He won't be paid any more if he does.*

Adrian sighed again. Raj and Center were putting him
through a course of study a good deal less agreeable
than the Grove's lectures on the Good and the Beautiful
. . . but their concept of the Just Order was a good
deal more empirically grounded.

He checked half a step. "I'll give him a bonus!" he
said. "Under the table, of course." Redvers' funds would
stretch to that.

*You're learning, son. You're learning.*

✧   ✧   ✧

"*Ufff!*"

The other man grunted as his back struck the hard-packed dirt of the corral. Esmond stepped back panting; he had a graze under his right eye that was seeping blood, and his left thumb had been painfully wrenched. The six men who'd offered to take their new employer on were in considerably worse shape, though some of them had shown a thoroughgoing mastery of informal all-in style.

"Any more fools among those looking for a job?" he asked.

There were thirty men grouped around the entrance to the corral. All Emeralds; none too young—most of them had a few years on him—and all fairly hard-bitten. Many of them wore sailors' knitted caps with tassels, and the Goddess only knew how they'd ended up so far from the sea. Sailing on merchantmen going foreign was the main way an Emerald could learn the use of arms these days, that and signing on with one or another of the Lords of the Isles as a mercenary . . . or as a pirate, not that there was much difference in that part of the world. A few did a hitch with the auxiliary light-armed slingers of the Confed forces.

"Good," he said, when no more volunteers stepped forward. He reached out his right hand, and his servant tossed a spear into it; the old Emerald pattern, six feet long with a narrow sharp-bladed stabbing head. "Now let's see who can use a sticker. Then we'll go on to javelin, sling, sword and knife."

The testing process lasted all afternoon, while the hot summer sun baked strong-smelling sap out of the eucalyptus trees that shaded the pasture beyond the corral. When he was finished Esmond's eyes looked twice as brilliant, staring blue out of the mask of reddish dust streaked with runnels of sweat. He gasped as he shoved his head into the bucket of water resting on the coping of the well, then poured the rest down his neck and tossed the bucket in for another load.

"Rejoice," he said dryly as his brother came up, a look of intense concentration on his face and a staff-sling in his hands. "Managed to bonk yourself on the back of the head again?"

"No, I think I'm getting the hang of it," he said seriously, his thin, intelligent face warming. "It's not that complicated once you grasp the basic theory."

Esmond snorted. "Weapons are something you have to learn with your skin and muscle and bone, not with your head," he said.

"Oh, I don't know," Adrian said mildly. "Knowing the basic principles always makes things easier to learn. Here, I'll show you."

The sling the younger Emerald held was a weapon popular because of its simplicity and compactness, but it needed as much skill to handle as a bow. There was a wooden handle four feet long, two silk cords of about a yard each—leather would have done, but not as well in damp weather—and a chamois pouch for the ammunition. Esmond blinked in slight alarm as his brother dropped an almond-shaped lead bullet into the pouch and let gravity draw the cords taut. Adrian's arms were well enough muscled, in a lean whipcord fashion; he'd be able to sling the bullet hard. Where it went was another question, and Esmond's fingers tightened on the single handgrip of the small round buckler he was carrying in his left hand.

"That tree," Adrian said. "Just below the forked branch." He whipped the sling in a single 360-degree circle before he released the free cord.

The gum tree in question was a hundred and fifty feet away. It quivered and there was a hard *thock*; the bullet itself travelled too swiftly to be seen, except as an arching blur. A scrap of bark detached itself, and

fell, exposing the lozenge-shaped hole in the pale wood
of the eucalyptus.

Esmond blinked again. *Dead center.*

"Not bad, little brother, not bad at all," he said. "I
wouldn't like one of those to hit my head." *Because it
would spatter my brains for yards.*

"Oh, it's not so hard. As I said, I understand the
principle . . . and when I throw, it's as if spirits were
showing me where the shot will fall. I'll be—we'll be—
throwing grenades," he went on. "They'll be more
effective than lead bullets."

"We just might make it," Esmond said, with a slow
smile.

"If Demansk comes in with his fourteen regiments,"
Adrian said seriously. "I'd say . . ."

He turned his head to one side, as if listening;
Esmond noticed because it was a habit he'd picked up
since they came to Vanbert.

"That the chances are about fifty-fifty if we—our
esteemed patron and his friends—enlist Demansk. Fifty-
fifty for a prolonged war rather than immediate disaster,
that is."

"Without him, fucking zip," Esmond said.

"Oh, not quite that bad. About one in twelve, really."

"Where's the master?" the steward bleated.

"Under house arrest, you fool. I have fifty men with
me. Food and wine for them, and send messengers to
the battalion commanders to meet me here immediately."

Johun Audsley's face was set like a death mask carved
in bronze. It turned with the mechanical precision of
a catapult on a turntable as Esmond bowed and saluted:

"My lord, what's the situation?"

"Who the daemons are . . . oh, the Emerald with the
toys. Well, boy, someone blabbed. Tows Annersun, at
a guess—he never could keep his mouth shut while he

was dipping his wick. Now the Speaker knows everything."

"Councillor Annersun told Speaker Jeschonyk?" Esmond said.

"No, you idiot, but he was sleeping with the man's daughter, and *she* told him. He moved fast, I'll give the old bastard that . . . stop wasting my time and get your Emeralds and their toys ready, for what they're worth."

"My lord!" Esmond saluted.

The Confed ignored him, sweeping past with his entourage; they all had the look of men who'd ridden far and fast, and several wore bandages that were seeping red.

Esmond stood frozen on the stairs for a full three minutes. *Amazing how many things you can think of at once,* he thought. On an impersonal level: disaster for the conspiracy. Jeschonyk alive, and most of the Council. They'd be mobilizing this minute, no matter what other parts of the plan had come off on short notice. Audsley had nearly twenty thousand men here and on neighboring estates, but less than a third of them were fully equipped, and their organization was poor. And . . .

*Nanya.* Left alone in the Redvers' townhouse, with the magistrate's guards, probably a force from the City Companies too. If the Speaker decided Redvers was too dangerous to live, they'd make a sweep of his household as well—

Esmond turned on his heel, clattering down the staircase and out through the service wing. His men were barracked in what had been spare housemaid's quarters; they looked up as he burst in, most of them sacked out on their straw pallets. Hands froze as they worked on gear, sharpened a sword blade, clattered dice ready to throw.

"Jusha!" he roared. "Full kit, get your mounts, I want first company ready to move in fifteen minutes with one led remount per man. Full satchels of grenades, and five packhorses with spares. Canteens, but no food or bedding—we're going straight into the fight from a fast route march. *Move!"*

He'd had the training of these men for four months now. The long room dissolved into chaos, a chaos from which order grew. He walked to his own room, a boarded-off cubby, and hauled down what he needed; a bucket of javelins slung over his shoulder, his helmet, war gloves with brass and lead covers over the knuckles. And a map of Vanbert; they might have to take an indirect route out.

"Ready, sir."

"Then let's ride," he said, striding out to the entrance and vaulting into the saddle with a hand on the pommel, ignoring the weight of weapons and leather hauberk. His hand rose and chopped forward. "Follow me!"

"No, no, no!"

Adrian Gellert turned and slammed the flat of his palm into the wall of the shed. The slaves looked up from pouring powder into small bronze kegs, then whipped their heads back to their work. The last four months had taught the survivors that handling powder was *not* something to do with half a mind. The sharp peppery-sulfur smell of the explosive filled the air inside the barn.

"No, no, tell me my brother's not as stupid as the hero of a street-epic!"

Adrian stopped, controlled his breathing and pressing his hands to his face. *Suicide,* he thought. *He can't possibly cut his way into Vanbert—riots, chaos, street fighting—and get out with Nanya.*

**probability of success 35%, ±7,** Center said.

Surprise flashed through Adrian's mind. Raj's mental voice cut in: ***If you're going to stage a raid into a major city, riot and insurrection make it a lot easier.***

A vision floated through Adrian's consciousness: East Residence, the capital of Raj's native land on Bellevue. Blue-uniformed troops fought from behind a barricade against rioters, volley-firing in silent puffs of off-white smoke. Men screamed and writhed and lay and bled before the improvised breastwork . . . and behind the soldiers a gang of thieves calmly loaded furniture and bolts of cloth and tableware from a mansion into a waiting cart.

"I've got to help him," Adrian said. "He's being an idiot, but he's my brother . . . how much does *that* improve the chances?"

There was a long silence in his head; he was conscious, somehow, of Raj and Center speaking at a level and speed beyond his comprehension.

*Tell him,* Raj said at last.

**probability of successful rescue attempt increases to 53%, ±5, with your participation and full support from raj whitehall and myself,** Center said. **however, this is an unnecessary risk to you, our operative, and does not advance the prime objective to any significant degree.**

That was a long speech, from Center. Raj's voice held a flash of amusement: *Center's learned to trust me when it comes to judging men. You're going to do it, son—I would, if I were you and I were alive—and we might as well give you all the help we can.*

Adrian nodded, startling the slave with the funnel again, and walked out into the bright morning light. "Fered," he said. "Gather the slingers. I need their help."

# THREE

There was an eerie familiarity to the streets of Vanbert, full of mobs and the bitter smell of smoke from things not meant to burn. *Like the visions*, he thought.

**scenarios,** Center corrected. **multisensory holographic neural-input simulations of probable outcomes calculated by stochastic analysis.**

*As you say*, Adrian thought. *Visions*. Raj chuckled softly at the corner of his mind.

That was the only humorous thing in Vanbert this day. Adrian's mounted grenadiers—a hundred men, freedmen new and old—looked military enough with their slings and shortswords to fend off ordinary mobs, even though they were obviously mostly Emeralds. Many of the mobs out today weren't in the least ordinary. He threw up a hand and the column halted with a ragged bunching in the mouth of an alleyway.

"Down with Jeschonyk!" the men in ragged tunics shouted as they ran past. "Down with Jeschonyk! Long live Speaker Redvers! *Long live Bull Redvers! Death to Jeschonyk!*"

The rioters weren't armed, technically speaking, although many of the belt knives they waved were considerably longer than was convenient for cutting your food. Some waved torches, others iron spits and pokers, or clubs made from pieces of furniture and the limbs of ornamental trees. A number were pausing now and then to pry up cobbles from the street; and there were *thousands* of these people. Here and there was a man with a sling draped around his neck; a fair number of the Confed Army's light-armed slingers were recruited from the urban poor. A spray of outrunners went before the rioters, pounding on the shuttered windows of shops. Every now and then a crash and a scream would echo back, a counterpoint to the snarling rumble of the mob. Adrian craned his neck. A hundred yards back was a wagon, full of skins of wine. Men in the livery of a noble's house slaves were handing them out to grasping hands, with a dozen guards in full armor to keep the distribution quasi-orderly.

He turned his head the other way as there was a check in the surging trot of the mob. A line of men from the City Companies stood there, two deep. Their right arms rocked backward at a barked command from a noncom, marked by the transverse red crest on his helmet.

"Throw!"

A curled tuba blatted to emphasize the order. Darts flew up, then down into the front ranks of the mob. The barbed points were designed to punch through shields and armor, and they were driven by lead weights behind the head and the throwers' strong arms. The front rank of the rioters shattered like a glass jar struck by a mallet, men falling dead or screaming and pulling at the whetted iron in their bodies. The slingers among them might have helped break that thin line of armed men, but they were too crowded to use their weapons.

**On the other hand, that mob doesn't have any**

*cohesion to lose,* Raj observed. **Only the ones in front, the ones who can see what's happening, can be frightened enough to run; and they don't have room to run.**

"Throw. Throw. Throw."

Scores of the men packed into the head of the mob were down. Others were throwing a rain of cobblestones, but those simply boomed on the big hemispherical shields. A snapped order, and the rear ranks of the City Companies raised theirs to make a roof. The javelins were gone; another rasp of command, and every man's right hand snapped up behind his left shoulder. A long slither, and the assegais came free, glinting bright and long.

The street was only twenty feet across. The City troops could advance almost shield to shield, stabbing. Confed armies had beat bigger odds, killing undisciplined barbarians until their arms grew too tired, and here the mob had no room to use its numbers against the flanks or rear.

"Jeffa," Adrian said, pitching his voice to carry over the roar of the mob. *Rhetorical training's some good after all,* he thought, licking dry lips. The snarl of the crowd touched something older and deeper than any training, something down at the base of his spine and in the scrotum. It felt warm and loose and weak, the touch of fear.

"Four throws and a lighter," he said, touching his mount's forelegs. The animal crouched with a blubbering snarl of uneasiness.

Adrian stepped forward, his men behind him. There was a short bubble of clear space in front of the alleyway, but that wouldn't last when the bulk of the crowd realized what was going on and tried to escape. There were enough of them that anything in their way would end up as another greasy smear on the filthy pavement of the alley.

"Ready . . ."

He unclipped his own staff-sling and put a grenade

in the pouch, the fuse hanging free. The other four slingers imitated him, spreading out so that their weapons wouldn't foul each other.

"Target is formation of troops," he said again, feeling a mild distant astonishment that his voice was firm and calm.

"Light."

The lighter went from man to man, touching his coil of quickmatch to the fuses. The fuses sputtered and bled blue smoke, but they were more reliable than the first they'd tried.

"*Cast.*"

He whipped the staff around his head with both hands and loosed at the quiet tone in his inner ear that was Center's judgement of the aimpoint. All *he* had to do was get the staff moving in the right plane. The cord flew free, and the grenades arched out. His headed towards the noncom commanding the blocking force, and exploded precisely at chest level. The others were within a second and a half of it, and only one shattered on the ground before it burst. That produced an effect he hadn't seen before, a sort of exploding fiery mist up to waist height.

The front rank of the mob was as panicked as the surviving soldiers; those were running—or limping or crawling—away from the blasts as fast as they could. The front rank of the mob *couldn't* run, although some tried to, turning and pushing at the solid mass of humanity behind them. Some of them were knocked over and trampled as the packed throng went forward, joining the City Companies soldiers as stains on the pavement. He saw a few of the more thoughtful picking up shields, helmets and assegais as they passed the bodies.

Adrian turned and looked at his slingers; they were grinning, laughing, slapping each other on the back. One was dancing the *kodax*, prancing and snapping his fingers.

"Shut up!" he said, his voice the crack of a whip. They did, falling silent and shuffling their feet, the mounted ones looking down at their saddlehorns. "Now we've seen what our weapons can do. Let's get moving."

"Sir, if you go, I'll follow you. I can't say how many of the men will, though."

Esmond looked at Jusha. His second-in-command was a grizzled middle-aged man, shorter than his commander but thicker through the shoulders, with a seaman's rolling gate and a scar that drew his upper lip off one yellowed dogtooth.

Esmond nodded silently, then looked back at the Redvers townhouse across the road. There were City Companies men outside the front entrance, blocking the street both ways, and the scouts said there were another hundred around the rear walls and wagon entrance. Magistrate's guards, too; not real soldiers— even the City Companies weren't *real* soldiers, though there were plenty of paid-off veterans in their ranks— but still armed men. *Say two hundred, two hundred and fifty in all,* he thought. *More than half of them inside, and the place was designed to be held against attack.* It was all blank exterior wall, three stories high here and ten feet even where it surrounded nothing but interior courtyard-garden. The narrow windows on the third floor here would serve the purpose of a fort's arrow slits quite well.

Esmond swallowed salt sweat. "Here's what we'll do," he said. "It'd be suicide just trying to storm the place— too many of them, they've got the position. So we'll tie them down with a diversionary attack; grenades first. Then I'll go in with a satchel of grenades, and toss them against the door."

That was set back into the wall facing the street, making a little alcove.

"One will be lit. You've seen what the stuff can do.

Then when the door's blown in, we throw more grenades through and go in on their heels—by the ashy banks of hell, man, it'll be like spearing stunned fish."

Jusha looked at him. "Hope you can get something from her that you can't buy for half an arnket any day," he sighed. "All right, sir; we ate your salt and took your weapons. Let's get ready."

"Didn't work, did it, brother?" Adrian said.

"No. What's *wrong* with the bloody things?" Esmond said, glaring across the street.

They were crouching behind the stone counter of a soup shop across from the Redvers mansion. Adrian could smell the bean stew still bubbling in the big vats, and the heat of the charcoal fire was almost painful on his knees and belly. Absently he tore a small loaf of bread in half and reached over the greasy marble to dip it in the soup.

"There's nothing wrong with the grenades," Adrian said. "You just weren't using them properly. The force of an explosion propagates along the line of least resistance."

Esmond was staring at him with tightly-held anger. "I recognize every one of those words," he said. "But they don't make any sense."

"The power of the grenades goes where it's easiest. Out into the open air, not into the solid door. You've got to put the explosion in a confined space for it to do much against doors or walls."

"Oh," Esmond said.

There were bodies lying in the street in front of the soot-stained walls of the great house; mostly magistrates' guards and men of the City Companies, but a few of Esmond's Emerald mercenaries, too. They'd been killed by darts hurled from the narrow third-story windows. Adrian's jaws worked mechanically as he examined the scene; Center drew diagrams over

it in green lines, with notes on distances and trajec-
tories.

"The street's a long javelin cast, even from a height,"
he said thoughtfully. "But it's possible for good slingmen.
That bronze grill over the main door, that gives into
the hallway, doesn't it?"

"Yes."

"All right, here's what we do."

Esmond looked at him again; not angry, but with a
sort of wondering curiosity. *Uh-oh,* Adrian thought. *By
the Maiden's Spear, I've started sounding like Raj.*

It *was* comforting to know he had an experienced
general living in his head, when it came to things like
this. Adrian had read a good deal of history during
his time in the Academy of the Grove, but it was
Esmond who'd been interested in things military.

"Jeffa," he went on. "The four best men. Target is
the third-story windows; on my command, not before.
The next two sections are to lob grenades right over
the roof—see if they can land them on the other side
of the ridge tree, and let them roll down into the
courtyard. Brother, you get your men ready—we won't
have much time."

He waited while the messages were passed down to
the clumps of men concealed behind shop windows and
planters; this side of the street was a mansion much
like the Redvers', but like many wealthy men the owner
had let out cubicles along the streetfront for stores. A
minute later a hissed word came back.

"They poured boiling water on my men," Esmond
said in a cold tone, his eyes fixed on the enemy.
"They're going to regret that." There was an angry red
weal down his left arm.

**Good man, your brother,** Raj said. **He's got a lot
to think about, but he isn't forgetting his command.**

"That they are, brother," Adrian said. "They're going

to regret it extremely." His voice rose higher. "On the three . . . one . . . two . . . *three*."

The slingers dashed out into the street. Javelins and darts arched down from the windows, but they skittered sparking across the paving stones. One or two stuck in the cracks between blocks, humming like malignant wasps. Adrian lit the fuse to his first grenade from a helper's torch, swung . . .

**now.**

Hours of practice had connected Center's machine voice to his own fingers. The cast was sideways, up at a slant. The clay jar spun through one of the gaps in the bronze grillwork over the main door of the Redvers mansion, and exploded just before it reached the wooden shutter inside.

*Crack.* Then *crack . . . crack . . . crack . . .* as three more arched into windows on the third story of the facade. The bleeding trunk of a man collapsed out of one slit opening, trailing tattered arms and a runnel of blood down the smoke-dimmed whitewash. The second gave only screams, but the third added a gout of flame.

"Must have had a pot of boiling oil over a fire," Adrian muttered. Louder: "Again!"

More grenades arched out, for the windows, and a dozen or more over the rooftree. His own snapped into the bulged framework of the bronze grill, and blasted a corner of it out in a shower of wood splinters and metal fragments that pinged and whined off the wall and the street. His next went through the gap, and a hollow roar told him it had exploded in the hallway within.

"Again . . . all right, let's go for it!"

Esmond and scores of his men joined him. They flattened against the wall, but no darts or boiling water or oil cascaded down from the windows above. Adrian lit another grenade and tossed it overhand through the shattered grill; it was one of the red-banded kind, the

ones with lead balls packed into the double shell outside
the powder. He could feel them slamming into the teak
of the door's interior.

Crossed spears tossed Esmond up. He gripped the
stonework edges that had held the grill, looked within.

"All clear," he said, and swung himself through
feetfirst with an athlete's impossible grace. They heard
him swear mildly on the other side, as he wrenched
at the warped bar, and then the doors were open.

Adrian looked through and swallowed. Men must have
been packed in here pretty densely, when the first grenade came through. More had been trying to drag away
the wounded, when that last one he'd thrown had landed
among them.

Esmond stood with blood splashed up to his knees,
like a statue of Wodep the War God poised with shield
and sword. His face held a stony unconcern.

"This way," he said, pointing.

The main staircase to the second floor ran up from
the other side of the vestibule courtyard. In ancient
times there would have been an open light well over
the pool, letting in water for domestic use. Here it was
a skylight, and the pool was ornamental . . . less so now,
since a grenade had evidently landed in it, and the
colorful swimmers were pasted across the columns and
mosaics. A wounded man had crawled as far as the
staircase, and was making a messy time of dying. Black
smoke poured down the landing.

"Oh, Maiden shield us, the place is on fire," Adrian
blurted.

"Well, what did you expect?" Esmond said harshly.
"Let's go."

"Wait." Adrian ripped a strip of cloth off the bottom of his tunic and dipped it in the water of the
ornamental pool before tying it around his nose.

"Good idea," Esmond said, following suit along with
the rest. "Half of you hand over your grenades and

follow us," he went on to the men. "The rest of you, keep a sharp lookout on the street for enemy reinforcements."

The water smelled rankly bad, but it was welcome as they forced their way up into the furnace heat of the second story. The fire had started along the streetfront, and the doors in that direction were belching gouts of fire. It was running fast into the northwest corner of the building, though, running along the tinder-dry cedar rafters and the laths of the plasterwork that made up most of the big house's interior partitions. *And the paint in the murals, that's linseed oil,* Adrian reminded himself. *And the tapestries . . . Maiden shield us!*

They crouched and went down the connecting corridor around the central courtyard, towards the suite of Redvers' wife, where her personal servants would be. Halfway down it was an improvised barricade of furniture, with the gasping, coughing forms of half a dozen City Company troopers behind it.

"We can—" he began. His brother ignored him.

"*Nanya!*" he shouted, like a battle cry, and leapt.

Adrian followed, sword in one sweating hand and buckler in the other. *This isn't my proper work—* he thought.

His brother struck. Adrian's eyes went wide; he felt Raj's surprise at the back of his mind as well. The sword moved, blurring with its speed, and a spray of red droplets followed it in an arching spatter across the pale stucco of the walls. A man screamed, looking at the stump of an arm taken off at the elbow. Another slammed backward as the edge of Adrian's sword ploughed into his forehead and then fell in a spastic quivering heap. As he wrenched the weapon free, Esmond kicked another in the crotch, then broke his bent-over neck with a downward blow of the shield rim. Adrian struck at a man backing away with his face slack in horror and the assegai loose in his hand. The City Companies trooper wailed

and fled, clutching a gashed forearm. He looked up to
see Esmond driving the remaining two Confeds before
him down the corridor. As he watched, one went over
backward at a slam from Esmond's brass-faced shield.
Esmond leapt high, came down on the man's ribcage with
both heels, managed to spring free in time to turn a final
assegai thrust with his shield. Then the sword sprang out
like a kermitoid's licking tongue. The Confed gaped down
at the blade through his torso, then slid backward as his
face went slack.

"Nanya!" Esmond screamed again, and dashed forward.

Adrian followed, stopping only long enough to snatch
up a canteen and rip a piece of cloth free. He wet it
and held it across his mouth and nose as Esmond ran
through gathering smoke and heat towards the family
quarters. The door there was locked. Esmond's sword
went straight into it; the steel snapped as he twisted,
but so did the mechanism of the lock.

Adrian was close behind. He saw what his brother
did, as the door swung back in a belch of flame that
singed their eyebrows. The women were huddled in the
center of the room, clutching each other, some of them
still conscious. They had time to see the men in the
doorway before a flaming beam and mass of plaster fell
across them.

"Nanya!" Esmond screamed a last time, foam on his
lips.

Adrian had to hit him three times across the back
of the head with his shield rim before Esmond slumped;
then he put his hands under his brother's arms and
dragged him backward, cold with fear that he'd struck
too hard.

But he'd *had* to hit him. Nothing but unconsciousness
was going to stop Esmond from plunging into that
room, and the very *gods* themselves couldn't bring him
alive out of it.

# FOUR

Dust. Whenever Adrian remembered the retreat to the west, it was the dust that came back, the acrid taste of it in his mouth and clogging his nose. After a while he got the knack of sleeping while he rode, nodding along in a half-doze. Shouting woke him.

He rubbed a hand over his face, smearing reddish dust and sweat. Esmond was standing in the stirrups, looking forward.

"Messenger just came in," he said, with a little more life in his voice than there had been over the past week. There was still something missing from it. . . .

*Youth, lad,* Raj said. *That comes to us all. He's just had it removed faster and more painfully than most.*

"And there go the cavalry," Esmond went on.

The velipadsmen were riding at the head of the column, where they could spread out to screen the infantry. Adrian blinked gummy eyes as he watched them fan out into the low rolling hills ahead; they were Southron barbarians, mostly, mercenaries serving for pay and adventure under Confed officers. *Screen* . . . he thought, watching their velipads trot into the ripe standing wheat like boats breasting a sea of living bronze— *Damn, I'm thinking in hexameter*—if the cavalry were being sent out to screen the main force, then the Emerald light infantry would too.

One of Audsley's tribunes rode up, fingers plucking nervously at the crimson sash that circled his muscled cuirass.

"Deploy," he said, pointing westward with his staff of office. "The enemy is approaching from the west in strength. No more than three miles distant."

"Three miles?" Esmond said sharply. "To their cavalry screen, or to their main body? How many? Who commands?"

The legate looked down his well-bred nose; he was about their age, a young spark of the nobility following his patron to war, and unused to such a tone from a mere Emerald mercenary.

"Justiciar Demansk commands," he drawled. "But that needn't concern you, Emerald; you won't be treating with him yourself, you know."

He reined his velipad about and clapped heels to it. Esmond snorted. "If Justiciar Demansk was ever involved in this—and I beg leave to doubt—he's certainly going to prove his loyalty to the State *now*. With our blood and bones."

**probability 97%, ±2,** Center said helpfully in the back of Adrian's mind. **probability approaches unity as closely as stochastic analysis permits.**

*I could die here,* he knew sharply. Suddenly he could see and smell and feel more vividly than ever in his life; the smell of trampled barley and dust, the heavy shamble of a half-armed Audsley "volunteer" a hundred paces back, the song of a shrikewing . . .

**probability 52%, ±3,** Center said. **as you were warned.**

"All men are initiates of the mysteries of death," he whispered.

"Death, *hell*," Esmond said, grinning through sweat-caked dust. He raised himself in the stirrups and called to his men: "*Those* poor sorry ignorant bastards are going to be doing the dying, aren't they, lads?"

The men cheered him. "Deploy, and remember the training! They've got nothing like our thunderbolts—or our guts. Deploy!"

Justiciar Demansk grunted as he looked up from the folding map table set on the little ridge. Trampled barley stems were glassy and a little slippery under his hobnailed sandals, and he was sweating under the bronze back-and-breast that tradition mandated for a general officer.

"Here they come, the fools," he muttered.

Audsley had been a competent commander once; how could he have gotten himself into this position? *Good Confed troopers are going to die because Audsley and his friends can't pay their debts*, he thought. *Meanwhile the Islanders raid the coasts and the barbarians stir in the southlands. What a waste.* Granted that the State was like a knot of vipers these days, all old good ways breaking down, but this . . .

This was a ratfuck waiting to happen, he thought coldly. One day—not too long from now—a strong man was going to have to seize the reins, or everything would melt down as the generals fought over the bones of the Confederation like crabs in a bucket. Either one strong man emerged to end the endless rivalries, or it would go on until the Southrons and the Islanders fought each other to see who picked the bones of civilization. *But Audsley is not that man.*

*Am I?* ran through his mind, and he pushed the thought away with a mental effort. Even if he was, this wasn't the time. Not yet.

His head swiveled from side to side, the silk neckerchief that kept his skin from rasping on the edges of his back-and-breast sodden with the heat and chafing him.

*Ten thousand men,* he thought. Two brigades of regular infantry, somewhat understrength; call that six thousand all up. The core of his force, and they waited in formation with ox-stolid patience. Companies deployed in lines three deep, each battalion with a company in reserve; the men were kneeling with their shields leaned against their shoulders. The helmet crests ruffled in the wind; here and there an underofficer walked down the lines checking on lacings and positions. *And three battalions as general reserve,* he thought. That ought to be enough. He could feel the regulars, ready to his hand like a familiar tool that a man grasps by instinct in the dark.

A thousand cavalry. Mercenaries, Southrons under Confed officers. They lacked any semblance of the strict order and silence of his infantry brigades. There was a general uniformity of equipment—mail shirts, kite-shaped shields, helmets, lances and long swords—but within that every man suited himself. They had some discipline, of course, more than any barbarian warband, which wasn't saying much. And he had to admit that they were highly skilled individual fighters, sons of the Southron warrior class for the most part. *Audsley doesn't have any cavalry at all.*

Forward of the main line his light forces were deploying, skirmishers with javelin, sling, bow, buckler and assegai. They didn't have the staying power of the heavy infantry, but with any luck they'd handle this battle alone.

He narrowed his eyes. Audsley had a core of men in regular formation, looking fairly well equipped—one full brigade's worth, say four or five thousand men. They'd be veterans, but not drilled much recently, and it was a scratch outfit. On the flanks shambled more of his supporters, *not* properly equipped and in no particular order; eight or nine thousand of them, but they were meat for the blade. Out in front were what looked like mercenary light infantry.

"Grind me away these rabble," he said, in a voice harsh with distaste and impatience. "Loose the velipads!"

*Let the Southrons earn their pay,* he thought. Every rebel they killed was one less to menace his precious trained men . . . *and every Southron who dies is one less to raid over the border a few years down the road.*

Gallopers spurted away from the command group. A few minutes later the cavalry on either flank began to trot forward, moving into open order. The Confed officers dressed their ranks, and then dust spurted as the trot turned into a canter and then a slow hand gallop. Lanceheads came down in a rippling wave.

"Here come the even-more-barbarous barbarians," Esmond said, his voice full of confidence. "God of the Shades, accept our sacrifice—even if it does have fleas."

Adrian didn't join the chuckle that ran through those of the Emeralds who could hear his brother; it rippled down the loose formation as men repeated it to their neighbors. His own mouth was dry as he watched the line of bright points boiling out of the dust . . .

*Intimidating, isn't it?* Raj's voice whispered. A vison ran through his mind: another battlefield, and *thousands* of men riding the giant dogs he'd seen before. Men in steel helmets and breastplates, big bearded yellow-haired men with fifteen-foot lances, some of them with great wings sweeping up from the backplates of their armor. The howling of men and mounts and the earth-shaking thunder of paws filled his mind.

Ahead—ahead and to the right of Raj's viewpoint—

men in blue uniforms and bowl helmets bent over the curious chariotlike device Raj called a cannon.

"Juicy target," one of them said, grinning and spitting through brown irregular teeth. He stood aside and gripped a cord that ran to the rear of the cannon. "Nine hundred meters, shrapnel shell . . . fire!"

Adrian blinked and nodded, smiling internally. A few of his slingers gave him odd looks, but it was only to be expected that a man who made miracles would be . . . odd, occasionally.

"Fuses ready!" The fuse men whirled the rods that held the slowmatch, and trails of bitter blue smoke cut through the air. "Light!"

Each touched the slowmatch to the fuse of a grenade, and the cords sputtered into life. There was a gingerly care to the gestures that put the round brown pottery shapes into the pockets of the slings; the fuses were supposed to be seven-second, but they weren't entirely reliable yet.

"Targets—"

The slingers raised their staff-slings, eyes picking out spots in the onrushing formations. The snarling fangs of the velipads were clearly visible now, and the shouting contorted faces behind the bar visors of the helmets.

"Loose!"

The slings had yard-long wooden handles, and the silk cords at their ends were as long again. Each man swept staff and cords around in a full circle that put the strength of their shoulders and torso into the cast, not simply their arms. The one-pound bomblets didn't have the blurring speed a lead shot did; those almond-shaped bits of metal could punch through a shield and kill the man behind it through a cuirass. The grenades *did* snap out quickly enough to make men look up and raise their shields.

*Crack. Crack. Crackcrackcrackcrack—*

Vicious red snapping sparks, faint in the midday sun, visible only against the puffs of dirty gray-black smoke. The velipads reared and whistle-screamed at the noise and the unfamiliar sulfur stink. What couldn't be seen or heard were the fragments of hard ceramic and lead shot that smashed out too fast for the eye to catch, and the shockwaves of the grenades. Then men and beasts screamed as fragments gouged into flesh. The order of the charge disappeared into sudden chaos. An armored man and heavy war-velipad weighed over a ton; at a full gallop they *couldn't* turn swiftly, or overleap the writhing heap of mangled flesh that suddenly appeared at the footclaws of the mount. The riders' efforts to turn their beasts simply added to the chaos as clawed feet skidded out from under the torquing weight that hindered them. Worse, the lancers further back in the formation could see nothing within the dust cloud ahead of them, and spurred their velipads forward.

And the second volley of grenades burst over the heads of the milling, thrashing mass. More velipads went down, to add to the bone-breaking weights rolling and kicking in the tangled barrier of flesh. Another volley, and another . . .

"They're running, by the Maiden!" Esmond shouted.

"That they are," Adrian replied, grinning, slapping him on his corseleted shoulder. He carefully avoided looking at the killing ground before him.

"D . . . ddd . . . demonic thunder!" the courier stuttered, his face the color of the whey that dripped from the pans when the dairywoman squeezed the curds to make cheese.

"Control yourself!" Justiciar Demansk snapped, shading his eyes with a hand; when that proved inadequate he swung up onto his velipad and stood in the stirrups.

*Something* had happened to his cavalry, and that was a fact. There was a huge cloud of dust; extraordinary noises were coming out of it . . . and so were Southron mercenaries, some of them lashing their velipads, others lumbering on foot, all of them in utter screaming witless panic.

"Runner," he said. "If those imbeciles attempt to interfere with the formation, give them a volley of darts."

An order which his regular infantry would follow with zeal and enthusiasm. Nobody liked Southrons.

Demansk's eyes scanned as much of the battlefield as he could see. "And a general order," he went on. "The enemy has some sort of incendiary weapon." The pirates of the Isles used those, naphtha and seabeast oil and quicklime, compounds that would burn even under water. "Remind the officers that it can't do more than kill them."

One could get away with a good deal in the Confederacy, in these degenerate days. Even his own class was not safe from the rot anymore. But running away in battle wasn't among the pardonable offenses, thank the gods.

"Here it comes," Adrian said, licking dry lips.

**look for a line of retreat,** Center's passionless voice said.

*What?*

***Do it, lad. This is a disaster waiting to happen,*** Raj confirmed.

"Esmond," Adrian whispered. "We should be preparing a line of retreat."

His brother looked back at him, his eyes sapphires in his dust-caked face. "Adrian," he said, "there are times when I think the Gray-Eyed gave *you* the general's gifts. All right, let's see."

He thought for a moment, called a pair of his underofficers, gave low-voiced instructions. They trotted off to the rear.

The Emeralds were on the right of the rebel

position, at the junction between Audsley's brigade of fully-equipped troops and the shapeless clot of the volunteers. The dust had died down a little, and out of it Demansk's army came marching. Light sparkled and rippled down their line, sunlight off the points of the darts they held in their right hands, off helmet crests and standards and the gray gleam of oiled links of mail.

"My, aren't they pretty," Esmond said.

Adrian found himself joining in the chuckle that ran down the ranks of the Emeralds. *I wonder if the rest of them are as nervous as I am,* he thought.

**Most of them,** Raj murmured. **The ones who aren't are stupid, overconfident, or very experienced.**

Adrian licked his lips, tasted the sweat running down his face from the light helmet, and spoke: "Pick your targets. Aim for officers and standards—standards, and the ones with the transverse helmet crests. Wait for it, wait for it."

"Now!"

The slingers were loosing as fast as their loaders could put lighted grenades into the pockets of their weapons. The projectiles arched out towards the first line of Confed regulars, and eyes went up nervously under the helmet brims. Horns screamed harsh bronze music, and the whole formation speeded up into a trot—not a solid line, but a sinuous bronze-and-steel snake that advanced in pounding unison, keeping its alignment across the slight irregularities of the barley fields.

*Crack. Crack. Crackcrackcrackcrack—*

The bombs exploded, and a two-hundred-yard stretch of the Confed line vanished in smoke and malignant red snaps. Screams sounded louder than the explosions, as sharp metal and ceramic sliced into human flesh.

. . . and out of the smoke marched the survivors, still moving at the same steady trot. Men double-timed up from the second and third ranks, and the whole formation rippled and closed as the gaps were plugged and the replacements effortlessly fell into alignment. Adrian could hear the harsh clipped commands of the officers and file closers, but no screams apart from the wounded men—and not all of those.

"Shit," Esmond swore feelingly. Then louder: "What a target! Give 'em more, lads."

Adrian whipped his own staff-sling around his head, aiming for a standard in the fourth rank of the nearest Confed battalion borne by a man with the tanned head of a direbeast over his helmet. The bomb flew faultlessly, exploding at waist level before the standard-bearer had time to do more than flinch. Smoke kindly hid what happened next, but he could see the pole with the upright gilded hand totter backwards and fall. Then the standard rose again; a trooper had scooped it up, bracing it on his hip as he trotted forward.

Esmond's head was whipping back and forth as he tried to keep the whole field under observation. He fell back half a dozen steps.

"The battalion in front of us is edging right," he yelled to his brother. "But any second now—"

*"Vanbert! Vanbert!"*

The shout was loud, and the rebel regulars to their left closed formation and raised their shields in a sudden bristling of vermillion-dyed leather and brass, turning their formation into some huge scaled dragon. The volunteers to the Emerald's right tried to do the same— most of them had shields, at least—but lacked the instinctive cohesion of real fighting units.

Ahead the attackers' formation rippled as well. Adrian felt the small hairs along his spine as he realized why; the whole front line was leading with the left foot, getting ready to—

*"VANBERT! VANBERT!"* the front-line troopers roared, pivoting forward as their throwing arms flashed up.

The sound of seven thousand men shouting in unison was like a blow to the gut. The whistle as seven thousand arms launched their lead-weighted darts made Adrian's testicles try to draw themselves up into his gut.

**Heads up, lad,** Raj's voice said, cool and steady at the back of his brain.

Not many of the volley struck the Emeralds—the grenades had cleared too much of the front line opposite them. Men went down, here and there; others cursed and flung aside their shields as the barbed heads with the ball of lead behind the points stuck and could not be removed. To their left, the volley struck the raised shields of Audsley's brigade, most of them glancing from the curved surfaces or the metal facing, some rattling off mail, some punching into flesh.

"That's torn it," Esmond said.

He was looking to the right, where the volley had ripped into the shapeless clot of half-armed volunteers. What happened there was like a glass jar falling on rock, only what it spilled was redder than any wine. Few of the volunteers wore armor, and none had the tight shield-to-shield formation that was the only hope of stopping most of the missiles.

"VANBERT! VANBERT!"

Another volley, and the Confed trumpets sounded again, a complex rising-falling note. The battalions facing the volunteers drew their assegais with a long rasping slither and began to double-time forward.

"It's time," Esmond said; his face was white about the lips—with rage, Adrian realized, and the effort of will it took to order retreat rather than stay here and die killing Confeds. He nodded to their right, where the scythe of Demansk's wing was about to rip into the edge of the unravelling rebels.

"You're right, brother," Adrian said. He raised his voice. "One more volley to discourage them, men, and we'll leave the Confeds to each other."

The bombs punched out, as accurate as the first round. Other men were helping the wounded who were still mobile, or giving the mercy stroke to the helpless. Adrian swallowed a bubble of pride; his mercenaries and freedmen and general rabble were steady with the many-headed beast almost within arm's length of them.

Esmond's light infantry spread to cover the grenadiers, hefting their javelins.

"Give them a shaft, then we go!"

Esmond turned, hefted his javelin and threw with a skill that made it seem effortless. It ended in the face of a Confed underofficer; the fan-crested helmet snapped back, and the volley that followed made them waver for an instant. The Emeralds turned and trotted away in a compact body, heading to the rear and to the west—behind the still-solid ranks of Audsley's brigade.

The same mounted galloper as before drew rein before them; Adrian could smell the rank omnivore breath of the velipad as it came up on its haunches, pawing the air before it with great blunt claws.

"Where do you think you're going?" the young Confed nobleman cried. "Back to your posts, you Emerald scum—"

*Thunk.*

Esmond's javelin punched through the light cuirass of linen and bronze scale with a sound like an axe hitting wood. The Confed goggled, and then his eyes slid down to the slim ashwood shaft in his gut. He slid free of the saddle with the same expression of bewildered indignation, as if he could not *believe* that a mere Emerald mercenary had dared to raise a hand against him.

"For every slight, for every insult, I will send a dozen of them to the Shades," Esmond muttered as he caught the velipad and swung into the saddle with effortless grace. "For Nanya, not all their lives are enough."

Adrian swallowed at the sound of his brother's voice, even now. There was a huge rasping slither behind them as Audsley's men drew their assegais in turn, then a banging clatter like all the smiths' shops in the world as the fight came to close quarters. He risked a glance over his left shoulder; the volunteers were going down like greatbeasts under a sacrificer's axe, but there were so many of them that it would take some time . . . and the dust and confusion were immense. Without Center to sketch images across his vision it would have all been a mass of steel and shouting and blood, patternless, Chaos and Old Night come again.

"When Demansk's men get through with the rabble, they'll curve in to take Audsley's regulars from the rear," he called up to Esmond. "If we get out of the bag in time . . ."

"Exactly," Esmond said, like an apparition of Wodep the War God on the restive velipad, his armor splashed with blood.

*Me too*, Adrian realized, daubing at himself. *Me too*.

"Strike sail," Adrian said.

The skipper of the *Wave Strider* shrugged. "Lay aloft!" he shouted. "Strike sail!"

The ship they'd hijacked was much like the ones their father had run out of Solinga for most of their lives: a hundred feet long and forty at the broadest part of the hull, fully decked, with one tall mast and a single large square sail. Adrian didn't think his father would ever have tolerated the skirt of weed that showed green against the blue water all around, or bilges that stank badly enough to overpower even the iodine smell of the sea. The swan's head that curled above them on the quarterdeck was standard, but the blue and gold paint was chipped and faded. For all that, the hull was watertight and they'd made good time from the west-coast port of Preble. Adrian licked dry lips, squinting out over the white-flecked blue of the Western Ocean; they hadn't had time to ship extra water or supplies, and with two hundred men aboard they were down to a cupful a day—green, slimy, sweeter-tasting than any wine.

The big yard came down with a rattle, and a curse from the Emerald mercenaries on deck who had to scramble out of the way. With the sail down, Adrian had a better view of the craft that was approaching them.

It was no merchantman. The hull was low and long and snake-slender, with glaring eyes and snarling teeth painted above a bronze ram that flashed out of the water with every forward bound. Outriggers held seats for oarsmen who would drive two banks of long oars when the mast was down. Right now it was rigged for cruising, the mast up and a sail painted the same blue-gray as the hull bent to it. Two light catapults stood manned near the bows, ready to throw rocks or jugs full of clingfire; two ballistae flanked the quarterdeck, with giant javelins ready to hurl. The knot of men by the steering oar was bright with plumes and gold and blowing cloaks dyed in the famous purple of the western islands. And the flag above them had the stylized cresting wave of the Lords of the Isles.

The other ship's sail came down like magic, neatly furled—a heavy crew, a warship's crew. Esmond came up beside his brother, shading his eyes with a palm. As he did, the oars flashed out of the other ship's sides and struck the water all together like the limbs of a centipede, slashing creamy froth from the waves. The slender hull jerked forward, then turned to present its ram to the merchantman's side in a smooth curve, turned by the oars as well as the twin steering oars; they could hear the *clack . . . clack . . . clack* of the hortator's mallets on the log that served as drum.

"Bireme," Esmond said. "Twenty marines, hundred and twenty oarsmen, thirty sailors. They can't be far from home. Royal ship too, I think, not a freebooter. Very well-trained crew."

Adrian nodded, although being a royal ship wasn't always much of a distinction, with Islanders. Any king's ship would turn pirate if the opportunity offered.

One of the officers on the warship's quarterdeck raised a speaking trumpet. He hailed them in Confed, accented but understandable.

"Ahoy there! What ship?"

"*Wave Strider*, out of Preble," the captain said. "Bound for Chalice."

"What cargo?"

The voice sounded suspicious; there were far too many armed men on the merchantman's deck, but she was equally obviously no pirate or longshore raider. That would make her cautious. Even a successful ramming run might leave the warship vulnerable to boarding; a little bad luck, a ram caught in the wounded ship's timbers, and the *Wave Strider*'s men could swarm aboard. That was how Confed ships had beat the Kingdom's fleets despite the Islanders' seamanship, grappling and turning naval battles into land fights.

Adrian stepped forward, speaking in the tongue of the Isles; he could feel Esmond stiffen in surprise. Which was natural enough, since as far as he knew Adrian spoke only a few words.

"Our cargo is brave men," he said. "Come to serve King Casull IV, Lord of the Isles, Supreme Autocrat, Chosen of the Sun God and Lemare of the Sea, against the thieves and tyrants of Vanbert. We are Adrian and Esmond Gellert, of Solinga."

The ships were close enough now that Adrian could see the officer's eyes go wide in a swarthy, hook-nosed face. The plume at the forefront of his turban nodded as he turned and spoke urgently with some others.

"They've heard of us, and not just through Father," Esmond murmured at his ear.

"Now the question is whether they want to get in good with the Confeds or poke them in the eye," Adrian murmured back.

The gorgeously-dressed officer turned back, sun breaking off the gilded scales of his armor. "The King, may he live forever, must hear of this," he said. "You will transfer to Slasher."

"Esteemed sir, we will remain with our men," Esmond said, in slower and more heavily accented Islander. "But we are very eager to lay our fates at the feet of the King, to whom the gods have given a great realm."

There was a moment of tension as stares met. The plumes nodded again as the Islander captain nodded. "Very well. Make what sail you can."

"Enter," King Casull said.

The audience chamber was small and informal, one wall an openwork lattice of carved marble looking down over the city of Chalice. For the rest it held a mosaic of sea monsters—most of them quite real, as Casull had learned in his years as a skipper and admiral, before the previous King had met an untimely end in the last war with the Confeds—an ebony table inlaid with mother-of-pearl, embroidered cushions, a tray of dried fruit and pitchers of wine and water. A girl in a diaphanous gown knelt in one corner, strumming a *jitar*, and two guards stood by the entrance, the points of their huge curved slashing-swords resting on the floor before their boots and their hands ready on the hilts. A stick of incense burned in a fretted brass tray, melding with the scent of the flowers in the gardens outside, and the tarry reek of the harbor below.

Two men came through the door with a eunuch chamberlain following, in robes even more gorgeous than theirs.

"O King, live forever!" all three cried as they prostrated themselves on the floor.

The silver aigrettes at the front of the two merchants' turbans clicked on the tessellated marble of the floor, as did the ruby in the eunuch's turban. *A palace chamberlain might lack stones, but not the opportunity to acquire precious stones.* Casull smiled slightly to himself at his own pun and made a gesture with one hand. Another girl rose with silent grace and moved to pour thick sweet wine into tiny cups carved from the gemlike teeth of the *salpesk*.

"Rise, my friends," he said genially. His father had once told him that even if you had to kill a man, it cost nothing to be polite. "Speak. Your King would hear your tale."

The merchants rose and sat cross-legged on cushions, raising the cups the slave handed them in a two-handed gesture of respect before sipping appreciatively. Both were middle-aged men with gray in their curled, oiled beards. *Enri and Pyhar Lowisson,* Casull reminded himself. *Brothers.* Their father had been a fish farmer, but the sons had made a fortune in trade . . . and in raiding, during the chaos of the wars with the Confeds. They'd served ably in Casull's own campaigns against islands that had fallen away from the Kingdom while his predecessor was occupied on the mainland, too.

"Know, O King, that we have long traded with Solinga," Enri said; he was the elder of the two.

Casull nodded. "Dried fish, textiles and spices for wine, grain and jerked meat," he said. "With sidelines in zinc ore, bar iron and general handicrafts."

The merchants blinked and bowed their heads in respect. "Go on," the King said.

"We have dealt, over the years, with one Zeke Gellert of Solinga," Enri went on. "He died last year, but we exchanged *tesserae* with him some time ago."

Casull nodded again, silent. He'd found that was more effective than talking, often enough. Tesserae were tokens—usually ivory—exchanged between guest-friends in the Emerald countries. The token was broken in half; when the other half was presented, the guest-friend was obliged to offer help and shelter to the man who brought it, and the obligation was hereditary. Or so Emeralds generally thought; Islanders were more . . . flexible. Still, it would harm the Lowissons' reputation in the Emerald lands if they turned away their guest-friend's heirs.

Enri moistened his lips and sipped delicately at the wine. "Well, O King, Adrian and Esmond Gellert have come to Chalice, claiming hospitality of us . . . and wishing an introduction to the King's self."

He hesitated, and the King spoke. "The Adrian and Esmond Gellert who took part in Audsley's rebellion in the Confed territories, yes," he said. "They are outlaws in the Confederacy—not the first time exiles from the mainland have sought the Isles."

*Although no other exiles have been preceded by such rumors,* he thought. Weapons like the lightning of the gods, thunder and fire that left men torn to shreds . . . *There may be something to it,* he thought. *Still, less than rumor paints, or Audsley would have made himself master in Vanbert.*

The conversation wound on, intricate and indirect; the three might all be self-made men, but they'd aquired polish as well as wealth and power on their journey up the slippery pole of rank. The Isles weren't like the mainland, where a man's life was fixed at his birth. Here a sailor or a peasant might end his days with a palace and a harem, if he had the luck and the *nous*; but equally, the pit of failure yawned before his steps all his days, and his rivals' knives were always sharp and ready.

Casull smiled and nodded. *Yes, you wish to share in any favor that may befall the Gellerts,* he thought. *Yes, equally, you wish to avoid the blame for any failure, if they are nothing but boasters. Yes, these desires conflict—for if you wait too long, you will surely lose. A beautiful dilemma.*

At the end, he clapped his hands. "We will grant these Emeralds the favor of an audience," he said. "Talk is cheap, and stolen goods are never sold at a loss."

His gaze sought the city that tumbled down the slopes from the palace to its circular harbor. *And I need any help I can get,* he thought. The Isles were far from united, and when they were the Confeds would still outweigh him by thirty to one. Skill and distance had kept the Islands independent, but . . . what was that old saying? Ah, yes.

*Quantity has a quality all its own.* He would seize any advantage that came his way with both hands, preparing for the inevitable struggle.

# FIVE

*Impressive,* Adrian thought, pausing in his restless pacing and looking up the slope of the volcano.

The mansion of their father's guest-friend was down by the docks—the Lowissons liked to keep in touch with the sources of their wealth. Like most buildings in Chalice it was made of stone blocks, like volcanic tufa plastered over and whitewashed or painted, with a flat roof where the inhabitants could sleep during the hot summers . . . or pace while they awaited the word of the King. Other buildings stretched up the steep slope, along roads cobblestoned or paved or deep in mud, narrow and twisting except for the Processional Way that led from the docks to the great blocky temple of Lemare, the Sea Goddess. The buildings lay like the dice of gods themselves, tumbled over the slopes in blocks of brilliant white, emerald green, purple and blue and crimson; they turned blank walls to the streets, centering around a myriad of courtyards large and small. A wall might hide anything; the mansion of a merchant prince, a teeming tenement house, the workshops of artisans. Over some one could see the tips of trees

97

swaying, and within could be beautiful gardens and fountains of carved jade splashing cool water . . . or flapping laundry and shrilling children.

The streets were crowded themselves, with near-naked porters bent double under huge loads, with chains of the Island dwarf velipads under similar burdens, with water sellers and sweetmeat sellers and storytellers, rich merchants in jewels and silk, swaggering crewmen from pirate galleys with curved swords at their sides and horn-backed bows slung over their shoulders, priests with their heads shaven and painted in zigzag stripes . . . Here a wealthy courtesan went by in her litter borne on the shoulders of four brawny slaves, crooning and feeding nuts between her teeth to a gaudy-feathered bird; there a scholar paused to buy a cup of watered wine, while his students gathered behind and broke into arm-waving argument, using the scrolls they carried to gesture—or to rap each other over the head. . . .

Chalice took in three-quarters of the circumference of the ancient volcanic crater that made up its harbor and gave it its name; the knife ridges above made a city wall unnecessary. The great expanse of the caldera was thick with ships, galleys spider-walking to the naval base on the north shore, fishing smacks, the lines of buoys that marked the outlines of fish farms. Above the buildings reared the slopes of other volcanos; the Peak of the Sun God highest of all, topped with eternal snows and trickling a long plume of smoke into azure heavens. The lower slopes were terraced for orchards of pomegranate, mangosteen, orange, fig; the upper bore dense green forest, the source of valuable hardwoods and ship timber.

Adrian turned back to his brother . . . and stopped a moment, shocked. *Esmond looks* older, he thought. *Thirty, at least.* There were deep grooves from the corners of his mouth to his nose, and his blue gaze was blank as he waited.

*What can you say?* he thought. The School of the Grove taught that the love of women was a weakness, disturbing the equilibrium that a wise man constantly sought. He didn't think that was what Esmond's grief needed to hear; and he'd obviously loved Nanya with exactly the sort of grand obsessive passion that Bestmun had denounced, the sort that had set a thousand ships to sailing and brought the wrath of the Gods down on the city of Windhaven in the ancient epics. *The problem is, he'd say it was worth it, even with the pain,* Adrian decided. *Thank the gods I'm free of* that, *at least.* It would have been more wholehearted if he'd been able to deny an element of wistful envy . . .

His host saved him the embarassment of speech. "Come," he said, smiling. "The King will hear you, most fortunate of men."

Adrian's eyes went to the volcano for a moment. The slopes of such mountains bore soil of marvelous richness . . . but anything a man grew there might be destroyed by fire and ash at any moment.

**We never said it would be easy, lad,** Raj said.

Adrian took a deep breath and bowed in his turn. "The King does us honor," he began.

"The King does us honor," Adrian said again as they sat awkwardly, unused to the cross-legged position.

"The King is finished with ceremony," Casull said, leaning back against the pile of cushions. "I can see men beating their heads on the floor of the throne room any time of the day—men with something interesting to say are much rarer, and I prefer not to have important news bellowed out in open *durbar*. Even the Confederacy can find the occasional able spy."

The day had turned warm; the King was glad enough of the peacock-feather fans stirring a little air across his face, and the fine mist from the fountain in the courtyard. The palace of the Kings of the Isles was a warren that had grown by accretion over four centuries, every new monarch adding something and few tearing anything down. This chamber was open at both ends, slender pillars with coral capitals giving onto the corridor and a terrace that looked over the outer gardens; the through breeze made it tolerable on these hot rainy-season afternoons. From the raised platform where he sat Casull could see past the Emeralds to the city, and to the black thunderclouds piling up on the eastern horizon.

*Luridly appropriate,* he thought.

"The . . . grenade, did you call it? The grenade was very impressive. At sea, such weapons could be decisive—at least for the first few times, when the enemy were unused to them, and had none themselves."

He spoke Emerald, the cultured version of Solinga's gentlefolk, not the patois of the sea. The younger Emerald's Islander was impressively fluent, but it wouldn't do to let him think he was dealing with a boor, a mere jumped-up pirate chief. Casull's mental eyes narrowed as he appraised this Adrian Gellert; outwardly he was very much a young Scholar of the Grove, but there was something else . . . *Harder than one might expect,* he thought. *And more perceptive—he misses nothing.*

The brother was more outwardly formidable. A fighting man, Casull judged, and not just an athlete. The reports from the mainland, and from the spies among the barkeeps, whores and gamblers who'd had contact with the mercenary troop the Gellerts had brought with them, all said he had the *baraka,* the gift of inspiring men in battle. Wits besides; and he certainly *looked* like an incarnation of Wodep, the ancient War God of the mainlanders.

The younger Emerald bowed. "O King, the grenades are the *least* of what can be done with the new . . . new *principle* involved in these explosive weapons."

Casull raised his eyebrows. The Emerald word meant *underlying cause*, and he didn't quite see how it applied.

"Speak on," he said mildly, quelling a restless stir by his son Tenny. *Let the boy learn patience; that's not the least of a ruler's virtues.*

"If my lord the King would deign to look at these— the first is what is called a cannon, for hurling iron balls and giant grenades; to smash ships, or batter down the walls of a fort . . ."

Two hours later Casull leaned back again. "Interesting indeed," he said. His eyes turned to Esmond. "And you, young sir, what have you to say?"

Esmond smiled, a gesture that did not reach the cold blue eyes. "My brother is the scholar," he said. "What I do is fight. I've managed to kill a fair number of Confeds, over the past six months. I intend to kill a good many more." His fist tightened on his knee; the scars and burns across the back showed white against his tanned skin. "For every slight, for every humiliation they've inflicted on me and my city, I shall take recompense in blood—and they owe me a debt beyond that. When the last trooper dies in the burning ruins of Vanbert and the Confederacy is a memory, then *perhaps* I'll consider the account settled."

Casull nodded thoughtfully; he'd seen hatred before, but none more bitter. *Pity,* he thought. A man that eaten with hate turned inward on himself; his luck might be strong, but it would run too swiftly, carrying out the current of his life. *But I can use him.*

He clapped his hands. "Hear the commands of the King!" he said, his tone slightly formal. The *wakil* leaned forward, pen poised over a sheet of reed-paper.

"It is the command of the King that the noble warrior Esmond Gellert's-son of Solinga, be taken into the forces of the King, to command the Sea Striker regiment; he shall rank as a Commander of Five Hundred—which

is about what they'll come to, with the men he brought
with him. The usual pay and plunder-shares."

Esmond bowed again, and this time his smile was
more genuine.

Casull turned his eyes back to the younger man. "You
shall have a chance to demonstrate your new weapons,"
he said. "It is the command of the King that Adrian
Gellert be accepted into the Court with the rank of
Scholar-Advisor, with the usual pay and perquisites. For
the purpose of building his weapons, he may exert the
royal prerogative of eminent domain, acquiring land,
and requiring artisans and merchants to furnish the
materials he needs . . . saltpeter, you said? And the
metals. He may use a royal estate to be designated
hereafter, and royal vessels, within reason. All goods and
labor to be paid for at fair market prices, of course."

A King of the Isles was theoretically absolute; in
practice there were always enough claimants that a
monarch who angered enough of the powerful merchants and ship owners would find that the despotism
was tempered by assassination and leavened by coup
d'etat. He certainly wasn't going to risk that for this
Emerald's untried notions. The potential payoff was
certainly huge, though.

"Ah . . ." Adrian looked uncertain. "My lord King,
this work will require considerable funds," he said.
"Even for demonstration purposes. How . . ."

Casull smiled at Enri and Pyhar Lowisson. "Your
patrons will, of course—out of patriotic duty as well—
loan you the funds at a reasonable rate of interest. No
more than fifteen percent, annual, compounded."

The two Islander merchants winced; that was the rate
for a bottomry loan, with no premium for risk.

"If the weapons are satisfactory, I will reward you
richly; and they shall have the interest doubled from
the royal treasury, as well as my favor, of course."

He beamed at the Emeralds and the two Islanders

as well. Unspoken went the fact that if the weapons
*failed* to satisfy they would get nothing, and the
Lowissons could try as best they could to get satisfaction
from their penniless guests.

Casull clapped his hands. "This audience is at an
end!"

"By the Dog," the mercenary officer said. "Has the
King sent us a pretty boy for a party?"

"The King has sent me here to command," Esmond
said. "Name and rank."

The mercenary turned crimson. "I'm Donnuld Grayn,
and I command here now that Stenson's dead, by the
Dog!"

Esmond rested his hands on his sword belt and
looked the man up and down. By his accent he came
from Cable, ancient enemy of the Solingians—not that
that mattered much, these days—and by his looks, scars
upon scars, he'd been in this profession most of his
thirty-odd years. And from the look of his bloodshot
eyes . . .

"Are you usually drunk this early?" he said. "Or are
you just naturally stupid?"

"Ahhhh," the man said eagerly, his hand falling
towards his sword hilt. "I'll see your liver and lights
for that, you mincing Solingian basta—"

The growl broke into a yelp as Esmond's thumb and
forefinger closed on his nose and gave it a powerful,
exactly calculated twist. As he'd expected, the mercenary
forgot all about his steel and lashed out with a knobby
fist.

Esmond's own hand slapped it aside, and his right
sank its knuckles into his opponent's gut with the
savage precision of the palaestra. As the man doubled
over, the Solingian stepped to one side and slammed
another blow with the edge of a palm behind his ear.
The mercenary dropped to the ground like a puppet

with its strings cut and lay wheezing at the victor's feet.

The victor looked up; there were a crowd of Strikers looking on, together with some of the camp followers and children that crowded the barracks. Some were smiling, some glaring, most wavering between the two.

"You!" Esmond said. "Name and rank, soldier."

The man stiffened. "Eward, sir—file closer, second company."

"Eward, get Captain Grayn to his quarters—he needs to sleep it off. Trumpeter," he went on, "sound *fall in*."

That took far too long, and he had to detail some of his own men to push the noncombatants out of the way. When it was finished there were about four hundred men standing on the pounded clay of the parade ground; it was surrounded on three sides by barracks, and on the fourth by a wall. Esmond paced down the ranks of the sweating, bewildered men, pausing now and then.

*Not bad*, he thought. About half-and-half javelineers and slingers. They all had linen corselets with thin iron plates sewn between the layers of cloth, shortswords, and light open-face bowl helmets. Most of them looked to be in reasonable condition, and King Casull certainly wouldn't be wasting his silver on deadbeats. From what he'd heard, a lot of them would be men who'd left the Emerald cities for reasons of health, or on their relatives' urgent advice; but war and the Confederacy had left a lot of broken men in the southern lands.

"All right," he said at last, standing in front of them with his left hand resting on his hilt and the cloak thrown back from his shoulder. "My name is Esmond Gellert."

A slight murmur. He noted it without the pleasure it might have brought him a few months ago. He'd always been proud of the fame he'd won as a competitor in the Pan-Emerald Games—if not for undying fame, why would men go through the rigors of the palaestra? Now it was like his appearance, something he noted with cold objectivity, a tool to be used. *And some of them will have heard about the war on the mainland, too.*

"You know—or you should, if you're paying any attention to anything besides booze, dice and pussy—that there's war coming. Probably with the Confeds." Another low murmur. "I've fought them myself, not too long ago; so have these men with me." He indicated his own followers with a toss of his head. "They're tough, yes, but they're not ten feet tall, and they bleed as red as any man when you stick 'em. The King wants this unit ready to fight, and by the Gods, it will be— or we'll all die trying."

He nodded at the last murmur. No use saying anything more; they'd be waiting to see if he was real, or all mouth.

"For starters, we're going on a little route march. Fall out in campaign order in twenty minutes. Dismissed!"

"Faugh, this stinks," Enri Lowisson said.

"Think of it as the smell of money," Adrian said, chuckling with delight.

The cave was halfway up the side of Gunnung Daberville, the main volcanic peak that loomed over the port of Chalice. From the entrance you could see down past jungle and orchard to the city itself, the bastioned wall, the near-circle of the drowned caldera that made up the harbor, and over miles of sail-speckled water beyond. It was what lay within that interested him, however, down into the depths of the fumarole that twisted like a frozen intestine into the depths of the mountain.

Thirty feet overhead the ceiling of the cavern was not of the same pockmarked gray-green rock as the rest of the cave. It was brown instead, lumpy . . . and it *moved* as the chitterwings nesting there for the day stirred uneasily at the light and heat of the party's torches. A soft pattering left gloppy white stains on the floor, adding to a layer that was probably four feet deep at least. That was the source of the rancid, ammonia-harsh stink that had several of the party breathing through pieces of their tunics.

"The stuff we need, the saltpeter, will be concentrated in the lower levels of this," he said, kicking at the hard dried surface of the chitterwing dung that covered the ground. "We'll dig it out, cart it down lower, then leach out the saltpeter in a system of trays and sluices."

"That will cost," Enri warned.

He looked backward, and Adrian nodded. The way down was near-as-no-matter roadless; if it had been easier, farmers would have come to dig the dung out for fertilizer, as they had with several caves lower down. The chitterwings went out in huge flocks at night, to feed at sea on tiny phosphorescent fish. At dawn they returned, to sleep, and to breed and nest in season—most of the females had tiny young clinging to their belly fur with miniature claws right now.

"It'll be worth it; there's more here than we'll need in a generation." He looked downslope as well, and suddenly a tracery of drawings was overlaid on it.

**so,** Center said. **and so.**

Adrian started and came back to himself, conscious of the curious stares Enri and his men were giving him.

"There's a way to make it easier," he said. "See how this ridge curves away down to the foothills?"

"Building a road?" Enri said. He shook his head. "I don't think that's practical."

"No, what we'll do is build a trackway," Adrian said. The words tumbled over themselves at the series of silent *clicks* just behind his eyes; suddenly Center's drawing made *sense*. In fact the principle . . . *Why haven't we thought of this before?* he wondered. *It would make so much easier.*

The problem was he knew the answer to that. *"Thought was not to be sullied with the base, contemptible concerns of men whose lives were warped away from virtue by cramping labor . . ."* Which, in effect, means anyone who isn't an absentee landlord; not something that would have come to him before Raj and Center took up residence in the rear of his mind, but it was his own thought.

"We'll lay down two rails of hard wood, spiked to cross-ties," he said. "Carts will run down it, on flanged wheels. When they're empty, they can be hauled up easily."

Enri winced. "Oh, that will *cost*. Sawyers, carpenters, the metal for spikes, all that cordage . . ."

"No, it'll turn a profit," Adrian said. "What we extract will still leave the sludge good for fertilizer, and think of what that fetches in the gardens around the city."

Enri brightened. "And, of course, the King will pay . . . eventually."


"Interesting!" the blacksmith said.

*Well, thank the Gray-Eyed Lady for that!* Adrian thought to himself. *At least I'm not getting "but such a thing was never done in the days of our fathers" so often here.*

The smithy occupied the lower story of a house near the docks, with the quarters of the smith's two wives, his children, the two apprentices and the three slaves to the rear, on the other side of the courtyard. It held a large circular brick hearth built up to about waist height, the bellows behind that, and a variety of anvils. The front entrance could be closed by a grillwork that was now hauled up, a little like a portcullis; the walls held workbenches, racked tools, vises and clamps, and more anvils of different shapes and sizes. It was ferociously hot—the smith wore only a rag-twist loincloth under his leather apron and gloves, and the slave working the bellows less than that. The smells were of hot oil from the quenching bath, burning charcoal, scorched metal, sweat.

"Interesting, the Lame One curse me if it isn't," the smith said. "This tube you want, now, it's to be sixty inches long?"

"Sixty inches long, and an inch and a quarter on the inside. I thought you could twist the bar around an iron mandrel, red-hot, and then hammer-weld it."

"Hmmm."

The smith went over to a workbench and brought back a sword. It was nearly complete except for the fitting of the hilt and guard; a curved weapon with a flared tip, more than a yard long, the type of slashing-scimitar that the Royal bodyguards carried. Adrian whistled admiration as he peered more closely at the metal; it had the rippled pattern work of a blade made from rods of iron and steel twisted together, heated, hammered, doubled back, hammered again . . . and repeated time after time until there were thousands of laminations in the metal.

"Look," the smith said.

He braced the point of the blade against the floor, placed his foot against it, and heaved. Muscle stood out like cable under the wet brown skin of his massive, ropy arms and broad shoulders. The blade bent nearly double . . . and then sprang back with a quivering whine when he released it.

"That's good steel," Adrian said sincerely; tough and flexible both.

The smith gave him a quizzical look, out of a face that looked as if it had been pounded from rough iron itself, with one of the sledges that stood all around the big room.

"You're not the common run of fine Emerald gentle-men," he said. "Never a one of them I've met who thought *how* a thing was made."

Adrian smiled. "I have unusual friends," he said. "Can you do what I ask?"

"Oh, certainly: Lame One be my witness. The thing is, friend, it'll take *time*. Three weeks to make a good sword blade—not counting grinding, polishing, and fitting; I contract those out. I'm not one for fine work with brass and ivory, anyway . . . say the same for one of these . . . what was the word?"

"Arquebus barrels," Adrian said helpfully.

"One of these tubes, then. And it'll cost what a good sword blade does, too."

"If I paid you extra, to take on more labor, could you do more?"

A decisive shake of the head. "No, sir. Guild rules." At Adrian's expression he went on: "But see here, sir, I like gold and silver as much as the next man, and I like to do something new now and then. What I *can* do is contract out. There are dozens of mastersmiths in the Brotherhood; not many as good as I am, if I do say so myself, but nearly. And there are plenty of journeymen we *could* hire away from their regular work, and who could do the simpler parts. Say . . . thirty in three weeks, with as much again every week after that. It'll go faster once we're used to it."

Adrian sighed. "Well, if that's all that can be done . . ."

**the artisan is not being entirely truthful,** Center pointed out. An image of his face sprang up, with pointers indicating temperature variations and the dilation of his pupils. **mendacity factor of 27%, ±7. i suspect that he is merely establishing an initial bargaining position.**

*Oh,* Adrian thought. He was the son of a merchant, but most of his life had been spent among the Scholars of the Grove. *What should I do?*

***Well, I wasn't a trader either,*** Raj's mental voice said, amused. ***But I did do a fair bit of dickering with sutlers. I'd suggest you say that's not enough***

*to make the project worthwhile. He'll scream and modify his terms; then point out that he and his friends will be able to sell the muskets elsewhere, too . . .*

"What is this, a flowerpot?" the brassfounder said.

"No, it's a weapon," Adrian replied, biting back the first words that came to mind. "The one the King has commanded me to build," he added.

"May the King live forever!" the artisan said, without taking his eyes off the model Adrian had had carved from soft wood.

The Emerald's hands trembled slightly as he pulled on it. Not enough sleep, he thought to himself as the model split down the middle.

"This is a—" He paused, frustrated. *What's "cross-sectional view" in Islander?* he thought.

**Lad, there's no word for it. There's no word for it in your language either,** Raj said.

"—what it would look like if it was cut down the middle?" Adrian said. *Have I changed so much in a year?*

He shook aside the obscure sense of instability that lay like a lump of cold millet porridge below his breastbone for a moment. The reasonable man did not doubt that he himself *was*, the School of the Grove taught.

The brassfounder was in a bigger way of business than any of the smiths; he was a merchant, as well as the manager of a workshop. Iron was much more common than copper, vastly more common than tin. You had to have long-distance contacts to deal in bronze. Hence the warehouse attached to his house, and the courtyard with its ruddy tile and fountain, that Islander symbol of status. The man's turban was of plain cotton, though, and the eyes below it were shrewd and dark.

"Like a tube closed at one end, then," he said, tracing the model. "You know, this trick might be useful for making preliminary models of castings of many types . . . and the metal outside the tube grows much thicker towards the closed end. What's this, though?"

"It's a thin hole going from the outside—this depression—into the tube at the breech end. The closed end," he added, at the man's frown.

"Hmmm. Well, with bronze, it would be simpler to *drill* that afterwards. And what are these little solid tubes at right angles to the main one for?"

"You'll find out," Adrian said, smiling slightly.

**Good. We don't want too much getting out too early, and I'd be surprised if some of these people aren't for sale,** Raj said.

*Or all of them,* Adrian replied.


"Well, you make pumps with close-fitting pistons, don't you?" he said.

"Of course, honored sir," the metalworker said. "By lapping—you use the piston head to do the last little bit of boring out, covering it with *naxium*—emery is your Emerald word, I think. That will give you a very close fit."

"Well, then, that's how we'll make this engine work," he said, forcing cheerfulness into his voice.

"Yes, but I really don't think it can be done with iron," the metalworker replied. "Iron is too hard—and too hard to cast, honored sir. By the Sun God, I speak the truth."

Adrian sighed and let his head drop into his hands. *My back hurts,* he thought; he was never, never going to get used to sitting cross-legged on cushions.

"All right," he said. "We'll start off by using bronze for the pistons. We want two, to begin with, six inches in bore and four feet long. But the piston rods will have to be made of iron—wrought iron."

"Hmm-auhm," the Islander—his name was Marzel, a plump little man with a snuff-colored turban—said.

He picked up the model Adrian had had made by standing over a toycrafter. It showed a single upright cylinder, with a piston rod coming out of its top. The rod connected to one end of a beam; the beam was pivoted in the middle, and the other end had a second rod that worked a crank, that in turn moved a wheel with paddles.

"I've seen wheels like this used to move grindstones," Marzel said. "This is the same thing in reverse, isn't it?"

*Gray-Eyed Lady, thank You,* Adrian thought. *Finally, someone who* understands *what I'm talking about!*

"Exactly!" he said aloud. "The steam pushes the piston, the piston pushes the beam up and down, the crank turns that into around and around, and the wheel pushes the ship—one on each side."

"Hmmm-auhm," Marzel mused again. "You know, honored sir, one could use this to move a grindstone, too."

*A hecatomb of oxen to you, Lady of Wisdom.* Aloud: "Yes, it could—think of it as a way of transforming firewood into work, the way a man or a velipad converts *food* into work."

Marzel laughed aloud. "Ah, you have a divine wit, honored sir!" He returned to the model. "So, let me see if I have grasped this. The steam goes through these valves *here*, at each end of the cylinder. As the piston moves, it uncovers these two rows of outlets here at the middle of the cylinder, letting the steam escape."

At Adrian's nod, the artificer turned back to the plans, tracing lines across the reed-paper with a finger and then referring back to the model.

"Honored sir," he said at last, "I love this thing you have designed—so clever, you Emeralds! Yes, I love the thought of making it. But I am not sure that it *can* be made, in the world of real things. In the . . . how do you Emeralds say it? In the world of Pure Forms, yes, this will work as you say. But it has so many valves, so much piping, so many *joints*, you see. Holding water in such a thing, for say the fountains and curious metal beasts in the Garden of Curiosities in the King's Palace, that is difficult. Holding hot steam . . . can fittings be made precisely enough? Even with the finest craftsmen? And these parts will be *large*."

Adrian nodded in respect for the man's honesty; and his courage, expressing doubts here in the palace rather than telling the royal favorite whatever he wanted to hear.

"I am certain that if any man can do it, Marzel Therdu, you can," he said. "And I am certain that it *can* be done." He spread his hands and smiled. "And my head answers for it, if it cannot, not yours."

Marzel rose and made the gesture of respect, bowing with palms pressed together. "Perhaps . . . Perhaps we would be well advised to try first a *model* of this thing, this . . . hot water mover?"

"Steam engine."

"Steam engine, then. Not a toy model, although that was useful. A *working* model, enough to drive a small launch, of the type rowed by ten men?"

**probability of success of steam ram project has increased to 61% ±7,** Center said. **as always, stochastic analysis cannot fully compensate for human variability.**

Adrian smiled; if that had been a human voice speaking aloud, and not a supernatural machine whispering at the back of his mind, he'd have sworn there was a rasp of exasperation in it—rather the way one of the professors of Political Theory in the Academy had spoken of the Confederacy of Vanbert's Constitution; it should not work, but it *did*.

"I think you are right, Marzel," he said. "If you could bring me the costed estimates, in . . ."

"Three days time, honored sir."

"Three days, that would be excellent."

They parted with the usual flowery Islander protestations of mutual esteem; this time they were sincere. As the Islander left, Adrian rose to circle the ship model on the table once more. It showed a craft halfway between a galley and a merchant ship, perhaps five times longer than it was wide. The bow ended in a ram shaped like a cold chisel, and there were neither oars nor sail. Instead two great bladed wheels revolved on either side, and the hull was covered over wholly by a turtlelike deck. Octagons covered that in turn like the scales of some great serpent, marking where the hand-hammered iron plates would go. The upper curve was broken by two smokestacks, one to the left and one to the right; between them was a low circular deckhouse, with slits all around for vision.

Esmond rose from the corner where he had been sitting silently. "Brother," he said gently. "Will this really *work?*"

"I don't know," Adrian said. "I *think* it will. The gunpowder worked . . ."

"Yes." Esmond paused. "I know I haven't been much help to you . . . much help since Vanbert," he said hesitantly.

Adrian turned and gripped his shoulders. "Oh, no— just saved my life half a dozen times in the retreat, got us all out alive, got us a ship, rushed around like Wodep would if he had enough sense to listen to the Gray-Eyed . . ."

"Brother, I'm worried about you," the taller of the Gellerts said bluntly. "I don't . . . I've known you all my life. Yes, you're the smarter of us, and yes, you're a Scholar the Grove could be proud of—but all these, these *things* you've been coming up with since Father died . . ."

"These *things* are our only chance of revenge on

the Confederacy," Adrian said, with a peculiar inward wrench. *I cannot tell the truth even to my brother, who is not only the brother of my blood but the brother of my heart,* he knew. First, Esmond would simply be horrified that his brother had gone mad. And even if he *believed,* would he *understand?* The concepts had been hard enough for Adrian, and he had two disembodied intelligences speaking directly to him.

He thrust aside certain fears that had come to him in the night, now and then. *What if I am truly mad? What if these are demons, such as the ancient stories tell of?*

Esmond's face hardened. "You're right," he said. "I thank the *gods* that you've stumbled on these things." A smile. "Forgive my weakness."

"I'd forgive you far more than a concern for me, Esmond."

The cry was a huge shout, like a battle trumpet. Adrian Gellert shot out of the low soft bed as if he had been yanked out with cords, not fully conscious until he realized he was standing barefoot on cold marble with the dagger he kept under the pillow naked in his hand.

*Nothing,* he thought. Nothing but the night sounds of Chalice, insects, birds, the soft whisper of water in the fountain that plashed in the courtyard below, a watchman calling out as his iron-tipped staff clacked on paving stones.

Then a woman screamed; that was close, just down the corridor. Adrian was out the door of his bedroom in seconds, feet skidding on the slick stones of the floor. One of the Lowissons' guards was there not long after him, likewise in nothing but his drawers, looking foolish with his shaved head showing—no time to don the turban—but a curved sword ready in his

hand. Adrian ignored him, plunging into his brother's
room. The door rebounded off his shoulder and
crashed against the jamb and Adrian's gaze skittered
about. The room was dark—even the nightlight in the
lamp by the bed had gone out. Then it grew a bright
greenish cast, as Center amplified the light that was
reaching his retinas. Even then Adrian's skin crawled
with the revulsion that brought, but there was no time
for anything but business now.

Esmond Gellert was sitting up in bed, his muscular
chest heaving and sheening with sweat. His eyes were
wide and staring, and cloth ripped in the hand that held
a pillow. An Islander woman crouched naked against
the far wall, sobbing.

"He was asleep!" she cried, looking blindly to the
door. "I did my best, I swear!"

"Go," Adrian said gently in her language, rising from
his crouch and letting the dagger fall along one leg.
"Go, now. This is not your fault."

She scuttled out, scooping up clothing as she went.
Adrian moved over to the bedside. "Esmond," he said
sharply. "Esmond, it's me. What's the matter?"

His elder brother shook himself like a dog coming
out of a river. "A dream," he muttered softly. "It must
have been a dream. My oath, what a dream . . ."

"What dream, Esmond?" Adrian said carefully.

"Nanya," he said. "The fire . . ." His face changed,
writhing. "They'll *burn*."

"Who will burn?"

"Vanbert. The Confeds. *All* of them. They're going
to burn, *burn*."

"Esmond, it's late. Do you think you can sleep now?"

Esmond shook himself again, and something like
humanness returned to his eyes. "What . . . oh, sorry,
brother. Bit of a bad dream. Yes, it's going to be a long
day."

✧          ✧          ✧

"The man will be impaled, otherwise," Casull said. "He is a criminal."

Adrian sighed; it was not something he wanted to do, but on the other hand . . . well, *he'd* rather be shot than have a sharpened wooden stake up the anus, if he had to choose.

King Casull was present, and his eldest son Tenny— a twenty-year-old version of his father, except that there was a trace of softness around the jaw, of petulance in the set of his mouth. There were a scattering of Islander admirals as well, ships' captains, mercenary officers, and an interested score or so of Adrian's own Emerald slingers. Three of them were serving as the arquebus' crew. Adrian squinted against the bright sunlight; the first target was floating on a barge twenty yards away, tied to a stake and with a Confed infantry shield set up before him. Royal guardsmen kept the crowds well away from this section of the naval dockyards.

"These have two-man crews," Adrian went on. "They load . . . thus."

He nodded to his men. The weapon was clamped into a tripod with a pivot joint. The gunner pushed on the butt, and the weapon spun around. He seized and held the muzzle, while the loader bit open a paper cartridge and rammed it and the eight-ounce lead ball down the long barrel. Then he spun it again, taking a horn from his belt.

"You see, lord King, the small pan on the right side? That is where the fine-ground *priming powder* goes. Then this hammer with the piece of flint in its jaws goes back . . ."

"Ah, yes," Casull said. "A flint-and-steel—the sort travellers use."

"Yes, lord King. The flint strikes this portion of the L-shaped steel, pushing it back from over the pan— the sparks fall down onto the powder—the powder burns, the flame goes through a small hole into the barrel and ignites the main charge."

He raised his voice a little. "Gentlemen, there will be a loud crack, a little like thunder."

There were alert nods, dark eyes bright with interest. *You know,* he thought, *this Kingdom of the Isles would seem to be a better place to start "progress" than the mainland. They're a lot less . . . hidebound, I think you'd say.*

**no,** Center said. There was more than the usual heavy certainty to its communication. **this culture is too intellectually amorphous.**

Adrian felt a familiar baffled frustration. Raj cut in: *Sure, they'll take and use anything that looks useful. But they're pure pragmatists. Your Emerald philosophers have gotten themselves into a trap—staring up their own arses and trying to find first causes in words, in language. But at least they* think *about the structure of things; so do the Confeds, when they think at all—they caught it from you. The Islanders just aren't interested; to them, everything you've shown is just a wonderful new trick, to be thrown into the grab bag.*

**accurate, if loosely phrased,** Center said.

*Hmmm,* Adrian thought. This time he felt the wonderful tension-before-release mental sensation of *almost* grasping a concept; it was like sex just before orgasm, only better. *But they have a lot of . . . what was that phrase? Social mobility?*

**correct,** Center said. **if anything, an excessive amount.**

*Sure, you can get ahead, here,* Raj said. *But you can't* stay *ahead. Everything here turns on the fall of the dice; the ruler's favor, a lucky pirate raid. This place is as unstable as water, while the mainland's set in granite. You can carve granite into a new shape, though; water will just run through your fingers.*

Adrian shook himself back to the world of phenomena; the mental conversation had only taken a few seconds, but he was attracting looks. Most of them were tolerantly amused; the Scholars of the Grove had a solid reputation for otherworldly abstraction.

*If only they knew,* he thought to himself. Aloud: *"Fire!"*

The gunner carefully squeezed the trigger. There was a *chick-shsss* as the hammer came down and the priming caught in a little sideways puff of fire and dirty-white smoke. Then: *Bdannggg* as the arquebus fired; the cloud of smoke from the main charge was enough to hide the target from Adrian's eyes for a second. Esmond gave a silent whistle of relief beside him; the bullet hadn't missed. Casull's eyebrows went up as well, and the Islander grandees were laughing and slapping Adrian on the back; eight ounces of high-velocity lead had smashed a hole the size of a fist through the Confed shield, through metal facing and plywood and tough leather, and then removed the entire top of the target's head in a spatter of pink-gray froth and whitish bone fragments.

Adrian swallowed. "So, you see, my lord King," he said. "Many such arquebusiers could sweep the decks of an enemy ship, beyond the effective range of archers."

"But not beyond the range of catapults and ballistae," Casull said. "Still, a dreadful weapon, yes. These . . . arquebuses? Arquebuses, yes—they can fire faster than catapults, and we can put more of them on a ship. The Confed marines have always been our problem, the Sun God roast their balls; we're better seamen, but as often as not they swarm aboard and take the ship that rams them."

"Lord King, I'm just getting started," Adrian said with

a grin. "Next is a much larger version of the arquebus, for use against ships and fortresses."

The King's dark eyebrows looked as if they were trying to crawl into his widow's peak. "Show me!" he commanded.

"This is the weapon," Adrian said, signalling. A half-dozen of his men dragged it over; a bronze tube seven feet long, mounted on a low four-wheeled carriage of glossy hardwood. "I call it a *cannon.*"

The barge teams in the military harbor were busy again; this time they towed out a small and extremely elderly galley. It was listing, and the dockyard workers had stripped it of most of its fittings; they anchored it to a buoy two hundred yards out in the harbor.

Meanwhile Adrian's men were busy around the gun. Adrian gave Casull a running commentary: "First, as you see, lord King, a linen bag full of the *gunpowder* is pushed down the hollow—the barrel. A wad of felt goes in next, to hold it in place."

The crew shoved the bag home with a long pole, grunting in unison as they slammed it down. "Now the gunner runs a long steel needle through the *touch-hole*, to pierce the bag, and fills the touch-hole and this little pan on top of the gun with *priming powder*—finely ground."

"And here is what the cannon will hurl," he said. The team paused for a second to let the King see what they were doing.

"A bronze ball?" Casull said. "Wouldn't stone do just as well, and be much cheaper?"

"We will use stone balls to strike fortress walls," Adrian said. Cast iron would have been better still, but the only furnaces capable of making it were in Vanbert, and not many of them. All the ironworks in the Islands were what Center called *Catalan forges*, turning out wrought iron.

"But this is a *shell*, lord King," Adrian amplified.

"You mean it's hollow?"

"My lord sees as clearly as the eye of the Sun God. It is filled with the gunpowder, and this"—he pointed to a wooden plug in the side of the metal ball, with a length of cord through it—"is the *fuse*. It is a length of cord soaked in saltpeter; when the cannon fires, the main charge lights it. Then in ten seconds, the cord burns through to the charge in the middle."

While they spoke the crew had been fixing the cannon's tackle to bollards sunk in the stone of the dock, and aiming it with handspikes and main force. The gunner glared down the barrel with its simple notch-and-blade sights, then stepped back and adusted the wedge under the breech of the cannon that controlled its elevation.

"If my lord wishes, he may fire the first shot," Adrian said, bowing. "If it please my lord King, please stand well to one side—the cannon will move backward rapidly when it is fired. And," he went on, raising his voice for the assembled dignitaries, "this time the noise will be *much* louder."

Casull was grinning like a shark as he brought the length of slowmatch at the end of the long stick down on the little pile of fine powder. It caught with a long *sssshshshshs*, and an appreciable fraction of a second later . . .

*BAMMMMM!*

This time some of the Islander magnates took startled steps back, mouthing curses or prayers. The gun leapt back until the breeching ropes brought it up with a twang, belching a cloud of smoke shot through with a knife blade of red fire. The wind had picked up, and the smoke swept to one side in good time to see splinters and chunks of frame pinwheeling up from the target galley. Then three seconds later there was another *crack*, muffled by the wood the shell was embedded in. A quarter of the light galley's side exploded outward;

when the smoke cleared from *that*, it was already listing to one side . . . and burning.

Casull gave a whoop and hiked up his robe in one hand, snapping his fingers and hopping through the first steps of a bawdy *kodax* dance; one could see he'd been a sailor long before he was King. His son stood blinking, red spots on pale cheeks; the buccaneer admirals and mercenary commanders were swearing, spitting, thumping each other on the back.

The King stopped first, pausing to turn and shake a fist to the east. "Now see who goes to the bottom, you turnip-eating peasants!" he shouted.

Then he turned to Adrian, eyes snapping. "What else have you for me, O Worker of Wonders?"

Adrian smiled thinly; the problem with getting the reputation for being a magician was that he had to live up to it, and when they expected him to be infallible . . . Esmond was looking hungrily at the burning galley and a slow, deep smile was spreading over his face.

"There are two other types of shot the cannon can fire, lord King," he said. "Solid stone balls, heavy basalt or granite. Those will pound down the walls of forts, as catapults might, but since they strike much harder from further away, they do it quicker. The other is *case-shot*. It's a leather bag full of lead balls, like the arquebus fires, but a hundred of them. Imagine them flung out in a spray, into a dense formation of men— a Confed infantry battalion, or a section of marines about to board."

Casull nodded hungrily. Esmond, from his expression, was imagining precisely that.

"Why didn't you make these for the Confed nobles you were working for?" the monarch asked.

"First, lord, I didn't have time. Second, they didn't take me seriously enough to give me what I needed. These cannon take a lot of bronze, and bronze is expensive—this one twenty-four pounder takes more than two *tons* of bronze."

Casull grunted as if belly-punched, losing a little of his joy. "That *is* something to think on," he said. "Not just the money, but the bronze itself—there isn't all that much around, we'll have to import . . ." He clapped Adrian on the shoulder again. "Still and all, you've done all that you promised and more. And there is still another wonder to lay the world at my feet?"

*Hardly ambitious at all, all of a sudden, isn't he?* Raj observed.

Adrian nodded—to both the entities he was communicating with. "Yes, my King. The next is a small taste of what a full-scale steam-propelled ship will be . . ."

He heard a *chuff . . . chuff . . . chuff . . .* sound. The twelve oar launch he'd converted came into view. Murmurs arose from the Islander chiefs; they *understood* the sea and ships. He could see them pointing out the rudder and tiller arrangement he'd rigged, debating its merits, and then there were louder murmurs as they realized that the launch was heading directly into the wind at seven knots, throwing back white water from both sides of its prow as well as the wheels that thrashed the harbor surface to foam on either side. Black smoke puffed in balls from the tall smokestack secured like a mast with staywires to fore and aft.

"Think of a full-sized ship, my lord," Adrian said. "Her decks covered over with a timber shell and iron plates, and with an iron-backed ram. No vulnerable oars, impossible to board, free of wind, tide and current . . ."

Casull was a fighting man who'd spent most of a long life waging war at sea, or preparing to.

"Tell me more," he said, breathing hard.

# S I X

"Pity you didn't get an opportunity to try out your new toys at sea," Esmond said.

"This will do," Adrian said.

The archipelago ruled—ruled more or less; from which they collected protection money, at least—by the Directors of Vase was considerably smaller than the one centered on Chalice. Few of the islands in it had enough area to grow crops, and they were low-lying and therefore dry, covered in open forest and scrub rather than jungle. To balance that there were mines, the fishing in the shallow waters round about was excellent, and they were a very convenient location for raids on the mainland. Vase was the largest, and the only one which looked like giving the Royal forces any sustained resistance.

"I can see why," Adrian said, bracing a hand against the mast of the transport, where it ran through the maintop. He'd been at sea long enough now to sway naturally with the motion of the ship, exaggerated by the sixty-foot height of the mast. They were both used to the bilge stink and the cramped quarters by now as well, and the unmerciful heat of the reflected sun that had tanned them both several shades darker.

"This is a tough nut," he said to his brother.

Esmond grunted agreement. "Harbor shaped like a U," he murmured, half to himself. "Steep rocky ground all around—absolute bitch getting men up those, never mind the walls at the top. Let's see . . . harbor wall just back from the docks, looks like it started out as a row of stone warehouses. Streets—tenement blocks, mansions, whatever, all bad—then the citadel itself on that low ridge."

Esmond squinted carefully, then looked down at the map King Casull's spies had provided. "Now, that's interesting," he said.

"What is?"

"This shows a ruined tower back of the rear wall of the citadel—unoccupied. Careless of them."

Adrian peered over his brother's armored shoulder. "That commands the citadel walls?" he said.

"Looks like. It's a thousand yards from the rear wall of the citadel, say a quarter-mile from the inner face of the works facing the harbor," he said. "Hmmm. Well out of bow and slingshot, of course, and you couldn't mount a useful number of torsion machines there."

He looked up, and for a moment his grin made him look young again, the youth who'd stood to be crowned at the Five Year Games. "But they don't know about your toys, do they?"

***Smart lad, your brother,*** Raj said. ***He's got a real eye for the ground. That's extremely important— nobody fights battles on a tabletop, and a rise of six feet can be crucial.***

"No, they don't," Adrian said, smiling back. *Oh, shit,* he thought to himself.

King Casull looked up at the burning fortress at the outer harbor mouth of Vase. It was a low massive blocky building, set cunningly into the rocky crags and scree, well placed to rain down arrows and burning oil and naphtha on any force trying to scramble up the gravel and boulder-littered slopes to its gates. That had helped it not at all when the shells from Adrian Gellert's mortar landed behind the battlements. A thick column of greasy black smoke rose, heavy with the scent of things that should not burn, a smell he was intimately familiar with comprised of old timber, paint, leather, cloth, wine, cooking oil, human flesh.

"How do you advise we assault the town and citadel, General Gellert?" he asked.

"If it please my lord the King," Esmond said, "we'll send in the *gunboats* now."

Those were waiting beside the royal galley, keeping station with occasional strokes of their oars. Ten of those to a side, with two men on each; the single cannon fired forward, over the bows; a long inclined wooden slide reached backward to nearly amidships, letting the weapon run in when it was fired or be lashed over the center of gravity when the gunboat was at sea. The crews waved respectfully as they saw the royal eyes fall on them.

"And we'll send the troop transports close behind. The cannon will fire solid shot until they've battered down a gate, or a suitable breach in a wall."

Casull nodded; it was often better to break down a wall, if you could—the rubble provided a natural ramp for assault troops, and gates usually had nasty dogleg irregularities and unpleasant surprises waiting for a storming party.

"That will give us the town," Esmond said. "But the guns are large—getting them up to the inner edge of the Directors' citadel, that will be difficult. Most of it's within bowshot of the walls, and all of it's within range of the boltcasters."

He nodded towards Vase. Two tall semicircular towers

rose from the edges of the citadel facing the town. That was a curve itself; the whole inner complex where the ruler resided was shaped like an irregular wedge of pie, with the palace and keep occupying the outer, narrow tip.

"Well, my lord King," Esmond said. "My brother and I have thought up something that may distract the men on the battlements quite considerably."

"Here you are, sir," the transport captain said.

Adrian nodded, modeling his expression on the one Esmond used. *Firm, confident, in charge, but not hostile or remote,* he told himself.

Men were going ashore in relays; the little semicircle of beach was too small to take the ship, or more than a few score at a time. *Three hundred men* didn't seem like too many, until he saw them all together like this. A hundred of the Sea Strikers had gone ashore first: Esmond's security detachment—light infantry with sword, buckler and javelin. The two hundred arquebusiers and grenade slingers were following more slowly, burdened with their heavy weapons and ammunition. Adrian heard a thump and a volley of curses from the netting on the side of the ship where men climbed down into the boats. *Long, clumsy* and *heavy,* he amended to himself.

Beyond the little cove rose stony hills covered in thorny scrub . . . and beyond those, the ruined tower where he was supposed to "amuse" the enemy and keep them from hindering the main assault. Adrian shook the captain's hand, adjusted his satchel of grenades, and swung over the bulwark himself.

"Feet here, sir," one of the Emerald slingers said cheerfully.

"What's that *sound?*"

"Ninety-*nine*, one *hundred*," Helga Demansk said, completing the series of sit-ups.

"Oh, *stop* that, Helga and come look," Keffrine said.

The woman who'd once been the pampered daughter of a Confederation Justiciar unhooked her feet from the back of the chair and padded over to the high barred window. If she stood on tiptoe, she could see some of the rooftops of Vase, down from the citadel. If she sprang up and gripped the bars, she could see a good deal more. She did, jumping nearly her own height and holding herself up easily, shaking tawny hair out of her eyes and peering against the bright light of morning reflecting off sea and roof tile.

"Oh, you're so *strong*," Keffrine said, batting her eyes upward. "Don't you think you should have a back rub, after all that exercise, though?"

"Can it, Keffie," Helga replied with a half-amused, half-exasperated twist of her lips. "I'm not that desperate yet."

"I can wait," the younger girl grinned. "Nobody's going anywhere."

Helga suppressed a shudder at that; even when the Director died, nobody in the hareem would go anywhere but into retirement . . . which meant they'd be shut up together until the last of them died of old age, and they'd never see another entire male until the day they did die—not even a loathsome toad like the Director. She pushed her mind back into the present, recoiling from the waste of years that stretched ahead. It could be worse; not so many generations ago, the hareem of an Islander magnate accompanied him to the tomb, with a cup of hemlock if they were lucky.

*I wonder what that noise is?* Helga thought. And: *Sky-Father Almighty, I'm* tired *of waiting.*

She hadn't thought that being sold into the hareem of a pirate chief would be tedious—other things, but not that. The Director of Vase was an old, fat, worried, overworked pirate chief, though, with the fifty concubines that custom and prestige demanded. After the brutality of the pirate crew—exactly according to legend—and the transit here, she'd thought that a deliverance . . . for the first four months in this velvet-cushioned, lavender-scented prison where nothing, absolutely nothing ever happened. There was a pool, where she could swim about six paces; there were a few chess sets and card decks; there were no books at all—it would never occur to an Islander chief that a woman would want to *read*. After a full year, only keeping up her training regimen and pretending she was going to escape had preserved her sanity and kept her from strangling someone at the seven hundredth repetition of the same inane gossip, the same shrill giggling at the same stupid jokes, the same fatuous cow-eyed flirting, the same . . .

Being summoned to the Director's quarters at least meant she got *out* for an evening, even if under guard. Usually the old heap of lard couldn't do anything anyway.

"Smoke from the harbor," Helga said meditatively. "And I think I can hear . . . yes, that's an alarm drum."

There was a section of garden and wall below the window, just visible. A dozen men trotted through it; archers, in brass-scale hauberks and spiked helmets, led by an officer with his saber drawn.

The young Confed woman released the bars and dropped back, her lips shaping a soundless whistle.

"War, I think," she said. "Wasn't there a rumor that the Director was having trouble with the King in Chalice?"

Keffrine nodded eagerly, blond bangs swinging around her ears and releasing a strong waft of verbena. Helga wrinkled her nose a little; she still didn't like the way Islander women slathered themselves with scent. That and cosmetics were the main pastimes here, along with intrigue and love affairs; one couldn't even dress up much, since tradition mandated hareem occupants wear filmy trousers and spangled halter tops.

"Isn't it *exciting*?" Keffrine squealed.

Helga sighed. *Well, what can you expect.* Keffrine was a gift from Sub-Director Deneuve, and born in *his* hareem. This sort of environment was all she'd ever known. *And I thought I'd led a sheltered life.*

"It may get more exciting than you'd like," Helga said. "Come on, we'd better go talk to the Eldest Sister."

The old bat was a harridan of the first order, but she'd been here since the Director was sixteen, and he *told* her things. If anyone knew . . .

"Yes, let's!" Keffrine grabbed her hand and pulled her out into the corridor, past arches and mosaics, into the main circular room where a dozen or so of the others lounged on couches, nibbled snacks, or paddled languidly in the pool about the carved youth whose seashell spouted warm scented water. The light from above was filtered through a fretwork stone dome.

Helga felt her heart beat faster. *More exciting than they'd care for,* she thought. *But any change is an opportunity. I've been here far, far too long.*

Keffrine was really starting to look tempting, for instance.

*Far, far too long.*

"Oh, what a beautiful, beautiful position," Simun wheezed.

Adrian nodded, breathless himself despite being twenty years younger and less burdened. The tower was ruined in the sense that some of the internal floors had collapsed, fire or rot destroying the beams. The central spiral staircase was stone, though, and still reasonably sound. So was the uppermost floor, and the crenellations were still waist-high. That would give the arquebusiers cover and excellent rests for their weapons; they were setting up now, with a little amiable squabbling for the best shooting spots. The infantry from the Sea Strikers had taken up ground around the tower's base, blending in to the maquis-covered slopes. The air had a slight brimstone smell from the black powder in grenades and cartridge boxes, and a wild spicy scent of crushed herbs from the ground around. It was warm now, and insects buzzed through the flowers; fliers darted by snapping at them.

Vase was laid out before them like a relief map, too— he could see men hurrying in and out of the two towers that anchored the citadel's harborward wall, others massing on the wall itself, still more movement in the narrow twisting streets beyond. Overhead the sky was a hot white-blue; he could even see the banners snapping on the gunboats in the harbor beyond, and the foam where the measured centipede stroke of their oars churned up the water. As he watched, a puff of smoke came from the lead craft. A measurable time later the flat deep *thudump* reached his ears, like a very large door slamming far away. A slightly louder explosion came from among the warcraft packed along the docks in front of the sea wall; they were firing shell initially, then. Smoke and fragments vomited up over the harbor defenses, and a slender galley began to burn and sink at its moorings, spine snapped. It couldn't sink far, in water only six feet deep under its keel, but that served to put the fire mostly out.

By the time the fourth round had hit, the remaining crews were scrambling ashore, tiny as ants as they swarmed through the sally ports next to the main gates.

"Ah, already spooked from the forts at the outer harbor, sor," Simun chuckled. "Ah, this is a fight how I loik it, sor," the middle-aged mercenary went on. "No risk, none of that there nasty hand-to-hand stuff."

Adrian smiled in turn. *Odd,* he thought. This man and he had as little in common as two beings of the same species, gender and nationality could, yet in a way they'd become good friends . . .

**Comes of risking your lives together, son,** Raj

thought, amused. *One of the things that, unfortunately, makes war possible.*

"Sort of a commentary on humankind, I suppose," Adrian muttered.

"What was thot, sor?"

"Just regretting you weren't a beautiful woman, underofficer," he said briskly.

Simun chuckled. "Well, then I'd be out of place here, eh, sor? Place for everything, yis, yis." He looked at the minarets, domes, gardens of the palace citadel ahead of them. "Though they say hareem girls smells tasty enough, yis. Hey, sor, you oughtn't to be doing that, now!"

Adrian ignored the hand that anchored the back of his weapons belt as he leaned over the crumbling sawtooth outer wall of the tower. "Simun," he said sharply. "Take a look there—do you see a mark in the ground there, leading from the tower to the citadel wall?"

The noncom respectfully but firmly pulled him back, then leaned over and peered himself. "Hmmm, now that you point it out sor, so I do, indeed. Old wall, mebbe? Hard to see why, though—just the one—tis not a walled way to this here tower, that would make sense, though . . ."

Adrian craned his neck. The line through the scrub was irregular, as much a trace-mark in the vegetation as anything, an absence of the low thorny scrub trees in the middle and a thicker line of them on either side.

He froze as Center's icy presence seized his eyes. For a moment the world became a maze of lines and points and moving dots, a glimpse of something too vast and alien for him to comprehend. Then it settled down to a schematic—clear white lines outlining the trace through the slope, and a cross-diagram beside it showing a tunnel with an arched stone roof.

**covered way, sunken to escape detection.** The

machine intelligence sounded inhumanly confident
. . . but then, it always did, even when confessing a
rare error. **since the tower went out of regular use,
the initial covering of soil has partly eroded from
the upper surface of the ceiling.**

"Yes, by the Gray-Eyed Lady!" Adrian said.

Simun was looking at him with mingled alarm and
expectation—the Gray-Eyed was also a Goddess of War;
more precisely, of stratagem and ploy, as opposed to
Wodep's straightforward violence. Adrian knew that the
Emerald mercenaries they'd brought with them thought
he communed with Her regularly; Esmond's new troops
were picking up the superstition rapidly.

"That's a tunnel—a covered way into the citadel,"
Adrian said.

"Oh, *ho*!" Simun said. "First in, first pickings . . . no,
sor, though, even Islanders, they wouldn't leave it
open—not when this here place ain't garrisoned, no,
no."

"We'll take a look," Adrian said. "Can't hurt."

Simun nodded. *Yes, I know Esmond set you as my
watchdog,* Adrian thought without resentment—after all,
he *was* the younger brother, and not trained to war. On
the other hand, curiosity was an Emerald characteris-
tic; where it concerned his trade, even a professional like
Simun had his fair share.

"Oll right, sor, but me'n the squad, we goes along."

"No argument."

"The city of Vase is under attack," the Eldest Sister
said calmly.

A chorus of squeals and giggles died down into
uncertain murmurs as the figure beside the head of the
hareem stepped forward—it was an entire man, one of
the few Helga had seen since she passed through the
door. A soldier, one of the Director's personal guard,
slave soldiers bought in infancy and raised in the

household; armored from head to foot in black-laquered splint mail, with a broad splayed nasal bar on his helmet that hid his face. He rested the point of his huge curved sword on the carpet and folded his hands on the hilt.

"Do not worry!" the stout, robed, middle-aged woman said. "In all things, we will accompany our lord."

Helga was standing well to the back, among the junior and childless members of the hareem—even then she took a moment to thank the Mother Goddess for *that* mercy. Although there was a rumor that all the pregnancies recently were the result of the Director sending in his younger brother under cover of darkness. . . . She was standing shoulder-to-shoulder with Keffrine, and felt the other girl suddenly begin to tremble. Helga decided that she didn't need to hear the rest of the Eldest Sister's speech.

"What is it?" she whispered sharply in her ear, then gave her arm a pinch to shock her out of the wide-eyed stare. "Keffrine, what is it?"

"Wuh—wuh—"

"*Keffrine!*"

A few others glanced at her reprovingly as her voice rose a little. That seemed to bring Keffrine back to herself a little; she dropped her eyes and whispered.

"They think we muh-muh-might *lose*," she said.

"What?"

"What the Eldest Sister said, about accompanying our lord."

"What, into exile? Ransom—"

The guileless blue eyes turned to her, and tears slid down the lovely cheeks.

"No. The Director's honor can't let other men touch his women. They'll cu-cu-cut our th-th—"

Quietly, hopelessly, Keffrine began to sob; she wasn't the only one, either.

*Cut our throats,* Helga Demansk realized; that was the end of the sentence. In more ways than one.

The plug at the end of the tunnel took on the flat, greenish-silvery look that Adrian's vision always did when Center was amplifying the available light. Something about extrapolating from partial data. . . . He shoved away the neck-tensing eeriness and instead tapped on the concrete and rubble with the hilt of his dagger, pressing his ear to listen. Only a dull clink came back through the ear pushed against the porous roughness, but Center spoke with mountainous certainty:

**the blocking segment is from five to eight and a half feet in thickness. beyond it the tunnel resumes with the same dimensions.**

A picture formed in his mind; the covered passageway on the other side of the block, and then a wooden door beyond that—thick with dust and cobwebs.

*How do you* do *that?* he asked.

**echolocation,** Center answered. **your auditory sensors receive much information of which you are not conscious. by calculating the time and angle of sound reflected through and beyond the solid material, i can infer the shapes and relationships of objects.**

*Oh.* Like most of Center's explanations, that raised more questions than it answered—sound could bounce? *Anyway . . .*

**one ten-pound cask of powder emplaced at the base will clear the obstacle,** Center said. **possibility of collapse of tunnel ceiling is 27% ±7.**

"Can't hurt, then," Adrian mused.

*Sure you want to do this, lad?* Raj asked. *It isn't your proper line of work, really.*

Adrian nodded. *My* brother *is out there, under the walls,* he replied firmly, swallowing through the dryness of his mouth and acutely conscious of the smell of wet stone and his own sweat.

"Simun," he said. "Get someone with a pick up

here—two men with picks, and one with a prybar. And a barrel of powder, and—" he consulted his unseen friends "—ten feet of quickmatch. Now!"

The distant thudding sounds were closer now, louder; like nothing so much as thunder. Beneath it Helga Demansk thought she could hear something far less uncanny than thunder from a clear blue sky; a snarling clamor of voices, and the harsh metal-on-metal sound of battle, with an undertone of the flat banging thumps that blades made on shields. The concubines were kneeling silently in rows according to seniority; several more of the black-armored Director's guardsmen had come in. One of them was pale-faced and had a bandage around his forearm; another was limping. The sunlight crawled past under the dappled shade of the dome, the water splashed in the pool, all infinitely familiar sights gilded with a nearly supernatural film of horror now.

Another man came in, the metal heel-plates of his military boots loud on tile and marble, muffled where he traversed colorful rugs. He looked at the guard commander standing above the Eldest Sister, swallowed, and gave a jerky nod.

"It is time," the commander said harshly.

"It is time," the older woman said calmly. "I shall go first, to show my sisters that there is nothing to fear."

She raised her chin. The soldier shook his shoulders back and raised the blade; sunlight broke off the bright edge as he took careful aim and swung with a huffing grunt of effort.

There was a wet cleaving sound. Blood splashed backward over the gilt mosaics of the wall, over young fleecebeasts gamboling in a spring meadow. Keffrine gave a breathless little scream.

"Time to get moving," Helga muttered to herself, and took one last deep breath.

✧          ✧          ✧

"All right," Adrian said to the worried arquebusier. "I'm leaving you the twenty best shots, with all the loaded weapons to hand. They should be able to keep up a respectable fire for half an hour or so, and that's all that we'll need."

The man nodded, saluted, and trotted away back up the stairs. Adrian looked at the other men near him: Simun; Tohmus, the commander of the Sea Striker detachment; the rest of his gunmen, now holding their cutlasses and targets.

"Everyone!" he said. "Be prepared for a very loud—"

*THACRACK!*

Smoke and debris vomited out of the mouth of the tunnel into the basement of the tower, shrouding its dimness and peppering them all with grit and small fragments of rock.

Adrian spoke again, his voice tinny in his own ears after the monstrous blow of the explosion in the tunnel's confined space. "Simun, Tohmus, no crowding. I'll go first."

He plunged in, coughing, waving a futile hand in front of himself. The breeze was strong from the seaward, from the blocked end of the passageway— previously blocked now—smelling of patchouli oil and flowers under the sulfur stink of the powder. The plug was scattered in toe-stubbing chunks for a hundred yards back from where it had spanned the tunnel, bits of it having bounced off the curves in the walls. Beyond it was the chamber Center's eerie sound-vision had shown, but the doors beyond were splinters hanging from twisted hinges. Ahead was a long sloping corridor, then a staircase with sunlight filtering down from above.

And barrels on either side; one was smashed, and the rich fruity odor of wine filled the confined space. Above the casks hung hams in nets, bunches of herbs, sacks of fruit . . .

"Gellerix's *cunt*," whispered Simun, beside him. "Anrew, Mattas, you pick six reliable men and *guard* this, you hear me?" To Adrian: "Sorry, sor—don't want to tempt the lads mor'n's right. And sor? Might be an idea to draw yor sword now."

Adrian did, gripping the little brass-rimmed buckler with his left hand. He peered around. "Storerooms . . ."

Center strobed one of the lateral corridors giving off the big arch-roofed cellar. There was an ironbound door set into the wall there, with a massive lock—rare and expensive.

"Simun, put that under guard too—I think it'll bear investigation. We'll keep going straight up," he said, indicating the stairwell.

Keffrine was still sobbing, her eyes squeezed shut and tears leaking out from under them. Helga waited . . .

. . . and a dozen women broke and bolted as the soldiers approached the front row. *Eldest probably knew they would,* ran through her; that was probably why she'd gone first, to spare herself seeing the indignity. The gathering dissolved into a chaos of running women and harassed, determined guardsmen. Blades began to flash, not in the orderly execution planned but in a frenzy, men slashing at figures that ran by or trembled and pled.

Helga moved herself; sideways, to where a tall fretted-brass brazier sent a coil of incense upwards. She gripped it by the base and heaved, toppling the man-high structure against the wall. Glowing embers scattered into gauzy hangings, and flames began to lick upward.

"Fire!" she screamed in Islander. "Fire!"

A guardsman had been approaching, blade in hand. He looked aside—no sailor or town dweller but had a healthy dread of uncontrolled flame—and when he

looked back he met the second brazier full in the face
as she swung it two-handed. Brass met flesh and bone
with a loud *thock*. Helga scooped up the falling sword;
it was a different shape from the ones she was used
to, and too heavy, but that didn't stop her short efficient
jab up under his chin.

"Come *on*," she shouted to Keffrine, and grabbed her
by one hand. Trailing the sobbing girl, she bolted for
the exit to the basement storerooms.

"Keep the men well in hand," Adrian said.

Screams were coming from the room at the head of
the stairs. *Women's* screams, but also men's shouts, and
the distinctive, unpleasant sound of steel driving into
flesh.

"Let's *go!*"

The noises ahead were loud enough that it was several heartbeats before anyone noticed the enemy surging
up through the passageway. Adrian had time to check
his rush a step in sheer astonishment at the sight before
him; a room floridly overdecorated even by Islander
standards, full of running, screaming women—*dying*
women—and soldiers in black-lacquered armor trying
to butcher them all. Dozens down on the floor, wounded
or dead; a nauseating mixture of smells: perfume, flowers, blood, shit . . .

And right in front of him, one of the women *fighting*
a pair of soldiers. An auburn-haired woman, one he'd
swear was Confed-born, not an Islander. Not doing
badly at all, either—

She beat aside a thrust, both hands on the hilt of
the long saber. The other soldier lunged as well, at a
smaller blond woman by the first one's side, and the
point of his blade slammed out her back. The redhead
screamed and slashed him across the face, blood and
a spark where the blade grated off the nasal bar of the
killer's helmet.

"*Get* the hell out of the way—sir!" someone shouted in Adrian's ear.

Men poured past him. He leapt forward himself, batted the saber of the man fighting the redhead aside and lunged with his own basket-hilted, Emerald-style sword. The black-armored man vanished in the melee; a second later Adrian saw him toppling into the fountain pool in the center of the room with a javelin through his neck. The fighting was brief, three mercenaries against an Islander here, four there—overwhelming numbers. The screaming didn't stop, and now he saw his own men chasing the women. They obviously didn't have butchery on their minds, but—

"You!" he said. One had grabbed the auburn-haired woman—girl—from behind, hands over her breasts. "You! Release that woman!"

"Wait yer turn—" the mercenary began.

**Get them in hand now, or you never will,** Raj said.

"Right."

Adrian took two steps forward and smashed the hilt of his sword into the would-be rapist's face. Bone crumbled under the blow, with a tooth-grating yielding feeling. He had time to see the woman's face go slack with surprise, and then he tossed her his sword to clear his hand.

He hooked a grenade out of his pouch, the ceramic cool and pebbly under his fingers. His other hand whipped the slowmatch from its covered metal holder on his belt, twirled it to make the lit end glow brightly, touched off the fuse. He waited three seconds, and then tossed it gently underhand into the pool.

*THUDUMP.*

Water—and bits of the dead man dangling over the fountain—sprayed through the room. The water prevented the fragments from being deadly . . . or not very deadly.

Silence fell in the echoing aftermath of the explosion. Adrian held the slowmatch next to the fuse of another grenade.

"If discipline is not restored immediately," he said, half-surprised at the calmness of his own voice under the enormous reined-in tension, "I am going to light this grenade and drop it in the pouch."

"We'd all be killed!" one of the Sea Strikers wailed.

"That's the idea." Adrian nodded. "We have a battle to fight, and it's *that* way. Anyone have a problem with that?"

"No, sir."

There was a general chorus of agreement, and men who'd seized women released them, forming up and heading for the doors.

"Simun."

The little mercenary came up, limping and pressing the tail of his tunic against a slash wound along one thigh—a vulnerable point in light-infantry armor, protected only by the studded leather strips of the military kilt.

"Simun, get some of the walking wounded together. Police this area, get the surgeon working . . . oh, he is."

The man had half a dozen of the more seriously wounded lying on improvised pallets, and twice that number of the hareem's occupants. Some of the hale ones were tearing up sheets to help him.

"Anyway, keep things under control."

Simun nodded. "Good choice, sor," he said. "Cut like this, Gellerix 'erself couldn't tempt me."

"I'll be with the unit," Adrian went on. "See you when it's over."

"I'm coming too."

Adrian looked around, startled, and met level green eyes. The auburn-haired girl offered him his sword; she'd taken a similar weapon from one of the dead, and

a small buckler. The filmy hareem costume was plastered to her, mostly with blood, and there were smudges
of it across her face where she'd bound back the russet-
colored hair with a strip of cloth.

"Miss—"

"Fuck that," she said. She was speaking Emerald, with
a slight Confed accent—upper-class Confed, he realized.
"I'm a . . . soldier's daughter, and I've been here an
Almighty Allfather-cursed *year*, and I'm going to *kill*
some of these Islander bastards."

"Soldier's daughter?" Adrian said.

"Name's Helga. My father . . . fought with Justiciar
Demansk's armies."

Things clicked behind Adrian's upraised eyebrows.
**She's really not bad with a sword,** Raj mentioned.

That meant she *wasn't* what she'd implied, the
daughter of some long-service Confed trooper. Women
of that class didn't train with the sword—certainly not
in the classic Emerald style. Some rich young women
did; it had been quite the craze for the last couple of
years, much to the scandal of the conservative nobility.
A few had even appeared in the Vanbert Games, first-
blood matches, until a reforming Justiciar had outlawed
the practice. *Noblewoman,* he thought.

**observe,** Center said.

A grid formed over her face, countour lines sprang
out. Justiciar Demansk's face appeared beside it, and
arrows sprang out to mark points of resemblance.
**allowing for gender, probability of close genetic
relationship is 97%, ±1,** Center said. **as near unity
as a hasty analysis permits.**

*And Demansk . . . one of his* daughters *was taken
in a pirate raid, and not ransomed,* Adrian thought.
Demansk had several sons, but that was the only
daughter he'd ever heard of . . .

The analysis had taken half a dozen seconds. "All
right, Miss Helga," he said crisply. "You may rest

assured of my protection." The courtly phrase seemed oddly out of place in this room of gilding and blood. "But keep close to me and don't get in the way."

"I won't," she said. The sword moved easily in her hand; it was the standard Emerald style, single-edged and with a handguard of bronze strips. "This may get in some other people's way, though."

"They've stopped retreating, sir," Donnuld Grayn panted.

"That's obvious," Esmond said, taking a bite out of the skin of the orange in his hand and tossing another to his second-in-command.

He squeezed the juice into his mouth, pitched the husk aside, and swished his hand in an ornamental fountain before drying it on the skirt of his tunic. The noise of combat grew in the courtyard ahead, and far and faint came the distinctive sound of one of Adrian's grenades. Esmond's grin grew; from the barely-glimpsed tower came another slow, aimed arquebus round. There was a shriek behind him—somewhere on the battlements that he'd bypassed when he took his men straight through the breach in the wall. Amazing what an entire oxcart full of gunpowder run into the ditch in front of the wall would do. The dry moat just focused the hellpowder's power on the stone.

*Little brother's been busy,* he thought, taking up his sword and buckler again, and pulling down the helmet he'd pushed up on his forehead. Trickles of tepid sweat ran down from the sponge lining, and the world shrank to a T-shaped slit of brightness . . . and he felt *alive.* Alive in a way he hadn't, except in combat, since Nanya died.

"Well, what are you lot waiting for?" he said as he came through into the next courtyard.

The Palace of the Directors of Vase was built to the same general plan as the King's house in Chalice, but it was older—older, and less less centrally planned, having grown slowly over centuries. Essentially it was a series of interlocking courtyards, sometimes separated by narrow service alleys, and sometimes as much as three stories tall. Some were elaborate with fountains and mosaics, others workaday storehouses, warehouses, workshops, guard barracks. The one through the arched gate ahead was one of the fancy ones, which was all to the good—the tall fountain in the middle would provide his troops with clean water, once they'd taken it.

"Keep *down*, sir," an officer said.

The men here were, behind the pillars of the arcade that lined the courtyard, moving only in short dashes between points covered by the stone. The movement got thicker as the hundred or so reinforcements he'd brought with him filed in among the stalled assault point element.

"They've got archers over there," the officer continued. *Maklin, that's his name*, Esmond thought. He'd made a point of learning all the officers' names, at least. "They're good, and they're not moving for shit."

Esmond nodded thoughtfully, looking at a couple of bodies out in the open. The black-fletched shafts were driven right through them, scale-reinforced leather corselets or not. From the angle, they'd been hit by men on the second-story balconies fifty yards to the east. Spearheads twinkled among the ground-story columns, ready to receive anyone who'd run the gauntlet of arrowfire across the open space. Many Islander archers used recurved bows, backed with strips from the mouthparts of sea monsters. They had a *heavy* punch, in expert hands.

"We need to get them distracted," he said. "Maklin, get twenty-five men down to each end of this arcade." The arches and pillars ran around all four sides of the courtyard. "Have them work towards the enemy, from pillar to pillar. Donnuld, back out and up, onto the second story—give those fucking bowmen something to think about besides sniping. Take a company."

Esmond waited with a cat's patience while the orders were obeyed. His mind and body felt light, tight, strong; it *was* like the Games, in a way.

"All right, men," he said when he heard the rising panic in the voices from the second story, across the way. An archer leaned far out to shoot at a man dodging from one pillar to the next; while he aimed and drew, a javelin sank into his back, and the body arched out to fall, *thump*, in the courtyard below.

"All right," he said again, raising his voice. "What are you waiting for, the enemy to send you enough arrows to open an archery shop? *Follow me!*"

With the last word he was sprinting out, dodging and jinking, as if this were the running-in-armor event at the Games. *There are times,* he thought, as a bodkin-pointed shaft chipped marble by his right ankle, *when straight up the middle is the only way to go.*

With a roar like the sea striking rocks, the troopers behind him surged out of cover on his heels. He kept well ahead of them until they were almost in contact. A volley of thrown spears came at him; he batted one out of the air with his shield as he curved around the fountain. Then he checked his pace, another, and the Strikers struck the line of Islander spears together.

One slammed forward, aimed for his belly. He swayed aside, his body moving in a single smooth curve, and then punched the boss of his small round shield into the face behind it. Bone crackled; he ignored the wounded man and turned his run into a lunge. The long sword in his right hand slipped into a throat; he twisted and jerked it free against the constriction of spasming muscle. Blood sprayed in an arc like water coming out of a hose as the man turned in a half circle before he fell. A saber slashed at him, motion caught out of the

corner of his eye; Esmond swept his shield around in
a circle, moving it without putting it in front of his face
and blocking his vision. The steel struck and sparked
on the studs in the surface of the leather, wrenching
painfully at the wrist of his left hand. Esmond stabbed
low automatically, stepped forward, beat a spear aside
with his sword and let the blade and shaft slide up his
sword and punched the man behind it in the face with
the guard.

"To me, Strikers!" he shouted. "Push 'em, push 'em!"

They *were* pushing them, in a heaving, thrashing
confusion that swayed backward a step, another step,
another, shouting snarling point-bearded faces and
spearpoints, curved swords, knives. Men locked chest-
to-chest, no room to dodge now, naked extreme violence, blows given and taken. Then they were under
the shade of the arcade's pillars, then past it, and
suddenly the combat broke into knots of men that
spilled out into a big room—an audience hall, like
Casull's back in Chalice.

"Rally, rally!" he called.

Beside him a signaler pulled a horn from his belt and
blew the call. The chaos gradually sifted itself into order,
men coalescing with their comrades, small bands being
overrun, until there were again two distinct bodies of
troops. His grew, as more men filtered in, and the Vase
troops retreated to stand in a clump around the high
throne with its backing of peacock-inlay feathers. Some
of them, he noted with glee, were standing guard at
the *rear* entrances to the room. Adrian was there, right
enough. *How in Wodep's name did he get over the wall?
Think about that later.*

Donnuld Grayn came panting up with his company;
a couple of them were waving inlaid bows and pear-
patterned quivers, or carrying silver-sheathed daggers
on their belts.

"Got those fucking archers," Grayn wheezed. "Couldn't

bear on us much, up there—good idea. Some sort of Director's Guard, I think—lot of 'em were Southrons, war slaves, maybe."

Esmond nodded. "We're through the rind and near the kernel. Let's see how determined this lot are."

"Not too much, I hope," the Cable officer said, rubbing his hands on his kilt to dry them. "Wodep bugger me blind, I've never seen anything like some of the rooms here—Director's palace, all right, a looter's delight."

"Let's get the fight finished first," Esmond said. "Surrender!" he called to the defenders.

A roar of obscene abuse returned, and a scatter of throwing axes, javelins and arrows; men snapped up shields around him as he ducked, and he could hear things clattering off them. One man backed into him involuntarily as a shaft went into his shield with a solid *whack*, the point showing through the tough layers of greatbeast hide and metal facing.

"Where's your leader, then?" Esmond called, straightening again. "Let him come out and face me—if he dares!"

The Emerald was distantly aware of a commotion at his back—Casull's name came through, but the King could wait. A man in his early middle years stepped forward from the crowd of Vase troops, a bloodied saber in one hand and a hacked buckler in the other.

"I am Franzois Clossaw, Director of Vase by right of blood," he called, wiping at a cut on one cheek with the back of a gauntleted hand.

His armor was plain but rich, and looked nicked and battered as the man himself; he had mustaches curled up into points like horns and a pointed beard, but the point had been slashed off at some time today, leaving him looking a little frayed at the edges. *Hmmm,* Esmond thought. According to reports, the Director of Vase was about seventy, and nearly twice this one's weight.

"I thought Antwoin Clossaw was Director," Esmond said in a conversational tone.

"My brother is dead, killed by your coward's weapons of magic. Until the Syndics of Vase can meet and settle the succession, I am Director—and no foreigner shall sit on the throne of Vase while I live!"

"That can be altered," Esmond purred. "I am General Esmond Gellert, commander of the Sea Striker regiment of Emerald Free Companions"—a little more elegant-sounding than *hired killers*—"and thrice victor of the Five Year Games, free citizen of Solinga. Let this be settled here and now."

Franzois swallowed, looked to either side. His men were apparently ready enough to make a last stand . . . but understandably not wildly enthusiastic about it.

"You guarantee the lives of my men if I lose?" he said.

Esmond nodded, and went on at the beginnings of a rumble behind him: "I can't guarantee the lives or estates of your nobles," he said. "That is in the hand of my lord, King Casull of the Isles—of *all* the Isles." The rumble turned to a purr. "But for your common soldiers, yes. Amnesty, and employment for those who'll swear allegiance. They fought quite well, all things considered."

"And if I win, we get safe passage to the harbor."

"Yes," Esmond said. "I so order my underofficers, in the sight of the Gray-Eyed Lady and by my own honor." That would be a hard promise for Casull to break; the regiment would be seriously pissed off if he did. The rumble was back, but he ignored it as he strode out.

"May I see your face?" Franzois said.

Esmond pushed his helmet back, letting the light fall on his features. The Islander smiled.

"Very much the Emerald hero," he said, taking a quick swig from a leather bottle one of his companions handed him. "My great-great—no matter—one of my ancestors fought against the Solingians at the Narrow Straits. He recorded that it wasn't a very good idea."

"My ancestors fought in the League Wars too," Esmond said politely. He took the time to lean his sword against his hip and carefully dry hand and hilt. "Both sides came off with credit, but the Fates spin the thread of every war."

He pulled the helmet back down and brought up sword and buckler, the small shield under his chin and sword advanced. Franzois nodded and took his own stance, slashing-sword up and back, leading with his shield. Esmond watched the way he held his weapons, the movements of his feet, the set of the thick blocky shoulders.

*Fast heavy man,* he thought; *that was rare, and dangerous. Sword's seen a lot of use.*

"Watch *out*, for Allfather's sake!" Helga shouted to Adrian.

The billhook crashed across the surface of her buckler. There was vicious weight and an urgent desire to kill behind the blow from the darkened alcove ahead, nothing like training back on the estate. Her left arm went numb for an instant, then gave a burning throb of pain that agonized from wrist and elbow right up into the shoulder. The weapon—a big straight razor on a six-foot pole, with a spike on top and a hook behind—slammed into the stucco of the courtyard wall, raining lime plaster and brick chips on her, leaving the billman bent over with the staggering surprise of *not* having his momentum stopped by his target. She stepped forward in a passing lunge, drilled reflex, sword out, her whole body taking off from the left foot and slamming forward behind point and arm, right foot coming down and knee flexing to add distance to the stroke. The soft heavy resistance as the point went in over the Vasean's collarbone was still an unpleasant surprise; so was the grating of steel on bone somewhere in the man's body.

So was the backstroke with the butt of the weapon, the iron ferrule thumping painfully into her thigh.

"Ow! *Pigfucker!*" she yelped, twisting and yanking to get her own weapon free.

The blood that splashed over her simply added to the drying, sticky mat that covered her from throat to shins; she'd learned to ignore the smell . . . mostly. With a grunt she braced a foot on the still-twitching body and pulled. There were ugly popping, rending sounds as she did, more felt through the hilt than heard through the ears.

"Don't you ever look where you're going?" she snapped at . . . *Adrian Gellert*, she remembered.

Confed folk wisdom had it that Emeralds had no bottom, no real guts; she'd seen enough today to make her seriously doubt that. It also held that Emerald wisdom lovers would step into a well while looking at the stars, and if Adrian was typical, *that* was pretty much true, at least. Her mouth twisted wryly as she fought to get her breath back. She'd had fantasies of rescue, of course; usually her father, or some handsome well-born young tribune in a crested helmet and figured back-and-breast. This slender young Emerald with the dreamy blue eyes and his air of listening to voices nobody else heard was a bit of a contrast, with his rumpled hair showing around his open-face helmet and bits of the iron plates wearing through the leather of his jack.

*Well, he's certainly good to have around,* she thought, looking out of the corner of her eye at the mercenary troopers crowding forward for the rush into the next courtyard.

Although *they* mostly weren't looking at her like a dog at a porkchop anymore. A couple of them crowed laughter at the sight of her tugging her blade out of the Islander.

"Good work, missy," one grinned. "The lord here needs someone to look after him."

She flushed and turned away at the laughter. "What *is* that stuff?" she asked, nodding at the satchel of round jarlike things at his side, each with its little tail of cord.

"I call them *grenades*," Adrian said absently—that seemed to be his usual manner of speech—and patted them. "They've got a powder inside that I found in certain . . . ancient records, very ancient. It has a number of uses."

"Like those thunder sounds we heard earlier?" she asked.

He looked at her, the absent-mindedness blinking away, and passed her the canteen someone had handed to him. She accepted it and took a pull; the wine that cut the water was nearly vinegar, but it was welcome in the gummy dryness of her mouth.

"Yes, as a matter of fact," he said; it was a second before she noticed he'd switched from his Solingian-accented Scholar's Emerald to a pellucidly pure dialect of patrician-class Vanbert Confed. "It *explodes*—that is, generates a lot of rapidly expanding gas—and pushes away whatever's around it. In the grenades, that pushes fragments of the casing out much faster than an arrow or a sling-bullet. If you put some in a bronze tube sealed at one end, it'll push out a *big* metal or stone bullet—big enough to smash ships or knock down gates and walls."

Helga whistled silently. "Now, won't *that* be useful," she said. "My father's men . . . men of my father's company, that is . . . would call it cheating, though. Not fighting fair."

Adrian shrugged. "I don't like fighting," he said simply. That made her blink again; not many men she knew would admit that—actual *men*, that is. The Emerald went on: "When I do have to fight, I fight to win. Fair fights are for idiots and Con— I mean, for those who are strong enough to be sure they'll win anyway."

Helga nodded slowly. "You know, that makes a lot of sense," she said, and felt herself obscurely pleased at the look in the Emerald's hazel eyes. "Of course, I'm a woman, and we can't afford some of the idiocies men get involved with."

"I see your point," Adrian said, and heaved himself away from the wall he'd been leaning against. "Now, I think there's a fight we—or I, at least—*do* have to engage in calling out."

The noise of combat had died down ahead; she cocked her head. "That's two men fighting," she said. "Odd, almost like a duel." With a quick urchin grin at the Emerald. "And you saved my life, but it looks to me like you need someone by you to return the favor—often."

"That's right, missy," one of the troops said.

"Hear her, lord," another chimed in.

Adrian straightened. "Let's get moving," he said. "Your munificent pay doesn't come for propping up walls." His eyes scanned around, and took on a hint of that distant look again. "This way leads to the throne room. Up one more flight, left, and that's the anteroom—they were probably going to try and get out right this way."

"How does he *know* that?" Helga whispered aside to a man with another satchel of grenades as the commander turned and walked briskly towards the landing at the base of a flight of stairs.

"You'll find Lord Adrian knows most anything he wants," the man said with unshakeable confidence. "The Gray-Eyed Lady speaks to him, y'see."

Helga felt her eyes go wide.

Esmond went into a stop-thrust, then recovered smoothly, turning it into a feint as Franzois beat it aside with his buckler and cut, backhand, forehand, boring in with a stamp-stamp-stamp and a whirling pattern that made a silver X of his sword.

*Right, let's see you keep* that *up,* the Emerald thought grimly as he backed. Normally he didn't think much of the Islander school of swordplay; all edge and dash and no science. Director-for-a-couple-of-hours Franzois was as good a master of that style as he'd come across, though, and thoroughly accustomed to using it against the more point-oriented Emerald blade-way.

He waited, point hovering, backing with an economical shuffle and his feet at right angles. Clang-ting-*clang,* and the saber knocked against his buckler, rang on his blade, shed itself from that with a long *scring* sound and deflected off his helmet and a shoulder piece with bruising force and there was the sting of a slight cut on his upper shoulder.

*Good steel,* he thought absently—to be that shaving-sharp after a long day's work. They had good smiths here in the Isles.

Franzois' face was a deeper purple now, his mouth open below the splayed nasal of his helmet. Esmond waited, backed once more . . . then *lunged,* with all the dense muscle of his weight behind it, the springing power of his rear leg, and a wrist locked to put it all behind the punching tip of the sword.

The Islander stopped, blade still raised for another slash. It came down and faltered weakly as Esmond's point ripped free of his inner thigh. From the sudden arterial rush of blood, he'd cut the big vein there. The Emerald stepped back and raised his sword again in salute.

"That was a brave man," he murmured as the body kicked and voided, the usual undignified business of dying.

"Esmond! Esmond!"

He jerked his head up suddenly. The chant had begun during the fight, but there was no room for it in the diamond-hard focus of a death duel. The men were yelling it, pumping fists and weapons in the air.

*"Esmond! Esmond!"*

The roar echoed back from the walls of the great room, bouncing back in confused waves of sound as the last of the defenders were disarmed and marched off. Not only his own Strikers were shouting it, but the Royal troops as well—only the knot of noblemen around King Casull weren't, and many of them were waving swords in salute as well. Even the King was, and smiling; there was a cut on his face, and blood on his sword—Casull was a fighting man whose praise you'd respect, and Esmond felt a sudden lurch as the truth of it rammed home.

*Well, dip me in shit!* he thought. *I not only won, I won big with the big boss looking on.* The news would be all over the Royal army and fleet by sundown, too.

Esmond bent, pulling off Franzois' helm. There was a purple-gold circlet around the dead man's brow; he paused a minute to hold the eyelids shut and close the staring gaze, then rose with the symbol of Vase's sovereignty raised high. The chanting gradually slowed, stopped, left a silence full of rustles and creaks and clanks as armed men shifted their feet and murmured to each other.

With sword and buckler in his right hand and the circlet in his left, Esmond paced across the throne room to where Casull stood. He went to one knee and held both forward.

"My lord King," he said, in slow, clear, carrying tones. "Vase is yours!"

Another roaring cheer. Cries of "Casull!" and "Esmond!" were mixed, together with "Hot damn!" and "Loot! Loot!"

Casull took the circlet, a wry smile on his face; he winked slightly as their eyes met.

"Well, you're a showman, as well as a fighting man,"

he murmured as he accepted the symbol of sovereignty. "Maybe you'll find a realm of your own someday; a man who's actor and fighter both is born to rule."

He straightened, took Esmond's sword and rapped him sharply on each armored shoulder.

"With swords such as yours, my throne is secure!" he cried. *From everyone but the people carrying those swords,* went unspoken between them—warning and mutual recognition at once. "Let the farmer-clods of the Confederation interfere if they dare—let all men take note that what we have, we hold, we and our valorous nobles and troops. Rise, Excellent Esmond Gellert!"

Esmond's eyes widened slightly, and his men redoubled their cheers. *Well, there's a step up,* he thought; he'd just gone from outland mercenary captain to the lowest level of Islander nobility. *Mind you, what the King gave, the King could take away;* and from the smolderingly jealous looks of the courtiers gathered about him, he'd also acquired a set of instant enemies. Casull's wry smile as Esmond rose—for an instant, until he noticed the added pain of the stiffening face cut—told the Emerald that the King was perfectly aware of *that,* too.

Casull paced across the room and up the dais to the Throne of Vase, turning to take the salute from the warriors who filled the great room to overflowing now.

"Hail to our lord King—King of all the Isles!" Esmond cried.

Helga Demansk watched the end of the duel wide-eyed, especially when Esmond Gellert pulled off his helmet after his victory. *Oh, momma!* she thought, glancing aside at Adrian. Yes, there was a family resemblance there, but . . . *Well, if the old stories about Emerald philosophers are true, I suppose the ones about the Five Year Games winners can be too.* Maybe even stories about god-fathered heroes, although like anyone

with a modern education she tended to believe—
consciously, at least—that the old gods were aspects of
the One, Who needed only to Be, not to do.

Looking at Esmond Gellert, it was easy to remember
things her nurse had told her, and old tales in books.
The other Emerald was a big man, but with none of
the beefy solidity she was used to in soldiers, or athletes,
for that matter. He moved like a big golden cat, and
his features might have been chiseled by a Solingian
sculptor of the lost golden age right after the League
Wars.

But there was something . . . something *missing* there.
A liveliness that was in his brother's eyes, even when
they were abstracted. It grew as the flush of combat
faded from his face, leaving it even more like a statue—
painted marble, with a deadness behind. Except that
marble did not conceal an ocean of pain. . . .

*Stop being fanciful,* she told herself. *Concentrate.*
Adrian had said she was under his protection, and oddly
enough she believed him. But *Adrian* might need
protection. Would the King protect him? Could his
brother? She stepped back a pace, hating the necessity
but wishing for a cloak, too.

"Adrian!" Esmond said, stepping forward and shoul-
dering nobles and ranking officers aside. A little life
returned to the carved planes of his face. "Brother! By
the *shades*, how did you get here?"

"Found an old access tunnel to that tower," Adrian
said, flushing with pleasure himself and clasping
forearms. "Blasted out the plug with some hellpowder,
and went looking for trouble—and found you, eventually."

Esmond laughed. "I *thought* it was something like
that. The Vaseans were retreating in pretty good
order—stood up to the guns pretty well, even your
sniping at their backs—and then they went to pieces."

"Men will, when they're attacked from the rear,"

Adrian said. "You managed to cover yourself with well-earned glory, I see."

Esmond laughed again; the sound was a little hoarse, as if he didn't do it very often. He caught the smaller man by the shoulder and pushed him forward unwilling, until they were before the throne. Helga slipped forward unobtrusively, absently knocking a questing hand aside with the rim of her buckler on its wrist bone, and ignoring the indignant yelp that followed.

"My lord King," Esmond said; not shouting, but pitched in a public-speaking mode copied from his brother's rhetorical training, and found useful on the battlefield as well—much likelier to attract attention than the usual roar, as conversation built up in the throne room.

"My lord King," he went on, grinning. "Here is my brother, Adrian Gellert, who has served you well—not only the devices which battered down the walls and gates of Vase, but by taking the citadel from behind through a secret passage and blocking the escape of Director Franzois."

Casull looked aside from a consultation with one of his admirals who'd brought him a tally of ships captured intact.

"Then he has served me well," the king said graciously, waving aside a surgeon who was trying to suture the slash on his cheek. "If the Director's heir—a pretender to this throne—had escaped, this victory wouldn't be complete."

He gave Esmond a slight, hard stare at that; if the Director had won the fight, Casull might well have had to let him go . . . which would have had much the same result, with the added disadvantage of the sort of colorful story likely to attract free-lances who valued a lucky commander.

"You'll not find me ungrateful," Casull went on.

"My lord King," Adrian said. "Forgive me if I claim

your gratitude so early, but there's a favor I *would* like to claim."

Casull's eyebrows went up; it was slightly boorish to take him up on his offer so early. "Ask," he said.

Adrian reached behind himself without looking around; Helga squeaked slightly as his hand closed on her shoulder and pulled her forward. The fingers were slender but unexpectedly strong, warm through the cooling blood on the fabric of her halter.

"My way here came through the Director's—the *ex*-Director's hareem," he said. "I'd have this woman assigned to me, if Your Majesty would be so kind."

Helga swallowed. *Hell, it's* got *to be better than the hareem,* she thought. Women in the Emerald lands were closer-kept than in the upper classes of the Confederacy, but vastly better than in the Isles . . . and Adrian hadn't made the slightest objection when she took a sword and came along for some payback. He'd even *thanked* her for probably saving his life—it would have driven most men she knew crazy, to owe a woman that.

*Although he has eyes in the back of his head, for a man who isn't paying much attention,* she thought, puzzled for a moment. His brother Esmond, you could *sense* that he saw with his skin, like a cat. Adrian, he gave off a feeling you could walk right up to him and bash him on the head; only you couldn't, he'd start and look up and be ready for it, from what she'd seen. As if someone was talking to him, and paying attention when he wasn't.

The King's words brought her back to her own personal reality with a thump.

"That's a little irregular, but since they're Royal spoils . . ." he said. Then he looked at Helga and laughed. "I see the former Director wasn't averse to a little perversion—that one looks like a boy with tits, or a field woman . . . no, those are acrobat's muscles,

I suppose. Well, she'll be athletic, if you like that sort of thing. But what by the Sun God is she doing with that sword?"

The King's voice was amused, a little contemptuous. Adrian's was blankly polite when he replied: "Killing Vasean soldiers, mostly, my lord King. Five . . ." His head went to one side. "No, six, with two probables, O King. Probably saved my life, as well."

The King laughed uproariously. "We can't deprive our master artificer of his *body*guard, then," he said. "By all means—"

"Excuse me, my Royal Cousin," one of the nobles said. A tall slender brown-haired man, he'd had time to shed his armor, but the padded leather doublet underneath was rank with sweat. "If I might?"

Casull nodded uncertainly, and the Islander noble came two steps down from the dais, giving Helga a slow head-to-toe.

"As you say, rather perverse . . . but interestingly. By ancient law," he went on, giving Adrian a cool glance, "officers chose personal spoils by rank—and I believe I outrank this outlander."

Casull's lips pursed in annoyance. He glanced around the circle of courtiers, and saw many nods and chuckles. *Of course,* Helga thought. An outlander, raised high so suddenly, was bound to arouse resentment—any Islander court was a snakepit at the best of times. And Adrian, unlike his brother, hadn't just pulled off a spectacular Wodep-like feat of public heroism.

"Unless," the noble said, "he'd like to fight me for her? No? I didn't think so." The noble had several skull-and-bones earrings, and he moved like . . . *Like Adrian's brother Esmond,* Helga thought. *No! I will not go back into another Islander hareem! No!*

The Islander stepped forward, and she tensed.

"Actually," Adrian said mildly, "I *do* object, and if necessary, I *will* fight you. But I appeal to our lord the

King, whose wishes you are quite obviously contravening, my lord . . . Sawtre, isn't it?"

Sawtre grinned, flushing and letting his hand drop to his sword. "Interfering in the affairs of *real* men, little Emerald manure strainer? Better to get back to your toys. We should all consider the consequences of our decisions, shouldn't we? You are what you do, after all. And we *know* what you are."

Adrian swallowed, shaking his head once and then again—*as if,* Helga thought under the rush of relief at his words and then horror at his prospects in a duel with this trained killer, *he was talking to someone again . . . and disagreeing with them.*

"I think you're forgetting something, my lord," Esmond said quietly.

"Yes?"

"Fogetting that if you harm my brother, in any way whatsoever, I'll kill you and piss on your grave," Esmond said, smiling himself. His eyes had taken on the same febrile brilliance they'd had during the duel with Director Franzois, and Sawtre checked for a moment.

"You don't dare, Emerald," he said softly.

"You'd be surprised what I dare," Esmond replied, his voice equally calm.

Behind him the men of the Strikers tensed, and exchanged glances with Sawtre's fighting tail. Those men began drifting towards their lord; one of them dashed out, to collect others of their band who were lifting their share in the sack of the palace.

"Excuse me," Helga said loudly. Sawtre's eyes did not waver. Helga tapped the edge of her buckler against her sword. "*Excuse me. You, the asshole in the arming doublet!*"

That brought amazed snickers from the crowd around the throne; even Casull, half-risen in annoyance and gathering apprehension at the sudden prospect of a battle royal before his eyes, turned to look at her.

The nobleman flicked her an annoyed glance. "Be silent, woman, or you'll get a worse beating than you would otherwise."

"Oh, *excuse* me, my mighty Islander Pirate Lord dumber-than-dogshit, but you're *forgetting* something."

"*What?*"

There was a slack amazement on Sawtre's hard face; he could not *believe* that this was happening to him, this public defiance by a woman. His hand went to his belt. Not to the hilt of his sword, as it had a moment before, but to the thonged crop that hung there.

"Forgetting *this*," Helga said, and thrust underarm.

Lord Sawtre's face went slack with an amazement even more complete than before. Even then, his hand began a movement towards his sword, struck the hilt, began to draw. *Hey, really good reflexes,* Helga thought— it helped keep her mind off the fact that she had just probably condemned herself to death. *I'd rather be dead,* she thought, at the thick wet butcher's-cleaver sound as the blade went in from below, just above the man's left hip. Sawtre's mouth and eyes went into identical Os of shock as she dropped her buckler, put both hands on the hilt, and ripped the blade upward with a twisting wrench of arms and shoulders and back.

It came free with a hard shit-stink following it, and the Islander noble dropped to his knees and clutched at the pink-and-red intestines spilling into his lap.

"*Be silent*, woman, you said?" Helga said, her voice breathy with exertion. "Try being silent about *this*, you velipad's ass."

The sword went up, and her right foot curled up and then slammed down to add emphasis as the blade fell— spattering red drops even before it struck the man's neck, and with white shreds of fat sticking in nicks in the steel. Sawtre flopped boneless to the ground, and blood spilled down, crimson against the marble white and malachite green of the steps.

For a long moment there was absolute silence; Adrian was staring at her and looking—again as if he was talking to someone. His brother was staring at her too, seeing her as a person for the first time rather than a symbol his brother was willing to fight for, and his eyes were wide with an expert's appreciation of what she'd just done. King Casull was frozen in a different set of calculations. His voice cut across the beginnings of a murmur:

"Well, it seems he *was* silent about that," he observed, leaning back in the throne and resting his bearded chin on the knuckles of one hand. "And you know—I've thought Sawtre was a velipad's arse myself, for a good long while now."

He chuckled, then threw back his head and laughed outright. Some of the courtiers chimed in immediately, and others took it up, until the whole room was roaring.

*Allfather of Vanbert, Greatest and Best—what a bunch of pirates!* Even after a year in the Isles, she forgot sometimes. . . .

Helga felt her shoulders begin to shake with reaction. Adrian laid his hand on her back again, gently— cautiously—but firmly.

"And now, if my lord King will excuse me," he said.

"By all means, my Iron Limper," Casull said, referring to the lame smith of the gods. "Keep the vixen, if you want her. I'd say not to turn your back, but—" he gave another shout of laughter "—that didn't do Lord Sawtre here any good, did it?"

He raised a hand and shouted over the court's merriment. "And now, my lords and gentlemen, we have a city to sack!"

"An' here's to lord Adrian, the favored of the Gray-Eyed, victory-lucky, best lord a fightin' man could follow!" Simun shouted, raising his cup.

The arquebusiers of the Lightning Band—they'd

come up with the title on their own—raised a deaf-
ening cheer. Adrian smiled and nodded; it was rather
like having a pack of pet direbeasts: alarming at times,
but it certainly beat having them against you. The long
palace hall was full of them, and of servants and
women—the latter volunteers, or mostly, considering
their alternatives—and the smells of food and wine and
hastily washed mercenary rubbed with scented oil, and
incense from braziers, perfumed lanterns, garlands. . . .
Light flickered on hard battered faces, on ranks of
bundles of plunder stacked against the walls, neatly
wrapped in canvas and inked with their owners' names,
and on the unit's equipment. They were ready to move
out in the morning.

"Here's to his brother, who's Wodep come again,"
Simun said loyally. "Yer can't go wrong with leaders
who're favored of the gods—smart, too."

"Long live lord Adrian, who taught us to wield the
lightnings!" someone else yelled.

"Long live lord Adrian, who's brought us to a place
where we can swim in gold!"

That brought a *really* enthusiastic cheer. The wine
cellar they'd gone through had turned out to be a
subtreasury or something, probably the ready funds for
the management of the Director's hareem. Strictly
speaking it should have gone into the general pot, but
everyone had agreed that that would be taking the rules
to a ridiculous extreme. It had come out to about a
year's pay for every man in the unit, not counting what
they'd picked up elsewhere the rest of the day.

"And now I'll leave you to your well-earned feasting,"
Adrian said.

There was another good-natured cheer. They didn't
resent him not taking part in the celebration; they'd
come to take a certain pride in the oddity of a Scholar
of the Grove commanding them, now that nobody could
doubt he had balls enough despite it. It had worked;

it was lucky; and if it wasn't broke, they weren't going to try and fix it.

"Won't be a gentleman's symposium, no, sir," Simun said. He leered cheerfully. "Watch out for 'er sword before you show 'er yours, too, sir!"

He left the chamber in a roar of bawdy advice, flushing and smiling a little. His own chambers had probably been a royal guard captain's rooms, up a flight of stairs, with half a flat roof as well, enclosed by a head-high wall except where a low balustrade overlooked the courtyard-drillyard, and set with plants in pots, tumbles of blossoming vine falling down to the brown tiles. The scent of the flowers was faint and cool, after the heat and smells of the main hall; the walls blocked out flames and sound from the rest of Vase, leaving only the stars above, many and bright.

"Ah—" he caught himself before he said *Lady Demansk*; the Gray-Eyed knew he didn't want Helga to know he knew *that*. "Freewoman Helga." There, at least he'd gotten across that he regarded her as a free citizen of the Confederacy, not a slave who'd changed owners. She nodded, taking note of the title, and he went on: "I've had some things gathered up for you, and you can have that chamber by the stairwell; we'll be leaving tomorrow."

"Well, yes, I'd sort of wondered about that," Helga said, stepping forward into the puddle of yellow light a brass globe full of oil with a cotton wick cast on the tiles.

She was wearing a clean tunic—man's clothing, but there was no doubt at all about the gender of the body within it. A garland of white-and-purple flowers crowned the long auburn curls that fell past her shoulders; it was hard to remember her turning the billhook meant for him, bathed in blood . . . *And fairly easy, too. All the gods witness, I was terrified.* Not half as terrified as he'd been challenging Sawtre, of course.

Adrian cleared his throat, glad of the night dimness. A voice drifted up the stairwell, followed by a tremendous shout of laughter, and then the jaunty notes of a *kordax* on the lyre. A line of torch-bearing men stamped out into the courtyard of this building, mostly leaning on their companions—women of the town, or boys in a few instances—and began weaving in a chain dance around the fountain and back into the hall. They were singing something, something with his name in it, but between distance, drink and the blur of voices far from used to singing in unison, he couldn't make it out.

*Interesting,* Adrian thought with a distant scholar's part of his mind. He'd never actually seen a victory *komos* before, although the old epics were full of them. This wasn't much like the descriptions the poets gave; they left out the bits about men who stopped to throw up, or just fell down paralytically drunk.

*I suspect that this is more like what they were really like, even in the War of the Thousand Ships,* he mused.

"Ah, um." *Oh, Gellerix, that's lame,* he thought and found his voice. "I'm definitely not going to force myself on you, Freewoman Helga," he said.

Helga smiled. "That's extremely gentlemanly of you," she said, with a polite nod and toss of her head. It wouldn't have been out of place at a dinner party at Audsley's house in Vanbert, except that most of his wife's acquaintances didn't have that much style. "But I assure you that force isn't required."

"Ah, um." *Oh, Gellerix.* "Ah, you really don't have to feel any sense of obligation, Freewoman Helga," he managed to choke out.

"You do *like* women, don't you, Adrian?"

Adrian felt a chuckle rising at her expression of sudden worry. "Well, yes. Don't believe everything you hear about Emeralds, my—ummmph."

"You're exactly the right height," Helga said as she

broke the kiss. "Two and one-half inches taller than me. . . . Look, Adrian, I'm not a virgin, my marital prospects are crap anyway, I've been locked up with sixty women for a year and I *don't* like girls . . . and I *do* like you. You're a fascinating man. You're also not someone my father picked, either—*I* like you, I said." Her smile grew. "Am I making myself clear?"

"Abundantly," he said, and scooped her up with an arm under the shoulders and another under the knees.

# SEVEN

"Preble," King Casull said.

His pointer tapped down on the map table. The greatbeast hide there showed an island covered in buildings, shaped like a peach pit with a stretch of blue water down the middle. Puff-cheeked wind spirits were drawn to represent the prevailing winds, and a line eastward showed the mainland coast. A few men stood around it: his heir, Tenny; Esmond; Adrian; and the Grand Admiral of the Isles, a half-brother of Casull who'd supported him in his thrust for the crown and had no sons of his own. A cooling evening breeze blew curtains aside to reveal the harbor of Chalice, crammed with shipping, a tarry reek penetrating even this far above the harbor. It was growing dark, but a flicker of red showed on the underside of the clouds that hung in the deep-purple sky—reflection of the lava in the craters above the city.

"We held Preble under my predecessor, Casull III, may his spirit rest with the Sun God," Casull went on. "Justiciar Marcomann took it away from us, along with the old mainland possessions of the Kings of the Isles.

169

It's barely half a mile from shore—you can see the old city, Sor, here—but it's a magnificent naval base and does a heavy trade. According to my spies, who are many there, there's only a small Confed garrison there, barely a battalion."

Silence fell around the table. The Crown Prince cleared his throat. "A strong party loyal to the Kings of the Isles has risen in Preble," he said. "They have extended an invitation to me, to come and free them from the tyrants of the mainland, and then to rule them as men are meant to be ruled."

"And not to pay the Confed tribute anymore," Casull added. "It's heavy; they don't really understand sea trade . . . farmers, really."

Adrian nodded in unison with Esmond. *No doubt a little gold from Chalice was spread around to get that Royalist party going,* Raj said. *But yes, on the whole, it looks like a good opportunity to test the Confeds.*

**probability of initial success is 77%, ±10,** Center interjected. **high degree of uncertainty indicates several factors, principally—**

*We'll discuss that later,* Adrian thought firmly. Aloud: "My lord King, perhaps we can take Preble," he said. "Can we hold it?"

Tenny's lower lip stuck out slightly. Adrian cursed himself silently; he should have framed that a little more tactfully. Casull nodded.

"That *is* the question," he said. "Normally, no. The island is too close to the mainland, to the Confed armies, and to their fleet. The fleet's laid up in ordinary"— meaning stripped and hauled up in boat-sheds—"but they can put it to sea fairly quickly."

"As sailors, they'd make good cowherds," Tenny observed. His father frowned.

"True, but don't underestimate their numbers, or their discipline, or the way their infantry fights once they get on your deck—previous Kings of the Isles have done that, to their cost." Casull III, for instance, had paid with his life for doing exactly that. "With 'zieur Adrian's new weapons, we *may* have a chance of holding it."

Adrian traced the narrow strait with a finger. "What's the depth, here, my lord King?"

"Ah, you see the problem. Shallow—full of shifting sandbars. Impossible to interdict with warships, but fine for shallow-draft barges carrying assault troops."

"They might try a causeway, then," Adrian said thoughtfully. "If they could round up enough peasants to dig."

Casull winced slightly. "That would be even worse. Damn them, they're always trying to turn sea into land."

"By the Lord of the Trident, they'll regret it this time," Esmond said confidently. "Most of Adrian's new weapons have the range to turn the straits into *hell* for them."

"So we'll put them into the hands of the Shades." Tenny chuckled, licking his lips. "And I will be King in Preble."

"Under me," Casull added dryly, and the Prince looked down. Patricide was an ancient tradition in the Isles. "By sending you, my son, I assure the men of Preble that they are to be free subjects, not a possession to be squeezed."

"What about the city militia?" Esmond said. "There ought to be . . . what, eight, ten thousand of them? In a city that size."

Casull nodded. "They will not be involved initially," he said. "Not if our plan goes as expected. Then they will have no *choice* but to fall in with us, and fight for us."

"Certainly, if the Confed thinks they were disloyal," Esmond said. "I take it, my lord, that the Strikers are to be the spearhead of this enterprise?" He bowed to Tenny. "Under your valiant son's direction."

"Of course," Casull beamed. "And your brother will be with you, to see to the emplacement of the new weapons to defend our new city. We will follow with the fleet."

The two Emeralds smiled and bowed to the King of the Isles. Adrian needed no voices from beyond the world to know exactly what the King was thinking: if the throw of the dice failed, he was out only one replaceable son and some Emerald mercenaries; if it succeeded, he had one of the richest cities in the Western Sea.

***That's how a King has to think, lad,*** Raj said. Adrian had an image of gray eyes, weary and amused. ***I never had to be*** **that,** ***for which I thank the Spirit of Man of the Stars.***

"When do we strike?" Esmond asked.

"As soon as may be. With the fleet gathered, Confed spies will swarm here like flies to velipad shit, and this is a logical step. I will feed them a dozen contradictory stories—that way even if they learn the truth, it may drown in a storm of plausible lies—but better still to strike before they decide to reinforce all their coastal garrisons."

Esmond nodded. "Then if my lords will permit, my brother and I will withdraw, to make our preparations. The Strikers will be ready to sail within three days."

"My Lightning Band within a week," Adrian said. "I will need time to modify some equipment and gather others."

"You gave her *what*?" Esmond laughed, cracking a nut in his palm.

"Well, it was what she wanted," Adrian said defensively.

"Flowers, a hare, jewels—but you gave her a *sword*?"

"Well, the one she had wasn't really very good quality," Adrian explained.

He was tired; they both were, with the load of work

they'd been doing. A light meal stood between their couches on a low table: cured fish, olives, oil, bread for dipping, watered wine. The room was plain white-wash with a pattern of leaves in blue around the upper edges, and a door gave out onto a garden full of lilacs. It might almost have been in Solinga, even the smell of the sea was familiar, if it weren't for a subtle wrongness in the noises, an undersmell of strange spices and rank lushness to the familiar reek of a port. Another table at the end of the room was littered with wax-covered board diptychs, scrolls, and scraps of reed-paper, models.

Esmond pulled a piece off a long loaf of bread. "Well," he said, with malice aforethought and a brother's cruelty, "it was a good enough sword to gut Lord Sawtre very effectively. If you finally had to take up with a woman regularly, and with a Confed woman, you at least picked one with some unusual talents." He laughed. "At least she's not Audsley's wife—or Justiciar Demansk's daughter."

His brother might not be a Scholar of the Grove, with an ageless machine and an ancient general's ghost at the back of his mind, but he was an Emerald and no fool—which was to say, a keen observer.

"*Wait* a minute!" Esmond said, half-rising. "Shit among the Shades, she *is* Demansk's daughter—the one captured by pirates."

"*Shut up!*" Adrian barked.

Shocked, Esmond fell silent for a moment. Adrian rarely spoke roughly; this time he fought for a visible instant to control his temper, something rare enough to make his brother's eyes go wide.

"You will *not* speak of that again," he said coldly.

"But why?" Esmond said.

"Because I don't want her to think I'm using her as some sort of angle against her father—which I'm not, by the way, and won't be."

Esmond's blue eyes blinked in bewilderment. "But why, brother if—oh, no. *Don't* tell me you've been scratched by one of Gellerix's cats and caught a fever!"

That was the slang term for being hit by love; any sensible Emerald regarded it as a form of infectious madness sent by the gods to plague mankind with suffering—the divinities could be remarkably petty and cruel, sometimes.

Adrian looked down and toyed with a dried fig. "That's one way to put it. You might also say that I like and respect her," he snapped.

"Adrian, my brother, please—think." Esmond stopped for a moment, and snorted. "Here I am, stealing your lines, like an actor . . . but really, think, brother. At least there's no question of marr—oh, Gellerix!" he broke off at Adrian's expression.

"Esmond, have you any conception of how *dull* most women's conversation is?" he snapped. "How dull most women *are*? It's not their fault, the gods know, most of them shut up all the time and uneducated, but—"

He stopped at Esmond's expression of bafflement. *Your Nanya was like a trembling dove,* he thought with kindly exasperation. *And the gods know, the Wodep in your soul would make that seem the sum of all womanhood to you. Me, I'm differently made, my brother.*

"She's—"

A dangerous glance passed between them, and an unspoken message: *You don't call her* used goods *and I won't say anything about Nanya, that's about it,* Adrian thought.

"Adrian," Esmond said slowly. "Demansk's daughter is going to be a Confed—not just by origins, she'll have been *brought up* on their old stories, walked past the death masks of Demansks who were Justiciars and Speakers back to when Vanbert was a mud-and-wattle village. How do you think she's going to feel when she finds out you're fighting to bring the Confederacy of Vanbert to the ground?"

*I should remind myself how smart Esmond is occasionally*, Adrian thought, wincing. His brother didn't have the temperament for a Scholar, but he had at least as much raw brainpower as his younger sibling, and a tremendous ability to focus.

"That's . . . for the time it has to be faced," he said slowly. "Look, Esmond . . . can't I have a few days? Just a few?"

"Of course," Esmond said. His eyes grew slightly haunted. "I know how brief that can be."

Feet clattered outside, and voices rang; one a high clear soprano. Helga Demansk swept in, wearing women's dress this time, a long blue robe with a fold of her mantle over her hair. That was tied back with a ribbon, and twisted into plaits.

"Adrian!" she said, handing her shopping basket to a maid. "It fits! Oh, hello, Esmond."

"Helga," he said, half-rising and bowing his head. "What fits?"

"The cuirass and helmet," she said. "They do good metalwork here, I've got to admit, even if they are pirate dogs." Adrian winced slightly, and looked around. "Oh, don't worry, Adrian," she went on. "They're *proud* of being pirates."

"But not dogs," he said.

"Are you going to tell me yet where this new expedition is headed?" she said, a green gleam in her eye. "Casull will have all the islands soon, at this rate."

"Are you so eager to slay men, lady?" Esmond asked.

This time Helga looked aside slightly. "Well, no," she said. "Not really. But it's . . . exciting, you know what I mean?"

"Unfortunately I do," Esmond agreed.

Helga reached into the basket. "*And* look at what I found," she went on more brightly. "A copy of the *War of the Thousand Ships.* I kept myself sane partly by reciting big chunks of it from memory, but it's been so long since I had anything to *read.*"

Esmond laughed. "You and my brother were made for each other by the gods, lady. Even when we were running for our lives, two pack-velipads full of scrolls followed us."

Helga chuckled, but scowled slightly. "That idiot Audsley got a lot of good men killed, from what I hear," she said. "Damned traitor . . . and of course he got his head handed to him when he met . . . Justiciar Demansk. Demansk is a *real* general, and he has the interests of the State at heart."

**correct,** Center said. **which is why with a high probability he would be hostile to our innovations. however, it would be advisable to gain a fuller psychostatistical profile of him—the subject helga demansk would be a valuable source of data.**

*Shut the hell up,* Adrian thought. He could feel Raj agreeing with him, an eerie nonverbal communication, like some ghostly equivalent of seeing expression on a man's face.

"Sorry," Helga went on after a moment. "Sometimes I forget you're Emeralds."

"Emeralds and Confeds are near-as-no-matter blood brothers here in the Isles," Adrian said lightly—which was true in one sense, and an outright lie in another.

Helga met his eyes and smiled, and worries seemed to dissolve themselves in time sweeter than honey. After a moment Esmond cleared his throat and stood.

"Well, I can tell when I'm the third wheel on a chariot," he said. "Tomorrow, then, brother."

"We're getting sort of close to the mainland, aren't we?" Helga said.

"That *is* the mainland," Adrian replied.

The galley had been under sail alone, one squat

square sail driving the lean hull eastwards. Adrian stood on the quarterdeck, with his arm and cloak around the woman beside him; he'd been still, because if he was still all he need see was the frosted arch of stars above, the ghostly arcs of the moons, the smells of salt water and sweat and tar and the mingling of jasmine and clean healthy woman that was Helga. If he did not think, his mind need not crack and bleed. . . .

"Sir . . ." began the ship's captain; he was Casull's man, and they were not authorized to be anywhere but on the approaches to Preble.

"Shut up, you," Simun said.

The Islander skipper looked at him, and at the scores of Adrian's arquebusiers sprawled about the galley's deck, sleeping wrapped in their cloaks, throwing dice in the hollow of an upturned buckler, chewing hardtack and dried fruit, or simply sitting patiently on their haunches. His crew numbered roughly the same, though all but fifteen of them were oarsmen and sailors, tough hardy men and handy in a fight, but no match for soldiers with swords and light body armor. And from the flat dispassionate stare of the little underofficer, they'd be perfectly happy to slit his throat, throw the crews' bodies after his, and turn pirate if this Emerald gave the word. They were *his* men, not the King's.

"Your orders, sir?" he said to Adrian.

"Beach the ship lightly," he said, then looked ahead. "There's shallow shelving water and soft sand there— just touch her."

The captain shivered and made a covert sign with his fingers. Those eyes . . . *They're not like those of other men. As if demons or spirits—or gods?—were looking out of them. Telling him things, that's what the tales say. He's not canny.*

He turned to give his orders to the steersmen and sailing master. The sail and yard came down with a muted thump and were furled; below the oarsmen

stirred in sleepy protest. There was a yelp or two as
the bosun's rope-end persuaders swung, and then the
oars came rattling out, poised, dipped down into the
dark star-reflecting water and bit. The ship turned
towards the black line of the shore, where low waves
and white foam and pale sand made a line in the night.
It was calm water, and the ship was a raider, built for
'longshore work. Behind him the sorcerer was talking
with his woman in Confed, a language the captain knew
only a few words of.

"Adrian," Helga said. "What's going on?"

The Emerald drew a deep breath. "I didn't tell you
where we were bound," he said. "Because I didn't want
to spoil things more than . . . earlier than I had to."

"You're bound to attack Confederacy territory," she
said, her voice quiet and level as her eyes.

"Yes," Adrian said.

"Preble? It's the logical target and weakly held."

Adrian felt a knife twist deeper. *This woman has
brains,* he thought. Some of the Scholars of the Grove
held that the only true love was between man and
youth, because only then could there be a meeting of
minds and not merely of bodies. He'd admitted the
theoretical force of the argument, but not anymore, not
anymore. . . .

"Yes."

"Adrian . . ." She stepped closer and put a hand on
his shoulder. He could barely feel it through the
shoulderpiece of his corselet, but a heat seemed to
gather beneath.

"Adrian, don't do it. You'll be killed, you can't
understand even if you win at first, the Confederacy
*always* comes back in the end, please, don't throw
yourself away—"

*She's thinking of me,* he realized with a glow of
wonder. He shook his head and went on:

"I've . . . got to back my brother. And I'm not going

to ask you to fight against your country . . . possibly against your father's own troops."

Shock turned Helga's face white. "You knew?"

"You favor him. And I knew about the raid." His hand came down on hers, where it rested on the bronze of the armor. "Helga . . . I didn't give a damn. Don't now."

She looked at him for a long slow moment. "I believe you," she said. "And you're not sending me back now as a gift to him?"

His mouth quirked. "Your father is notoriously patriotic. Who was that ancient Confed general, the one who executed his own sons when they proposed surrender . . . ?"

"Louis deVille," she said automatically. "That was in the war of King Peter."

*The one who came up with the phrase Petric Victory,* a scholar's corner of Adrian's mind remembered. That was long before the Confed conquest of the Emerald lands, when an Emerald—or half-Emerald— general could still invade there himself. But he'd won no concessions, although he'd carried half a dozen bloody fields against the nascent Confederation's army. The problem was that they could replace the men, and he couldn't.

"Well, if deVille was ready to sacrifice his sons, I think your father—much though he must love you—will sacrifice a daughter for Preble. I'm not going to be buying any favors from him with you."

Her eyes searched his. "How well you must know him," she said. "Is there nothing you don't know?"

"I don't know how to come by what I want most in the world and still keep my honor," he said.

The tears that glittered in her eyes stayed unshed; he'd found the one argument that would weigh heaviest with someone raised in the household of a Confed noble of antique virtue. *The fact that it's the miserable truth is sort of a bonus, I suppose.*

The cry from the bow was soft but carrying. "She shelves."

"Avast oars!" the captain called. "Brace for grounding!"

Adrian and Helga did, with an arm around each other as well as a grip on the rigging. The ship surged softly, and half a dozen crewmen dropped over the bow to hold her steady; the water was to their waists. For all its length and wicked bronze-sheathed ram the galley was absurdly light, a racing shell of thin pine planking.

The man and woman walked to the bow, hand-in-hand, in silence. Adrian vaulted over into the cold water, caught Helga by the waist and lifted her down. She was a solid armful, with the light corselet on her and the rest of her kit. Arquebusiers of the Lightning Band handed down the servant he'd bought her in Chalice, and a light duffel.

"There's enough here to see you safely to Grand Harbor, and the Confed garrison there," he said, tucking a soft heavy purse of chamois leather into her belt pouch. "And . . ."

"And?" she asked, chin up.

"And I may not be the Confederacy's enemy forever," he said in a rush. "When—if—that happens, may I come to call?"

She smiled with a courage that wrenched at his heart. "Yes," she said. "I will so petition my father." A moment's urchin grin. "I told you what my marriage prospects are, didn't I?" Solemnly: "Stay alive, Adrian."

"I'll do my best. Yes, best I go. Gods go with you."

He watched the two figures walk up the beach, towards the tree-lined trail a hundred yards inland; it shone white in the moonlight, a wanderer's ribbon across the moor that bordered the sea here. Then he turned and accepted a hand; others boosted him back to the deck. He stood there, unspeaking, while the crew pushed off and the oars bit, backing water and turning the galley's prow to the west.

✧      ✧      ✧

Esmond Gellert decided that the waiting was the hardest part.

The *Briny Kettle* was no warship, no sleek galley lavishly equipped with oars. She was a tub, a merchant-man that carried grain and fish and oil and general cargo along the western coasts, out to the Islands, down south to the barbarian country. The only oars she had were half a dozen sweeps on a side, used only for working in and out of awkward ports. For the rest she was a deep-bellied teardrop, with a swan's head curving up over the quarterdeck and steering oars at the rear, one tall mast in the center, and bluff-cheeked bows up front. At five hundred tons she was quite large, and that and her high sides and substantial crew, plus a couple of dart-casters, was usually enough to discourage pirates. Longshore raiding paid better anyway, usually.

"Yeah, waiting's the worst," Donnuld Grayn said.

Esmond started slightly. "Hell, I didn't know I was talking."

The older mercenary grinned gap-toothed, and offered a skin of well-watered wine—one part to three. "This business, you spend most of the time being bored, and a few minutes out of every hour shitting yourself," he said philosophically. "When you're not being seasick, that is . . . this tub pitches worse than a galley."

The *Briny Kettle* carried no cargo but armed men; five hundred of them, packed like cured fish below decks, or lying flat on deck to ride concealed from anyone else—anyone, for instance, like the inspector in the little customs galley that was coming alongside. Its dozen oars easily matched the long slow rocking-horse pitch of the merchantman, avoiding the bows where a creamy V of white water pointed towards the low dark bulk of the city ahead. Reddish lights glimmered on the water from some of the lights there, and from masthead lanterns on the clustering ships docked to it, and from sentries pacing on the high crenellated walls.

"You're late, Sharlz," the official called out, holding up a lantern.

That glittered on the water, on his bald scalp and big-nosed face and on the gold hoop in one ear. He was an Islander himself, not a Confed—Preble was officially a free city in alliance with the Confederacy, although the Confed prefect here would have a lot more say than the council of magnates.

"Tide and wind and a woman's mind, Juluk," the captain said, scratching at his hairy chest where the open shirt showed a mat of grizzled hair; he was a very tall man, enormously tall for an Islander, and his nose was a beak that made even the customs officer's look moderate.

"Where from, this trip, and what cargo?"

"Chalice. Ornamental stone, fig brandy, dried tentacle fish and hot peppers, indigo in cakes, conqueror root, and coffee," he replied calmly.

"Ah. Any sign the King in the Isles is getting stroppy?"

"Not that I saw—but I keep my head out of such things."

"Well, good for you," the customs man said. "Keep it under seal until tomorrow, eh?"

"You eat shit too, Juluk—am I going to start breaking bulk in the middle of the night?"

"I could come aboard and inspect now, Sharlz."

Captain Thicelt unhooked a purse from his belt and tossed it across the gap that the customs boat's crew kept open with fending oars. "The usual sweetener—and you don't need to share it with your boss, out here."

"Not all of it," Juluk said, weighing it. "Sail on."

They came to the entrance of the narrow canal that split Preble from north to south—a natural channel between two skerries, when this had been a dwelling place of fliers and seabeasts, rather than men. A semicircle marked the harbor, wharves and jetties three-deep with ships, some as large as theirs, others of all sizes down to fishing smacks. Their masts made a lifeless, leafless tracery against the sky, an angular forest that creaked and rustled and swayed. Light died as ships and buildings dimmed moons and stars, and the clean smell of the sea gave way to the ever-present stink of a major port. Plops and rustlings came from the water, and once a pair of huge silvery eyes glinted—the scavengers that feasted on the filth, and inconvenient bodies, and drunks who fell off gangways at night.

"Strike sail," the captain of the *Briny Kettle* said, and turned to Esmond. The Emerald could see the sheen of sweat on his face by the dim reflected lights of lanterns and sky, and smell it. "Out sweeps to the canal entrance . . . All yours from here on, excellent sir General."

Esmond clapped him on the shoulder. "Good work," he said. "You've earned what the King pays you—and more besides. Don't forget to come and see me about it after the city's ours."

A grin split the tall Islander's face. "That I'm not shy about, you'll find, excellent sir."

Even this late at night dock-wallopers were ready with a team of heavy greatbeasts. They caught the cable the sailors threw, hitched their team, and began hauling the ship through the sea gates and into the town.

Paved roadways lined both sides of the canal, from one half-moon harbor to the other; behind them warehouses loomed, linked until they formed seawalls of their own, preventing any enemy from storming into the city from this open water. Heavy iron grills closed the occasional roadway that led deeper into the town; iron chains could close the canal at need, as well.

Men were waiting halfway down the length of the canal, men with shuttered lanterns that they blinked briefly. They surrounded the laborers, and Esmond caught a gleam in their hands—probably long knives in one, and gold in the other. He knew which he'd have taken if he was a sleepy municipal slave on night watch at the harbor. They backed away, followed by their bewildered greatbeasts, and more lines flew to the roadway. Willing hands grasped them, drew them tight. Timber crunched against stone.

"For the King and the gods," a voice called softly.

"For Prince Tenny and liberty," Esmond replied.

He vaulted easily from the rail to the pavement four feet below. "General Esmond Gellert, with the Prince's troops. You're ready?"

"Enry Sharbonow, Suffete of Preble. Ready and more than ready. This way."

Esmond turned. "Disembark according to plan," he called. "No shouting, and I'll geld the first man that breaks ranks!"

*Except him, of course,* he thought sourly, as Prince Tenny jumped ashore in a swirl of purple cloak and clash of silvered armor—plumed spired helmet, back-and-breast, engraved armguards . . . The half-dozen friends-cum-hangers-on he had with him were just as gorgeous, or had been before some of them got seasick. Tenny, to give him credit, didn't look nervous as some of them did, either. *Brave, or too stupid to understand the risks, or both,* Esmond thought.

The Prebleans went to one knee before the Prince. He smiled and signaled them to rise. "Be at ease, my friends," he said, in a trained orator's voice. "Soon the night of Confed tyranny will be lifted—as the sun rises, so will a new, independent city of Preble."

Several of the Preblean conspirators seemed inclined to answer the Prince's speech with ones of their own. Esmond was relieved to see that Enry wasn't one of them.

"Your Highness, welcome to your loyal city," he said. "This way, please—the garrison doesn't patrol, but they're not blind and *somebody* will alert them if we don't move quickly."

The Strikers had formed up rapidly, and with as little noise as five hundred armored men could when moving on flagstones in the dark. Esmond fell in at their head, beside the banner and the commander's runners. Donnuld Grayn grinned at him out of the side of his mouth.

"Think the Prince'll screw things up really bad?" he said, *sotto voce.*

"Hopefully, not until we've taken the town," Esmond said. "By the way, I wasn't joking about taking the balls of anyone who starts chasing coin or skirt."

Grayn nodded. "You'll have to take 'em off the man dead, after I'm through with him," he said. "Probably will be one or two idiots—keeping hired soldiers in line in an enemy town, at night, ain't going to be easy."

"This *isn't* an enemy town. It's supposed to be *our* town, and we're taking it from the Confeds."

Grayn's grin grew wide. "That's not a distinction your average trooper is real interested in," he said. "But they'll understand my boot up their backside—and don't worry, sir, they're not going to upset a good thing. You've won us a couple of hard fights now; if you say paint ourselves green and hop around like kermitoids, most of the men'll do it."

"They've got the gates *open*?" Donnuld said incredulously.

"Wouldn't have believed it either, if I hadn't seen it myself," Esmond said.

Enry Sharbonow coughed discreetly; he was a discreet man, middle-aged and slim, with a pointed beard and a small gold ring through his nose; the cutlass at his side looked to have seen some use, though.

"We arranged a party for the commandant and his officers," he said. "As proof of our loyalty to the

Confederation, you might say. They're all away at the
Town Guildhall right now. And we sent in a wagonload
of wine and roast pigs and fairly high-priced girls so
the men could have a good time too. Some of the girls
are getting a bonus, and they saw to the door."

"Brilliant." Esmond grinned. "I hope you'll do as
much for my men."

"Oh, of course, excellent sir," Enry said. "And we
won't spike the wine with cane spirit, either."

Esmond laughed aloud. Colorless and tasteless, but
if you tried to drink it like wine . . .

"All right," he said, unfolding a square of reed-paper.
"Donnuld, Makin, as far as I can see there's nothing
to prevent us going straight in the front gate. The
barracks are in a square around a paved court with a
well, the usual arrangement; Confed regulars on these
two sides, this is the command block, and here's where
the light infantry are stationed. Half of the men are
out in the square, eating and boozing, and half are back
in their barracks screwing their brains out, or vice versa.
They've been at it for a couple of hours, more or less.
Makin, you bottle up the light infantry. We'll try and
get them to surrender. Donnuld, you take care of the
men in the square. I'll secure the barracks and the
headquarters."

It was no use trying to get Confed regulars to give
up, unless they bashed their heads in first. That was
one of the reasons Confed armies usually inflicted
heavier losses than they suffered, even when they lost—
they rarely ran away, and it was in rout and pursuit that
the real killing was done. One could spear a running
man in the back while chasing him, but he couldn't fight
back.

He looked up at the Preblean conspirator. "What
about the commandant and his staff?"

"Oh," Enry said, "I don't think you need worry,
excellent sir."

Esmond winced mentally; the wine servers stepping up behind men relaxed and unwary, only this time with curved daggers in their hands, instead of flasks. That had happened to the commanders of a famous Emerald mercenary unit serving in Chalice, just after the Alliance Wars, although the men had mostly been able to fight their way out—quite an epic. In a way it was fortunate, reminding him of the thin crust he walked, over an active volcano. He was never safe here, never . . . and it was no consolation that the local magnates played the same game among themselves. They were Islanders; they *liked* it.

It was strange. He hadn't really been *happy* since Nanya died; but it wasn't like he was *numb*. He could still feel some things just as well; he could be afraid, anxious, angry . . . hatred was stronger than ever. It was as if some *section* of his psyche had been cauterized.

*And I can still fight,* he thought. And now he could fight Confeds, not just Islander pirates. *I was wrong. I can still be happy . . . in a way.*

He drew his sword. "Walking pace," he said. Men running were more alarming than men walking. "Follow me."

Esmond turned the corner, walking lightly on the slimed cobbles. The streets here were narrow between banks of four-storied tenement houses, canyons of darkness with only a narrow slit of stars and moons above. The bright lights from the Confed garrision buildings were almost blinding by comparison, although the broad square of light there was narrowing quickly.

"Shit—charge!" Esmond yelled.

So much for being subtle. The doors were still open, but they were swinging closed; a section of frowsy-looking Confed regulars was doing it, under the direction of a noncom, a brick-built bristle-headed graying man with legs and arms like gnarled, scar-slashed tree trunks. He was wearing a scarlet dress tunic rather than armor and transverse-crested helmet, but there was no mistaking exactly what he was—and drunk or sober, he wasn't going to leave that door open. It was sixty yards between the alley where the Strikers had been waiting and the barracks gate . . . they'd have plenty of time to drop the bar in place before the first Emerald mercenaries reached them. It wouldn't save them—the force had grappling hooks and ropes and the wall was low— but it would turn the battle into a bloody dogfight.

Esmond's body reacted with automatic reflex, turning his run sideways as the javelin went back over his right shoulder. One skipping sidestep, two, and arm and back and shoulder moved with the smooth inevitability of a machine. The javelin disappeared, arching up into the night. He'd practiced throwing at the mark, stationary and moving hoops, nearly every day of his life since he went into the boys' palaestra at six.

The Confed noncom looked up at the whistle of cloven air just before the long narrow steel head of the throwing spear punched into his throat above his breastbone. Eight inches of it disappeared, and the point crunched into his spine between the shoulder-blades. He toppled like a cut tree, with only a single galvanic jerk as his heels came off the ground.

That paralyzed the men pushing at the door for a crucial two seconds; few of them had the noncom's experience, and they'd all been drinking wine much more potent than they thought it was. Time enough for twenty or thirty other Strikers to throw; they weren't Five Year Games victors, but they were closer, and there were a lot of them. Falling bodies knocked the gates wide again, and the Strikers burst through, roaring.

The courtyard had been set with trestle tables and lighted with tall iron tripods holding baskets of burning pinewood. Most of the Confed soldiers were sprawled about the picked-clean remnants of the pigs, bowls and cups in their hands, some of them with women in their laps, others watching a convoluted act involving four nude dancers and a very large trained snake. It took them gaping seconds to react, and none of them had weapons other than their eating knives at hand when hundreds of fully-armed alert soldiers poured through.

The first rank of Strikers launched their javelins and drew their swords; the second rank threw over their comrades' heads and plunged after them. Confed soldiers were dying—not only soldiers, Esmond vaulted over a whore in spangles and body paint, whimpering and pulling at the spear through her gut—and others were running, probably for their weapons. Some tried to make stands, grappling with the Emeralds or snatching up stools and eating utensils.

Esmond plunged through the chaos, over flagstones slippery with wine, spilled food, already wet with blood. Sword and buckler moved in clear, precise arcs; he seemed to be wading through honey, in a strange amber world in which everyone else moved very slowly, and he had more than enough time to do whatever was necessary. A solid wedge of men were following him, shields up and swords out. . . . A scrim of bodies marked the entrance to the barracks, men trying to get in, others trying to get out with snatched-up shields and assegais. The one in front of him stumbled and went down with a spear in his back, and then Esmond was facing an armed man at last.

The big shield with the crossed thunderbolts of Allfather of Vanbert on it—Allfather Greatest and Best— punched at him. The tip of the assegai glittered, held low and point-up for the gutting stroke. Esmond spun to the side, light on his feet as a dancer, hooking his buckler around the far edge of the oval shield and wrenching sideways to pin the Confed's spear arm against the frame of the door. His sword hilt went up high, like a beast fighter dispatching a greatbeast in the Vanbert arena after he'd teased it with the cape. The point punched down, in over the collarbone—unnecessary, the man hadn't had time to don his mail shirt, but you didn't think in a fight, you reacted on drilled reflex.

A wrench and jerk and the Confed went down. Esmond's foot and point snapped forward in a longe-lunge, skewered a thigh, pulled out with a twist to open the artery. He slammed his shoulder into another hastily-raised shield, and he was through the door. A Striker crowded through behind him, and in the dim light of the oil lamps he could see swarming confusion within, whores running and shrieking and the more sensible ones hiding under cots, men ripping weapons down from racks or stumbling in drunken bewilderment and getting in the way of their more sober comrades . . . and more of *his* men coming in the tall open windows. Barracks didn't run to glazing, but you wanted plenty of ventilation in this climate.

"*Strikers!*" he shouted. "*Strikers to me! Down Vanbert! Down Vanbert!*"

The Strikers were mercenaries, yes. They were also Emeralds almost to a man, and if there was one battle cry in all the world Emeralds could agree on, it was *that*.

Half an hour later, Esmond tucked his helmet under one arm and walked into the shrine room of the Confed headquarters, stepping over the bodies of the knot of men who'd died on its threshold. The slash on his thigh would make the leg stiffen in a little while, but for now he ignored it as he lifted out the ebony pole, with its golden wreath and hand and campaign-ribbons. He carried it himself onto the colonnaded porch that overlooked the courtyard, and the assembled Strikers roared his name as he held it high.

"Men!" he shouted, when the noise had died down a little. "So much for the invincible Confederacy!"

Another roar, with heartfelt emotion behind it this time. "Strikers," he went on. "We're soldiers loyal to

our salt. But we're Emeralds, too. This—" he waved
the standard "—has fouled the land of the Hundred
Cities far too long. This war is against the Confederacy."
A hush, then. "You know the gods favor my brother
and me."

Nods. *Or at least, my brother's productively crazy
. . . hands of the Shades, maybe the gods* do *talk to
him. Something does.*

"The gods foretell the fate of the Confederacy—they
tire of it. Vanbert shall *burn!*"

Wild cheers, and Donnuld Grayn looking at him with
a raised eyebrow—the expression looked a little odd
on the scarred, beaten-iron face.

"And think of the loot stacked up *there*," the mercenary shouted.

This time the cheers split the night.


"Where the hell were you?" Esmond asked.

"I had an errand to run," Adrian said, walking down
the gangway.

Esmond peered behind him. "Where's Helga?"

"As I said, I had an errand," Adrian said, and forced
a smile. "Look, let's forget about it, okay? Business."

"Certainly, brother," Esmond said. "This is Enry
Sharbonow, Suttete of Preble, Chief Minister to the
sovereign, Prince Tenny of Preble."

Adrian bowed, returning the Preblean magnate's more
elaborate salute. "Everything went well? Where's the
Prince?"

The northern dock of Preble was busy enough,
although most of it seemed to be ships loading for
departure—Adrian could see an entire household, from
a portly robed merchant to veiled wives and a dozen
children to skinny porters under huge bundles wrapped
in rugs. They were scuttling up the gangplank of a
freighter, and they were far from the only ones he could
see. There was a smell of smoke in the air, as well.

"Things got a little out of hand," Esmond said. "There aren't many Confed civilians left in town, either. We're letting some of the non-Prebleans leave."

Enry spread his hands. "The Confeds are not—were not—popular here," he said.

Adrian nodded. They never were; the first thing that happened in a country taken under Confed "protection" was a tribute levy, and then officials to collect it. The Confed Council didn't like hiring bureaucrats much: too many opportunities for political patronage with implications at home. They put tribute and tax collection up for competitive bidding; that might not have been so bad, if it weren't for the fact that the successful bidders had no fixed fee. The winning syndicate made its profit by collecting whatever it could above the amount it had paid for the contract, with the Confed army to see that nobody objected. Then Confed merchants swarmed in, to buy up goods and property at knock-down prices as the locals frantically tried to raise cash, and Confed bankers to loan at fifty percent interest, compounded, to those who *couldn't* raise the cash. If anyone defaulted on the loan, they'd sell every stick and rag he had, and march him off to the auction block, and he'd find himself hoeing beans on some Confed Councillor's estate outside Vanbert.

The nod was general; everyone knew how the system worked. "Funny," Adrian said. "The Confed peasants go into the army, because they can't compete with the big slave-worked estates . . . then they go out and get the Councillors the money and slaves they need to set up the estates in the first palace."

"Nice work if you can get it," Donnuld Grayn said. "Meantime the civvies ran down and killed maybe a thousand of 'em last night, once word got around we'd taken out the garrison." He smiled, a nasty expression. "Sort of commits 'em, don't it? What's that Confed saying?"

"'I am a Confed citizen; let kings tremble,'" Adrian said. "They're *not* going to be happy at a massacre."

Enry Sharbonow shrugged. "I put my arse above the stake when I enlisted in Prince Tenny's cause," he said. "Now everyone else in town is in the same boat."

"Where's Prince Tenny?" Adrian asked.

Enry coughed discreetly; it seemed to be his favorite expression. "He is occupied with setting up the Royal household," he said. "In his mercy, he has decided to take into his harem the now-protectorless females of the Confed commandant and his officers, or some of them."

Adrian winced slightly. **One of the drawbacks of this business,** Raj said at the back of his mind, **is that you usually end up working for some son of a bitch. Politics attracts them.**

"Well, we've got business to attend to," Adrian said. "I suppose I should start setting up the artillery?"

"Too right," Esmond said. "I don't think the Confeds are going to wait long to try a counterattack—some refugees will have made it out, over the wall and swimming if no other way."

"Sir!" One of the Strikers came up, panting. "Lord Esmond, Confed troops are putting out in small craft from the shore—barges, some ladders."

Enry made a small, appalled sound. Esmond nodded. "Numbers?"

"Fifteen hundred, sir."

The blond Emerald slapped Enry on the back. "Not to worry. That's the local commander, trying it on in case this is just some sort of pirate raid. Your militia ought to be able to see them off; there's seven or eight thousand of them."

"If they turn out," Enry said, taking a deep breath.

"Wait for it," Adrian said.

"Sor," Simun whispered back, "why don't we have the arquebuses up here? They're such *lovely* targets!"

**technological surprise,** Center whispered. **you may define this as—**

"Because we don't want them to know about the arquebuses until we really need them," Adrian said.

"They'll have heard."

"That's not the same thing as seeing something for yourself."

The landward edge of Preble had a narrow strip of sand studded with crags and boulders below the city wall, which was big ashlar blocks, enclosing a concrete and rubble core. It was crowded with men now, crouching down below the crenellations or behind the tarpaulin-covered torsion catapults. They were keeping surprisingly quiet, for civilians; nervously fingering bows, spears and slings, but not talking much. Esmond's Strikers probably had something to do with that; they'd kicked and clubbed a few noisy ones into unconsciousness to begin with.

Adrian turned his eyes from the mass of robed figures, from gleams of starlight and moonlight on eyes, teeth, the edge of a blade, out to the sea. The Confed flotilla was led by two light war galleys, each towing a string of barges; for the rest there were fishing boats, small coastal traders, a merchantman or two. They were crowded with men as well, probably the local coastal garrison; this area had been taken away from the Islanders by Marcomann only a decade or so ago, and it still resented Confed rule.

He turned to his brother. "Wasn't there a military colony around here?"

Esmond nodded. "Paid-off Marcomann veterans," he said. "Allied Rights settlement. I wouldn't be surprised if the governor had mobilized them."

Adrian nodded in turn; that was what a military colony was for, after all. They'd be ready enough, too; a successful revolt would let locals who'd had their land confiscated to make farms for the ex-soldiers get their own back, literally and metaphorically.

The ships were close enough to hear the rhythmic grunting of the oarsmen under the creak of rigging and wood. Adrian peered into the darkness, and suddenly it took on a flat silvery-green light.

"They've got ladders on those galleys," he said. "And on the barges—ladders with iron hooks on the ends. And what look like modified catapults. I'd say they're rigged to throw grapnels with rope ladders attached."

Esmond grunted. "Standard operating proceedure," he said. "Looks like the local commander really is going to chance the walls being lightly held." He cocked a sardonic eye at the militiamen. "Enry has earned his corn—I hope King Casull is paying him generously. He's had agents out all day, pointing out to the locals exactly what'll happen to them if the Confeds retake a city where six or seven hundred Confed citizens were massacred."

"Forward, sons of the Emerald! You fight for your homes and families, for the ashes of your fathers and the temples of your gods!"

The poet had said that about the League Wars, when the Emerald cities had turned back the Kings of the Isles. It was just as true here. In the open field, all the determination in the world wouldn't have stopped the Confed's armor and discipline; but fighting behind a wall, all the militiamen really needed to do was not run away.

"Ready," Esmond said. "Ready . . ."

The barges were coming forward, awkwardly, the oarsmen too cramped to pull efficiently. The square raftlike craft dipped at the bows, as armored men crowded forward with the ladders.

"Now!" He stood, waving a torch—three times, back and forth.

Brass trumpets rang along the wall. The men of Preble—sailors, craftsmen, shopkeepers—stood and shot. Arrows hissed out towards the Confed troops in a dark blurring rush, hard to see in the faint light, but appallingly thick. Flights of javelins followed, not very well thrown but very numerous, and sling-bullets, rocks, cobblestones. The Confed troops roared anger and surprise, with a chorus of screams from wounded men under it. Shields snapped up in tortoise formation, overlapping. At this distance some arrows drove right through the thick leather and plywood; rocks broke arms beneath them, crushed helmets. The catapults on the wall and its towers fired their four-foot arrows, pinning men together three in a row. A rock hurler sent a fifty-pound lump of granite skimming over the quarterdeck of one of the galleys, taking off the head of the captain as neatly as an axe and crushing the steersman against the tiller.

"Damn, they're still coming," Esmond said.

Men picked up the ladders of the fallen and ran them forward; others set the points of assegais against oarsmen's backs, to encourage them to keep rowing. Others beached their craft and jumped ashore, whirling grappling irons. A ladder thumped home against the crenellations of the wall, and then another. Men toppled off the rungs, and others replaced them; archers and slingers were replying from the invasion craft, concentrating their weaker fire on the crucial space around the heads of the ladders.

Four militamen came hurrying past Adrian, their rag-wrapped hands on the carrying handles of a huge bronze pot that had been bubbling quietly over a charcoal brazier. Adrian swallowed at the familiar scent of hot olive oil.

They reached the parapet and heaved the cauldron up, poured. The screams from below were unearthly loud and shrill, as the boiling oil ran over men's faces and through the links of their mail shirts. He could see Confed troopers throwing themselves into the ocean and drowning as they tried to extinguish the clinging agony.

"All right, Lightning Band," he called in a high carrying voice. "Let's see them off."

Adrian stepped up to the parapet, taking a grenade out of his satchel and lighting the fuse. One of the galleys was not far away below, more Confed troopers clambering over the pile of dead men in the bows to reach the grapnel-throwing catapult. Adrian waited a second for the fuse to catch fairly and then lobbed it overhand, an easy throw. The sputtering red spark of the fuse arched through the night; the clump of men suddenly turned white as faces went up to see what was coming at them.

With malignant, unplanned precision the grenade burst just above head-height, sending fragments slicing into the faces. Men scattered, screaming. Other red sparks were arching out from the wall, lobbed by hand or thrown with the sling at craft still trying to come up to the wall. Adrian threw two more; one rolled under the quarterdeck of the galley, and when it burst, pine planks shattered and began to burn. Several others of the invasion flotilla were burning as well, lighting the surface of water dotted with the heads of swimmers and men clinging to bits of wreckage—those must be oarsmen and sailors; anyone who went over the side in sixty pounds of armor wasn't coming ashore unless he walked along the bottom.

"Go back, you fool! Get your men out of here!" Esmond was shouting as he threw another javelin. "Order a retreat, gods condemn you!"

Adrian listened to the voices at the rear of his mind. "Their commander is probably dead," he said grimly. "There's nobody to order a retreat, and his underofficers are operating on their last instructions—press the attack."

"Wodep!" Esmond said. His eyes on the carnage below were full of a horrified pleasure. Adrian could read the thoughts on the shadowed face: *They're Confeds. But they're brave men, too.*

Even Confed discipline could take only so much. One by one the barges and fishing boats backed away, set sail or began to thrash the surface of the narrow channel with frantic oars. On a few of the craft fighting broke out, men who wanted to live in frantic close-quarter struggles with those determined to follow their orders regardless. Neither of the galleys was going anywhere; they were both outlines of yellow flame on the dark water, with men going up like torches or jumping overside. Some climbed the masts, scrambling frantically higher as the flames licked at their heels, screaming as the rigging burned through and the pine poles toppled over towards the water. Some of the water was burning too, pools of olive oil flickering with sullen orange-red.

"Gray-Eyed Lady," Adrian whispered.

The screams from below were drowned by the cheers of the militia, dancing and shrieking their relief and incredulous joy at beating back the Confed attack. They capered along the parapet, shaking fists and weapons, some lifting their robes and waggling and slapping their buttocks at the retreating enemy. The narrow strip of beach and rock below the walls was black with a carpet of men, a carpet that still crawled and moaned slightly. Adrian looked up at the stars for relief from the sight, and started.

"It's a full hour," he said wonderingly. "I'd thought fifteen minutes, thirty at the outside."

"Time flies when you're havin' fun," Simun said beside him, shaking and blowing on a hand scorched by a fuse that burned too fast. "We ought to get some men down the wall, sor—salvage them mail shirts 'n helmets. Better than some of our lads have—better than almost anything the milita here got. Must be seven, eight hundred we could get at."

"I suppose so," Adrian said quietly, looking down. *If you can accomplish the work, you should be able to look at the results,* he told himself.

"Victory!" Enry Sharbonow said, coming by with a train of servants carrying wineskins. "Oh, excellent sir, honorable sir—here, have a drink."

Adrian took a flask, swallowing rough red wine, unwatered.

"A great victory," the Preblean said.

Esmond lowered his own skin, looking around at the cheering milita; his own men were cheerful enough, but much quieter as they leaned against the parapet and watched the Confeds flee.

"I'd call it more of a skirmish," he said. "Come and tell me about our victory in a month or two."

# EIGHT

"Sun-stabbed by spears of *brazen* light," Speaker Emeritus Jeschonyk said. "*Brazen*, you see. Not *bronze light*."

One of his aides frowned. "That would be an irregular use of the pluperfect, though, wouldn't it?"

A babble of controversy erupted in the hot beige gloom of the command tent. Justiciar Demansk cleared his throat.

"Speaker," he said. Eyes turned towards him. "I think it's a dialect form, actually—Windrush Plain Emerald, archaic, of course." It would have to be; the poem they were discussing was eight hundred years old, an epic on the Thousand Ships War. Bits and pieces of it might go *back* to the Thousand Ships War, half a millennium before the poet. "In any case, Speaker, I think that at the moment we have more pressing, if banausic, concerns."

"By all means, Justiciar," the Speaker sighed, willing to listen to reason. He was a square-faced square-shouldered man, dressed in the purple-edged wrapped robe of his office, in his sixties, not a soldier recently himself, but still vigorous. "What do you recommend?"

201

When Demansk ducked outside the tent, one of his aides fell into step beside him. The man was a hundred-commander technically, but also First Spear of Demansk's First Regiment, the highest slot that a promoted ranker could reach. Within, it sounded as if they'd gone back to the irregular pluperfect. *Sometimes I wish we'd never let the Emeralds civilize us,* Demansk thought. *Particularly, I wish they'd never taught us literary criticism.* Rhetoric might be the foundation of civility—everyone agreed on that—but it did get in the way, sometimes.

"Get 'em to discuss business, sir?" he said, his voice still slightly rough with the accent of a peasant from the eastern valleys.

"More or less. We're putting in an attack as soon as we can get a causeway built. It's only half a mile, and shallow water. Meanwhile we'll get the fleet in Grand Harbor operational."

The promoted ranker shrugged mail-clad shoulders. "You get my men on solid ground next to the enemy and we'll thrash the wogs as soon as we get stuck into 'em, sir," he said. "But by the belly of Gellerix, we can't walk on water—or swim in armor, either. Not half a mile, not a hundred fucking yards, sir."

They reached the gate and took the salute of the watch platoon; Demansk trotted easily up the rough log stairs to the top of the openwork wooden tower, the left of the pair that flanked the gate. From there he could see out to Preble—the Speaker's camp was on the shore opposite the fortified island. One of the small ships the local commander had used in his abortive attempt to retake the city was still burning on a sandbank directly below the city walls. *Not encouraging.*

The camp itself *was.* Jeschonyk had brought four brigades, twenty thousand citizen troops, regulars, and nearly as many auxiliaries—slingers and archers and light infantry, of course; cavalry wasn't going to be much use here and he'd mobilized only enough for patrolling and foraging. The camp was a huge version of the usual marching fortress that a Confed force erected every night; a giant square cut into the soft loam of the coastal plain, with a ditch twelve feet deep and ten feet wide all around the perimeter. The earth from the ditch had been heaped up into a wall all around the interior, and on top of that were stakes pegged and fastened with woven willow. Each wall had a gate in the middle, flanked by log towers and guarded by a full company. Sentries patrolled the perimeter, and the rest of the men were hard at work. Four broad streets met in a central square for the command tent and unit standard shrines, and working parties were grading them, laying a pavement of cobbles and pounding it down, cutting drainage ditches along a gridwork throughout the camp. Orderly rows of leather tents were up, the standard eight-man issue for each squad; picket lines set out for the draught animals; deep latrines dug; even a bath-house erected. Smiths and leatherworkers and armorers were already hard at work, repairing equipment and preparing for the siege works.

Demansk felt a surge of pride; this whole great city, this expression of human will and intelligence and capacity for order and civilization, was the casual daily accomplishment of a Confed army. If they were ordered to move, they'd take it all down before breakfast muster—no use presenting an enemy with a fortress— and do the same again the next evening after a full day's march. And if they were here for a couple of months, it would be a city in truth—paved streets, sewers, stone buildings.

Then he turned and looked at Preble. *I hate sieges.* Sieges were an elaborate form of frontal attack, which was a good way to waste men at the best of times. With a siege, all the Confed army's advantages of flexiblity and articulation were lost. Against an Emerald phalanx . . .

well, you didn't have to run up against the pikepoints. Draw them onto broken ground, have small parties work in along their flanks, disrupt them—then they were yours. Islanders were like quicksilver; if you could get them to stand still for a moment, a hammer blow spattered them, no staying power. But behind a stone wall, even a townsman with a spear could become a hero. You had to go straight at him, and climbing a ladder left you virtually defenseless.

*If we can get the causeway close, we can batter the wall down with catapults.* The problem with that was that the defenders could shore it up, or build a secondary wall within while you were battering—ready to mousetrap you as you charged in over the rubble. *Or we could undermine, use sappers . . . The butcher's bill is still going to be fearsome. And if it takes too long, we'll get disease, sure as the gods made the grapes ripen, we'll have disease.* That *really* frightened him. He'd seen dysentery go through armies like the Sword of Wodep too many times.

"Sir!"

An aide came trotting up. "Sir, Justiciar Demansk— we've got a . . . a person, sir, who claims to have urgent news."

Demansk's eyebrows went up towards the receding line of his close-cropped grizzled hair. "A *person?*" he said.

"Claims to be a relative of yours, sir." The aide's aristocratic features curled slightly in disdain. "On the off chance that they might have some information I didn't have them whipped out of the camp, sir."

The Justiciar lowered the hand he'd been shading his eyes with as he peered towards Preble. "By all means, let's see this . . . person . . ." he said.

*Anything that could distract me from this would be welcome. Even a dancing ape.*

A small slight man came trotting up the log stairs of

the tower, with an Islander woman at his heels. *No, wait a minute,* he thought. He looked at bare legs and arms, at the way the stranger walked. *That's not a man, it's a woman in armor.* What looked like Emerald light-infantry kit, bowl helmet with cheekguards, linen corselet with brass shoulderpieces and probably iron scales between the layers of cloth. A trooper was carrying a sword and shield and pair of light javelins behind them, puffing along. . . .

This *was* out of the ordinary. Then the stranger took off her helmet, and long tawny-auburn hair fell free, nearly to her waist.

Demansk's eyes went wide. "Helga!" he said . . . almost sputterings.

"Father!"

"What are they doing?" Enry Sharbonow said, squinting.

"They're getting ready to build a causeway," Esmond said. He pointed. "See, they've got a good hard-surfaced road right down to the water's edge. They've almost certainly got local pilots and fishermen who can tell them exactly what the shoals are like. Now they're starting. See those lines of log pilings, a hundred yards apart? Those mark the edges. Between them, they've got working parties, their troops and whatever civilians they can round up, unloading those oxcarts full of rock—boulders, up to sixty pounds. See how they're passing them hand to hand? They'll pile those up until they get above the surface, compact them, then cover with a layer of smaller rock. By the time it's safely above high-tide level, they'll have a section of first-class paved road."

Enry swallowed. A little beyond him Prince Tenny lounged with elaborate unconcern, nibbling on a honeyed fig and fingering a set of healing scratches along one side of his bearded face.

"And those wooden things they're building, a little further back?"

"Well, that's a little far to see, but I'd say they're probably siege engines. Catapults, of course, heavy ones. Siege towers—wooden fort towers on wheels, covered in hides or possibly metal plates, so they can roll them up to our walls and climb protected. Solophonic ladders—big counterweighted things like a covered bridge on a pivot, sort of the same thing. Fire raisers. Metal-shod battering rams under heavy roofs, also on wheels, for forcing a breach. When they get the causeway close enough, they'll use the catapults and archers to keep our heads down while they complete it—batter a hole in the wall, if they can. If they can't, they'll roll the Solophons and siege towers up to the wall and storm it, while the battering rams knock sections of it down and make ramps for their assault troops."

Enry's natural olive skin had gone very pale, a sort of doughy white color. "What are we going to *do*?" he said.

Esmond took a fig from the silver tray being held up for Tenny, popped it into his mouth and chewed with relish. "Oh, there are a few tricks we can try," he said cheerfully, and cocked an eye at the sky. "No moons tonight."

"You shouldn't be here," Esmond hissed into the darkness.

"Neither should you," Adrian said.

"Sirs, with respect, shut the fuck up," Donnuld Grayn said, pausing as he tightened the strap on a greave. "We're getting close."

*We shouldn't,* Esmond thought. *Typical Confed arrogance.* When they sat down to besiege a place, they expected the defenders to sit tight and cower, waiting for inevitable doom, so what point was there in taking elaborate precautions?

At least, that was what the Preblean scouts had said, swimming in after sculling across the strait on inflated sheepskins. None of them had been caught, so either the Confeds were extremely confident or fiendishly clever at misdirection.

Esmond showed teeth, white in the darkness against skin covered with burnt cork. *Now, fiendishly clever is something that might be applied to an Emerald, or even an Islander. But to a Confed? No, no . . .* systematic, *yes.* Methodical, *yes. But fiendishly clever? Rarely.*

"I'll show them fiendish," he whispered, chuckling, and looked back along the boat.

It was about thirty feet long, the Preblean sailors at the muffled oars, the men his own Strikers with some of Adrian's specialists for luck. That dampened his mood, slightly. He might have known that Adrian wouldn't send his men along and not go himself; he wasn't a professional, but he thought like one, sometimes—as if soldiers' ghosts were whispering in his ear.

That checked him for a moment. *I suppose I am a professional now,* he thought. Not an athlete or a weapons trainer, but a general. *But not a mercenary. I have a cause.*

"Row off," the Preblean at the tiller oar said softly. "Row soft, all . . . raise oars and let her glide. *Not* raise it upright, Rawl, you stupid bastard; ten lashes for that."

The high timber wall of the causeway's edge loomed ahead of them. The Confeds had driven the logs into the sand and mud of the channel bed at an angle, slanting outwards. That made it easier to climb as the boat came alongside; he leapt, got a grip, swarmed upwards. Rope nooses flew up from his and the other boats, but Esmond ignored them as he poised crouching at the top. According to the scouts' reports, the sentry ought to be . . .

*There.* Pacing stolidly along, and no more than fifteen paces away, now. *Have to get him to turn around.*

"Hey, you Confed donkey fucker," Esmond said, in a conversational tone. "Did you know that your mother used to suck my dad's dick, and for free?"

The Confed soldier whirled at the sound, gaping. Esmond's arm whipped forward; it was an awkward position to throw from, but a clout shot at this distance—there were fires in iron baskets further in towards the shore. Iron crunched through the mail shirt the trooper wore, and he pitched over backwards. Esmond dropped four feet to the surface of the causeway; this section was half-complete, and loose rock shifted and crunched under the hobnails of his sandals.

The sentries died, quickly and with relative quiet. Men were forming up around him; others were coating the logs that ran along both sides of the causeway with oil and tallow brought along in leather sacks. More were handing up small wooden barrels from the boats.

"Ready, General," Donnuld panted.

"Follow me."

The Strikers followed. Behind them were Preblean archers; he'd picked them himself, from men with good sea-beast hornbows and plenty of experience. Forward . . . *Yes. They really didn't fortify their construction yard.*

Siege engines reared about him in the dark, like monstrous beasts in a child's nightmare. More sentries died, but a few survived long enough to sound an alarm. They'd have to work quickly.

Adrian and his men ran to the larger engines, the siege towers and heavy catapults. The kegs of gunpowder went underneath them, hastily buried. Esmond let his nose guide him to stacks of timber, mostly fresh-cut pine oozing sap.

"Right here, boys," he called.

Covered firepots were brought out, torches lit and whipped into flame. Esmond thrust one under a stack of four-by-six timbers and shouted glee as the wood began to catch. Others of his men were kicking over barrels and pots of pitch and tar, throwing long coils of rope onto growing blazes; the archers were sending fire-arrows buzzing about, into piles of cordage and wood further in, into tents and heaps of sailcloth and fodder. Esmond was whirling another torch around his head when a lead-weighted dart whipped by his ear close enough for him to feel the draft, going *thunk* into a timber and whining with a malignant buzz like an enormous, very pissed-off bee.

"Fall in!" he called. Beside him the signaler sounded his horn, and the bannerman waved the flag. "Fall in! Everyone else back to the boats!"

The Strikers formed up at the head of the causeway— most of them, at least, and anyone too hopped up or too stupid to remember the signals he'd gone over at great length deserved what was going to happen to them. Happy arsonists ran by, climbing the wooden edges of the causeway and sliding down to the boats or into the water, whooping. The Confeds were reacting at last, though; he could see blocks of them working their way through the burning equipment, and the fires were making this area as bright as day.

"Discourage them," he said to the Preblean in charge of the archers. The man nodded and turned to his own command: "Loose!"

The archers drew to the ear, thumbrings around the strings of their powerful composite bows. A cloud of yardlong shafts whickered out, vanishing from sight into the darkness and smoke above, then whipping back down into the gathering Confed ranks. A dozen men went down, silent or jerking or screaming and ripping at the barbed shafts in their flesh. More shrugged aside slight wounds, or started when armor or shields deflected the steel raining down out of the night.

"Keep it up," Esmond said, teeth showing. "Pour it on!"

The Confed noncoms were hustling their sleepy men into battle order, shoving, bellowing orders. The formation began to shake itself out into the dreaded double line of the Confederation, shields up, darts rocking back ready on thick muscular peasant arms. Here and there a man fell as an arrow or slingstone went home, and the formation rippled as it closed up to maintain the precise one-yard gap between each soldier. In a minute, that living wall would begin to walk . . .

*Except that in less than a minute . . .*

*BWAMMMP.*

"Yes!" Esmond shouted.

Dirt, flame and splintered wood vomited up from beneath one of the siege towers. Shattered along one side it began to sway, leaned drunkenly, and then fell— four stories of heavy timber, crashing down across the back of the Confed formation.

*About three hundred of them,* Esmond thought. *But—*

*BWAMMMP.*

The other siege tower writhed as half a dozen ten-pound kegs of powder went off beneath it; this one disintegrated where it stood, showering the wavering Confed troops with heavy bone-cracking lumps and baulks of timber.

"*Charge!*" Esmond shouted.

The trumpeter sounded it, but the Strikers were already running forward, howling. A cloud of javelins surged out before them, and the archers fired over their heads. When they struck the Confeds, they struck in a solid line abreast, struck men whose formation had already been shaken. A rippling series of explosions shook their nerve even more, as catapults leapt into the air in fragments and rained down out of the dark.

"Wodep's thunderbolts!" a Confed trooper bawled, and threw down his shield.

The noncom behind him killed the man before he'd taken his second panic-stricken step, but then the Emeralds were upon them. Esmond threw at point-blank range, and the javelin crunched through the Confed's face to knock his helmet off as the point met the inside rear with an audible *clank*. He punched his buckler into another face, stabbed a throat, brought the buckler around to break the wrist that held an assegai and then stab downward into a thigh. The Confeds shattered the way a clay winejug might when dropped on solid stone . . . and spattered red in the same way, too.

"Rally!" Esmond shouted, and the trumpeter blew it again and again. Some of the men were reluctant; one or two were so victory-drunk that they careened off into the darkness. "Rally!"

"Fall back to the boats," he went on.

"Feels good to see their backs, by Wodep," Donnuld said, as they jogged back.

Behind them the Confed siege works and timber stores were fully involved, a cone of bright orange flame rising into the spark-shot night and underlighting its own black cloud of smoke. *Glorious, glorious destruction,* Esmond thought, feeling the savage heat of it on his face.

They reached the edge of the causeway, slid down into the boats. Esmond took a torch and tossed it at the oil-soaked wood as they left; flames ran across the timbers in a sheet of orange-red, adding to the hellish symphony of flames.

"It won't be as easy the next time," he said, chuckling. "But I think we'll come up with some way to annoy them."

He started as Adrian nodded beside him. "We haven't shown them most of our surprises yet," he said. "*Techno-logical* surprise."

"What's technology?" Esmond asked, curious.

"That's what the Confeds are about to find out, brother."

"What am I going to do with you?" Demansk asked his daughter.

She lounged back in the camp chair and sipped from her clay cup. "Velipad piss . . . well, you're not going to marry me off, not after all this."

Demansk flushed and hit the table with a fist, making the jug bounce. "You don't speak to your father like that, missy!" he growled, his voice filling the tent like a direbeast's warning. "And a tent is not a place to discuss family matters at this volume."

They were both speaking Emerald, but so could any Confed citizen with any pretensions to education. The ranker guards outside probably couldn't, and there probably wasn't anyone else within earshot . . . probably.

"Sorry, Father," Helga said, dropping her eyes. "I'm just trying to put the best possible face on it."

Demansk sighed and rubbed a hand over the gray-and-brown stubble on his chin. Small insects were coming through the laced opening of his tent and immolating themselves in the oil lamps with small *spppt* sounds and a disagreeable smell; the scent triggered old memories of camps, running back to his earliest manhood. Helga had been conceived in a tent like this, to his second wife; she'd accompanied him on several campaigns down around the southern border, when he'd been one of the senior officers overseeing the building of the wall against the barbarians.

"Your mother was a lot like you," he said heavily. "Perhaps if she'd lived . . . maybe that's why I've indulged you so. Too much, probably."

He sighed again; with commendable self-command, Helga held her piece. "Oh, we could patch up some sort of match. . . ."

"You'd have to pay heavily, and I wouldn't be getting

any prize, Father. I'd rather be a spinster. It isn't as if you don't have grandchildren already, and besides . . ."

"Besides, there's this pirate," Demansk said dryly.

"He's not a pirate!"

"Mercenary, then," Demansk said, with a slight wry smile. "Emerald rebel, surely."

"Redvers was the rebel, and he was Adrian Gellert's patron," Helga said reasonably. "A client has to follow his patron, doesn't he?"

"Well, that's the tradition." Demansk gestured at the wine jug, and Helga poured for them both again, adding dippers of water from the bigger clay vase by the door. "I think sometimes it would be better for the State if it wasn't."

Helga chuckled. "Father, you're not rebelling against the Customs of the Ancestors yourself, now?"

"Our Ancestors were a bunch of pig farmers," Demansk said bluntly. "My grandfather used to be out every day, weeding the fields beside his slaves. Times have changed; Audsley's rebellion, Marcomann's dictatorship, the proscriptions . . . things are falling apart." His gaze sharpened. "And evidently my daughter has been driven mad by a scratch from one of the cats that draws Gellerix's chariot, and has become besotted with a rebel."

Helga shook her head. "Adrian's not . . . not really a rebel. His brother, Esmond, yes—Esmond would bring the whole Confederacy down in ruins, and everyone in it, I think, if he could. Adrian's more . . . reasonable."

"Reasonable and learned," Demansk said, keeping his voice casual. "He's the one that came up with this damnable hellpowder stuff, isn't he?"

Helga laughed ruefully. "You know, Father, the reason Adrian put me ashore was that he didn't want me to be forced to betray the Confederacy. And here you are, trying to worm *his* secrets out of me! I'm between the mad velipad and the direbeast."

"If you don't want to talk about it . . . I suppose I
*do* owe this man something for getting you out of Vase,
and for putting you ashore."

"There's not much for me to say," Helga said. "I don't
know how the hellpowder is made—Adrian didn't tell
me, and it's a close-kept secret. So are the other
weapons."

"Other weapons?" Demansk said sharply.

"There were all sorts of rumors, and I *saw* what
happened in Vase—the city wall pounded to rubble, and
the gates of the citadel smashed like kindling."

"Hmmm." Demansk rubbed his chin again. "I suppose . . . larger barrels of hellpowder thrown by
catapults? That *could* get nasty, very nasty, especially
in siege operations, or at sea—and here we're faced with
both!" He slammed a fist into the arm of the folding
camp chair, hard enough to make the tough wood and
leather creak. "I spend my whole life learning the trade
of war—not leaving it to the underofficers, but really
*learning* it, the way Marcomann did, damn his soul to
the Ash Fields—and this whippersnapper of an Emerald
turns it upside down, all at once. A *philosopher*, a
rhetorician!"

"Father . . . I don't think Adrian really *is* a rhetorician,
not anymore. He studied rhetoric, and he's very good
at it . . . but what he mostly seems to be interested
in now is . . . is the . . . way the world's put together."

Demansk's eyebrows shot up. "A *natural* philosopher?
Hmmm. There haven't been any of those since the
League Wars! If this hellpowder is what comes of it,
I'm glad there hasn't been. Still, the wine's out of the
jug now, no use trying to put it back." His shrewd green
eyes fastened on his daughter's face. "Just what do you
think this Adrian fellow will do, facing us now."

"Facing *you* now," Helga snorted. "Jeschonyk couldn't
find . . . what's the soldier's expression?"

*Couldn't find his dick with both hands and a hooker*

*to help,* Demansk thought automatically. Still, however much of a tomboy she was, there were things you didn't say to a daughter.

"Couldn't find his arse with both hands on a dark night," he chuckled aloud. "Not quite fair. He has enough sense to leave details to experts, and he *listens* . . . occasionally. But he's set in his ways even for a man of his generation. And I asked you a question, missy."

Helga's chin went up. "Adrian will do what you least expect, and when you least expect it," she said proudly. "His brother's a good soldier and a demon with a sword but Adrian . . . thinks about things."

Demansk shuddered, a little theatrically. "Allfather Greatest and Best, this business is bad enough without *scholarship,*" he said, and then cocked an eye. "Rumor has it that the gods talk to your Adrian."

He hid his surprise when Helga looked distinctly uneasy; she was as skeptical as any young noble— the way the younger generation openly said things that were whispered in his younger days shocked him, now and then. In his grandfather's day they'd been killing matters.

"I'm . . . not altogether sure about that," Helga said. "Sometimes . . . sometimes I'd catch him murmuring to *somebody.* Somebody who wasn't there."

Demansk grunted. "Perhaps he's mad, then."

"I don't think so, Father. Madmen hear voices, but if Adrian's listening, it's to someone who tells him things that are *true.* Or at least very useful."

*That's a point, a distinct point,* Demansk thought.

He was lifting the cup to his lips when the alarm sounded out across the camp.

# NINE

"This time they're being cautious," Esmond said, bracing his feet automatically against the pitch and roll of the ship.

"How so?" Adrian said curiously, peering towards the shore, where the causeway swarmed with workers and troops, like a human anthill.

"They're putting in a wall with a parapet and fighting platform along the edge of the causeway as it goes out, see? And they've got their building yard completely surrounded with a ditch-and-stockade, *and* they've brought out those two fighting towers—they'll push them out as the causeway proceeds. The catapults on them outrange anything a ship can mount, and they've got archers packed tight in there too. They can shoot from shelter."

"Hmmm," Adrian said. "*Not* good, brother."

**similar situations tend to produce similar solutions,** Center said.

*Meaning what?*

**Center tends to get a little oracular now and then, son,** Raj thought with a chuckle.

217

*Well, that's appropriate.*

**What he—or it—means is that this isn't the first time these tactical conditions have come up. Back on Bellevue, I got a reputation for originality partly because Center kept feeding me things that other generals had done, back on Earth before spaceflight. I've studied more since Center and I have been . . . together. There was a man named Alexander . . .**

"Adrian? *Adrian?*"

Adrian shook himself, stopped squinting at the eye-hurting brightness of water on the purple-blue sea, and looked at his brother.

"Sorry."

"I know Scholars of the Grove are supposed to be detached, but we have a *problem* here." A scowl of frustration. "Or are you still mooning over that Confed girl?"

"Yes, but that doesn't mean I can't think of practical matters," Adrian said, slightly annoyed.

*I've been getting that* detached *business since I was fourteen,* he thought. One of the earlier Scholars had had the same problem from his family, and had cornered the olive-oil market for a year, just to prove a philosopher could also outthink ordinary men in ordinary affairs.

"Don't think of it as a *problem,*" Adrian went on aloud, with a smile he knew was a little smug. "Think of it as an *opportunity.*"

He began to speak. Esmond's eyes narrowed, then went wide. When he'd finished, the older Gellert spoke:

"Well, I will be damned to pushing a boulder up a hill for all eternity. That *just* might work—and it's a little longer before we have to let them know about the rest of your surprises. Captain!"

Sharlz Thicelt hurried over. "Sir?" he said.

Esmond looked up, frowning a little—there were few men taller than he—and spoke:

"What are the prevailing winds like here, this time of year?"

"My General, they vary. Usually from the northwest, particularly in the afternoons—an onshore breeze, very tricky. It dies at night and backs in the morning, though. Of course, the Sun God alone can predict the weather on any given day; at times there are strong offshore winds, particularly if we get a summer thunderstorm, and—"

"Thank you very much, Captain Thicelt," Esmond said hastily; the Islander loved the sound of his own voice—something of a national failing in the Islands as well as the Emerald cities. "That may be very useful. Very useful indeed."

"Odd," Justiciar Demansk said, shading his eyes with one hand. "Those look like merchantmen."

The causeway had made two hundred yards progress, and the siege towers were half that distance from shore. Already the inner surface looked like a paved city street, flanked by fortress walls; attempts at hit-and-run sniping hadn't been more than a nuisance. *And we've sunk one of their galleys.* That had been the stone throwers on the siege towers. Nine stories of height made a considerable difference in one's range; when they got out to Preble, the tops would overlook the city wall by a good fifteen feet, and the archers and machines there could sweep the parapets bare for the infantry. Thousands of workers hauled handcarts and carried baskets of broken rock out to the water, and the sound of it dropping into the waves was like continuous surf. Masons worked behind them, setting up the defense parapet, and where it hadn't reached yet the workers were protected by mantlets—heavy wooden shields on wheeled frames. All was order, and rapid progress. At this rate, they'd be out to Preble in less than a month. And the troops would be *royally* pissed at having to work this hard for this long—it was worse than road-building detail, itself always unpopular. Added to what had happened there during the uprising, and the fact that Jeschonyk didn't even intend to try and keep the men in hand, and it was going to be a very nasty sack.

Demansk felt a *little* sorry for the inhabitants of the island city. The Confed occupation had been enough to drive anyone to distraction . . . although not, in his opinion, to suicide. Which was what came of massacring Confederation citizens; the ones spared for the mines would be the lucky ones. Jeschonyk was talking about a special Games for the captured adults; a Games Without Issue, pairs forced to fight to the death and then the winners matched with each other, with one survivor left to be poled.

He took an orange out of the helmet he had balanced on one knee and began to peel it with methodical care. *We've really got to do something about provincial government,* he thought. Every time there was a political crisis at home there was a revolt *somewhere*, and it was all because of the tax-farming system. *They're our subjects, we've got to stop treating the provinces like a hunting ground.* As it was, a provincial governor *had* to extort to the limit, to stand off the lawsuits that would be launched when he retired; for that matter, anyone who crossed swords with the tax-farming syndicates would be sued into bankruptcy or exile.

The Preblean flotilla was approaching the causeway from the northwest, with the sun behind them and to their right, and the wind directly astern. *Hmmm,* he thought. *Four galleys, and they're each pulling a merchantman. Could they be trying an assault?*

No, they weren't insane, or that desperate yet. He had a full brigade of troops ready to hand, with more to draw on—the working details had their equipment stacked and he'd drilled them in moving rapidly to kit out and fall in.

"Then what *are* they doing?" he asked.

*Helga's got me spooked, with her tales of that damned Emerald she took up with,* he thought sourly. *This is the modern age, not the plain before the walls of Windhaven during the Thousand Ships War. The gods do not don mortal disguise to fight in mortal quarrels, if they ever did.*

Still . . . "First Spear," he said. "Get your outfit standing to."

"Yessir!"

*That* would be done competently, he knew. He squinted again, then stiffened as the rebel flotilla came into closer sight, just outside catapult range from the siege towers. The galleys were casting off their tows, turning, their oars going to double-stroke; heading away, then halting and backing water, their sterns to the causeway. The tubby deep-hulled merchantmen were sheeting home their big square sails, though. Heading straight for the causeway . . .

No. Their crews were diving overside, climbing into small boats and rowing like Shadesholm back towards the galleys. One paused, just close enough to see, and pumped a hand with an outstreched finger towards the Confed forces. The four ships came on with the tillers of their dual steering oars lashed and the wind steady on their quarters, faster now, little curves of white foam at their bluff bows. And smoke, smoke curling up from under their deck hatches.

"Messenger!" Demansk barked. "The towers are to open fire on the ships—rocks. Knock down their masts, or sink them—immediately. I'll have the rank off the commander who lets them get through. *Move!*"

Demansk was a man who rarely raised his voice. The man ran as if the three-headed hound of the Shadow Lord were at his heels, and the Justiciar ground his teeth in fury.

*Emeralds,* he thought. No discipline; he'd fought them

from Rope to Solinga, talking less and hitting harder. But they were . . .

"Sneaky. And these Gellerts, they're sneaky even for *Emeralds*."

The tendrils of fire licking up from the hatchways of the ships were growing even as he watched, pale in the bright sunlight, but full of promise and black smoke.

"Burn, you Confed bastards!" Esmond whooped.

Beside him on the raised stern of the galley, with his head on the curling seabeast stemhead, Adrian winced slightly. A rock from one of the tower catapults splashed into the water a hundred yards astern; either someone there was getting vindictive or they were *really* bad shots. More fifty-pound rocks were striking the fireships sailing in at six knots towards the Confed siege tower, knocking bits off their railing, making holes in the sails, some of them crashing through decks or striking masts. The holes in the deck simply gave the fires spreading belowdecks among the barrels of pitch and tar and sulfur and oil and tallow more air, miniature volcanoes shooting up after each hit. One ship's mast did fall over; the high stern of the merchantman was still enough to keep it drifting steadily before the wind towards the tower, although it turned broadside on.

"Haven't a prayer of sinking them," he said.

You could sink an ordinary galley by catapult fire, if you were lucky. They were lightly built, racing shells of fragile pine, quickly made and quickly worn out. Freighters had oak frames and much thicker hull planks and frames. They were built to take strains and last; many sailed for thirty or forty years before they had to be broken up. The only real way to sink one was to ram it, or burn it . . . and these weren't going to burn to the waterline until long after they hit the causeway.

"They're bringing up men with oars," Esmond said.

Adrian could see them too; someone had been bright enough to rig a pump, to keep them covered with water. They'd never be able to stand the heat, even so. Probably.

"We'd better discourage that," he said. "Captain Sharlz, if you could bring us broadside on?" He turned and looked down onto the gangway of the galley: "Simun! Six arquebus teams—target the men trying to fend off."

"Sir, yessir!" the underofficer shouted back, as the galley heeled and turned in its own length, oars churning and then going to a steady slow stroke to keep the craft on station.

*Puduff. Puduff. Puduff* . . . Sulfur-stinking smoke drifted back to the poop. Men fired, stepped back for their loading teams, stepped forward again, intent on their work. The first six rounds brought one man down—good practice, at this extreme range. The four-ounce balls and seven-foot barrels gave the arquebusiers more range than any torsion catapult, though.

"Bastards don't know what's hitting them," Esmond chuckled.

***That they don't,*** Raj added. ***There's no reason for them to associate a bang and a puff of smoke with someone getting killed. But they'll learn.***

They did, as more of the men getting ready to fend off the fireships went down. Confed troopers trotted up, raising their big oval shields to hold off whatever it was that was killing their comrades. Adrian could see the bronze thunderbolts on their facings glitter as they raised them; another row behind held them overhead, making a tortoise as they would for plunging arrow fire. Habit, but it was also habit that kept them so steady. Even when the first soldiers went down; the arquebus balls knocked men back, punctured shields, smashed through the links of mail.

This time Esmond winced; Adrian sensed he wasn't

altogether happy at seeing personal courage and skill and strength made as nothing by a machine striking from twice bowshot.

"'Strong-Arm! How the glory of man is extinguished!'" the elder Gellert murmured; a king of Rope had made that cry from the heart, the first time he saw a bolt from the newly-invented catapult.

"Progress," Adrian replied. Then: "Cease fire!"

The first of the fireships would ground not ten yards from its target. The Islander sailors had done their work well.

"Ungh."

A man not two paces from Justiciar Demansk went down, grunting like someone who'd been gut-punched. Unlike a gut-punched boxer he wasn't going to get up, not from the amount of blood that welled out around his clutching fingers. *Better he bleeds to death now,* Demansk thought with a veteran's ruthless compassion. *I'd rather, than go slow from the green rot.* A puncture down in the gut *always* mortified. He could smell shit among the blood-stink, even from here.

"That went right through his shield," he said aloud.

"Fuckin' right it did," his First Spear said. "Sir, you've got to get *out* of here! You get killed, who's going to command this ratfuck? I can't, and them bastards in the command tent, most of 'em *can't*."

Demansk shook his head. Jeschonyk actually had half a dozen reasonably experienced advisors—one good thing about the past twenty years of Confederation history was that the upper classes were full of men who'd seen red on the field. He turned in exasperation, keeping his voice low:

"I can't expect the men to hold steady under this if I don't—"

*Ptannggg.* Another trooper went down in front of him, a hole punched through his shield. Justiciar Demansk found himself on the rough stones of the causeway as well, blinking up at the First Spear's horrified face.

"Where's the velipad that kicked me?" he muttered.

His hand went to where the pain was, the left side of his torso, and then he jerked it away from metal burning hot. When he looked down there was a trough along his flank, ploughed into the thick cast bronze of his breast-and-back muscled cuirass. Lead was splashed across it.

"The Justiciar's dead! The commander's dead!" some-one was wailing.

That pulled him out of his dazed wonder. He took a deep breath; there was a shooting pain in his ribs, but nothing desperate, no blood on his breath or grating of bone ends.

"I am *not!*" he said. "Get me up, gods condemn you!"

Hands pulled him up; he walked up and down behind the ranked troops, letting them see him.

*Some way of making hellpowder* throw *things,* he realized. *Throw them farther than a torsion catapult can, and too fast to see. That's what those puffs of smoke on the galley are.*

Another thought brought his eyes wide, appalled. "First Spear!" he snapped. "Get those men with the oars away from there."

"Let it ground, sir?" he asked, puzzled.

"We can't stop it." Still less push it around the front of the causeway, to drift harmlessly downwind. Some-body out there—those *damned* Gellerts—had probably timed this very carefully. "Have the battalion retreat—get everyone else out behind us. Walking retreat, shield-wall formation, but be damned quick about it. Move!"

He turned himself and began to walk to the rear. He'd been campaigning most of his fifty years; there was nothing in him of the need to prove his courage that had driven a young tribune to lunacy, so long ago.

And the First Spear was partly right; nobody else was going to do this job better, if he couldn't.

"They're bugging out," Esmond said, disappointment in his voice. "Someone got a rush of thought to the head."

Adrian nodded tightly; he wasn't grieved that fewer men would be burned alive. The first of the fireships was almost in contact with the sandbank the causeway was being built on . . . almost . . .

"There!" he said.

The comandeered merchantman touched, lurched forward and then stopped dead. With a long slow crackling audible even over the growing roar of the fire, the mast toppled forward, to lie with its burning sail over the rock of the causeway. It fell towards the tower, but did not quite touch it—men were leaning out of the upper works of the siege tower, reckless of arquebus bullets, and pouring water down the layers of thick green hides that made up its outer skin. Any moment now . . .

*BUDDUFFF.*

The force of the explosion was muffled by the hull of the ship, and the weight of combustibles lying above it. That confinement increased the force, as well. The burning deck of the fireship vanished in a spectactular volcano of flame, burning planks, beams, and dozens of barrels of flammables; many of them had ruptured in the hull as well, and added their sticky, fast-burning contents to the cone of flame that leapt upwards. It wasn't aimed at anything in particular, but the breeze bent it south and eastwards . . . and most of it fell across the wall of the siege tower. Buckets of water became utter irrelevancies, and so did the layers of hide—they dried out and began to burn almost immediately. When the explosion cleared, the whole flank of the tower was already burning, and smoke was pouring out of the arrow slits and catapult ports all along the other side of it. Men jumped too, men with their hair and clothes aflame. A few were running from the other side, but not many could have made it down the ladders. The tower was a chimney now, sucking in air from the bottom and blasting it out the top and every opening along the sides, the thick timbers and internal bracing adding to the holocaust.

The next three fireships drifted into the red heart of the flames and exploded almost immediately. Adrian felt a huge soft pillow of hot air strike his face, making him fling up a hand as his eyeballs dried. When he blinked them clear the first tower was falling onto the flaming pillar of the second, nine stories of burning timber avalanching down unstoppably. The second tower cracked, shedding men and planks and hides; part of it hit the shallow water beyond, but the thick stump of it remained to burn with the whole of the first. Pieces of flaming wood flew through the air for hundreds of yards, well into the walled camp where the Confeds had crammed their carpentry supplies and naval stores. Fires started there, too; he could hear trumpets and drums as officers tried to organize fire-fighting parties. It would be difficult, though—the way to the nearest water supply was thoroughly blocked by the conflagration on the causeway.

There, stone would be beginning to crack as it glowed white-hot. Esmond was laughing, and the crews of the galleys were joining in—even the rowers were grinning through their oar ports on the outriggers, and the soldiers and sailors on deck were dancing, snapping their fingers and making obscene gestures towards the shore.

"A thousand men lost, there," Esmond said, slapping his hand exultantly on his swordhilt. "A thousand men, and a month's work, and all those materials. Lovely."

Even against the wind, Adrian thought he could

catch a whiff of the smell. He gagged slightly and nodded.

"That will set them back a little," he said. "But I think we're going to be real, real unpopular over there now."

"Well, then," Esmond said, clapping him on the back. "We'll just have to continue closing the door in their face, won't we?"

"It's called a 'trebuchet,' " Adrian said to the carpenters and blacksmiths and shipwrights. "And it's a form of catapult."

He was standing on a platform of rammed rubble behind the city wall, the section nearest to the Confed's causeway. Everyone had been up there, and seen the redoubled efforts—this time the blocking wall along the sides was like a small city's, and the towers pressed forward to the edge of construction were squat monsters sheathed in plates of beaten iron and brass, glittering like malignant serpents in the bright sunlight.

The craftsmen crowded around to look at the man-tall model he'd built. It had two heavy tripods, linked by an iron axle. Pivoting on that was a beam, anchored about one-third of the way along its height. The short end of the beam held a box full of rocks, itself pivoting on an iron bar driven through the outermost part of the beam; the long end had a leather sling on its end, holding a fist-sized ball of rock.

"How does it work?" one carpenter asked after a minute, baffled. "There's no twisted sinew, no bow neither—how does it throw things?" He made a sign with one hand. "More of your hellpowder sorcery?"

Adrian smiled soothingly. "No, this is pretty straight-forward," he said. "I'll show you. Simun."

The underofficer motioned two arquebusiers forward. The other hundred were on the wall, happily potting men through the wooden shields that the Confeds moved forward to protect the working parties. They'd doubled and redoubled the thickness of planks on those, until they could barely move them over the uneven ground of the forward working surface, but the odd ball still penetrated. More still hit men *behind* the row of shields, or on exposed limbs, or struck the working parties that tried to move the mantlets forward. Other gunmen waited patiently for one of the trapdoors on the siege towers to open and spit a catapult dart at the city. They were just within extreme range . . . extreme catapult range, that was. The arquebuses were comfortably within *their* range, and a dozen fired every time the Confeds made the attempt. Men died within the tower, but that was secondary—a four-ounce ball travelling at nine hundred feet per second did unpleasant things to a torsion catapult's frame and fixings whenever it struck.

Simun chuckled, looking over his shoulder, then signed to the two men. They hauled on ropes running through a block and tackle, and the long arm of the miniature trebuchet came down until he could slip an iron hook into a ring driven into the wood just above the sling. The load in that now rested, just touching the ground.

"Here, sor," he said, handing a lanyard to Adrian.

"So, we pull this—"

*Thwack.*

The heavy basket of rocks pulled the short arm of the trebuchet down. The long arm moved more quickly, leverage driving it. The sling added to the momentum, and the rock blurred across the fifty yards to the wall in a streak of vicious speed. It cracked into the granite facing hard enough to spall off a foot-square flake. The craftsmen and sapper officers gave long, admiring whistles.

"The thing is," Adrian went on, resting a hand on the model, "that we can build this as big as we can get timbers for—and Prince Tenny and the Syndics have authorized us to demolish buildings, even temples.

We're a shipbuilding city, here, so we've got plenty of men used to working to these scales, and with heavy cables and pulleys. We'll need winches to pull down the throwing arm, but when it's ready we can throw really *big* weights; we can throw them on a high arc, to lob over the wall, and we can throw them all the way to shore, or nearly—dropping them right on the Confeds' heads."

A circle of beatific grins broke out as the image slowly sank into the consciousness of the onlookers.

"Shark-Toothed Sea Lord," one said, awed. "Like it was raining boulders, eh, lord? But how do we aim it?"

"We can move the whole frame around for direction," he said. "That won't be easy, but we can do it if we're careful how we build the underlying platform and if we apply plenty of manpower. For distance, we just fire ranging shots, adding or subtracting rocks from the basket on the short arm—that's where the impetus comes from, you see. We store up . . ." He halted; the Islander he was using had no word that precisely corresponded to "force." "We store up the ability to throw by hauling up the basket, you see. Then when it comes down, all that, ah, *strength*, is transferred to whatever we're throwing all at once. By altering the weight, we alter the strength—as a man does when he's throwing a rock by hand."

A few seemed to grasp what he was driving at. There were blank looks from the others, and he removed his hat and sighed. Sweat ran down his forehead and stung in his eyes; it was hot, and the stone buildings everywhere around reflected the heat.

"We can do it," he said. Center had filled his mind's eye with images of what the trebuchet could accomplish, and precise step-by-step instructions in making it. "And when we do, it'll ruin the Confeds' whole *day*."

Men on the wall looked down, grinning reflexively at the laughter around Adrian. It spread spontaneously along the parapet, until the wall was ringing with cheers. Morale in Preble was *very* good.

"Enjoy it while you can," Adrian muttered below his breath.

Out there, the resources of the Confederacy would be moving, moving—slow at first, like an avalanche did. But very heavy in the end.

Experience had shown that the base of the causeway was safe from the weapons on Preble's wall . . . and if you stayed low, from the ones on the galleys harassing the quarter-mile length. Justiciar Demansk stood, scowling and watching the stone stream forward, the dead and wounded trickle back. A solid line of guards was detailed to check that nobody came back without a real wound; they leaned on their shields, stolid and bored and glad they weren't out at the sharp end right now. The smell of sweat was heavy on the air, the smell of velipad and greatbeast dung, the dusty odor of cracked rock and the salt-silt of the shore.

*At least we're getting plenty of time to drill the new recruits,* he thought. That was the one good thing about siege operations, even this gods-cursed one. He ground his teeth as he watched the sails of a convoy of merchantmen appear on the horizon. Preble would be eating well; intelligence said they had six months' supplies, *and* they could import grain—from the Southern continent, through the freeport at Marange. As long as they had money, and they had plenty of that, too. Melting down the Temple treasuries, from what he'd heard; when that was done, there was always the King of the Isles.

"We're certainly not going to starve them out as long as they hold the seas," he said. "So, how do the men feel, First Spear?"

"Pissed off and scared, sir," he replied promptly. "They want to get stuck into those damned rebels out there, but they're starting to think that every time it *looks* as if we're getting anywhere, the fuckers come up with another trick. Sir."

Demansk nodded sourly. *I can't think of anything else they could do,* he mused.

They'd planted iron-tipped stakes in the shallow water a hundred yards out from both sides of the causeway, using conscripted local sponge divers. *No more fireships, thank the gods.*

The *arquebuses*—spies and prisoners had brought the name back from Preble—could punch through shields, but not walls or reinforced mantlets, or the iron plates on thick timber of the new siege towers. The trickle of casualties from the towers was getting worse as they got closer to Preble, and so was the continuous sniping from galleys ranging along the causeway, but the Confederation had a big army. Soon enough they'd be within effective catapult range, and a little after that of archery. The Confed army had a lot of mercenary archers, too. The new towers were an absolute bitch to move, they were so heavy they'd had to use iron-plated wheels under them, but as a side benefit they ought to be fairly immune to battering rocks from catapults, as well.

"What am I missing?" he muttered.

"Sir! Heads up!"

Demansk felt his eyes go wide with surprise as he saw the tumbling dot rising from behind the walls that fringed the peachpit shape of the island city. *I'm getting to absolutely* hate *feeling that expression on my face,* he thought angrily. It was a rock, obviously. And equally obviously it was *huge*, a quarter of a ton, far heavier than anything a catapult could throw—could have thrown, before the gods condemned him to this nightmare operation. Once more he felt the ground shifting below his feet, as the certainties of a lifetime—of uncounted lifetimes, back to the times of the heroes—crumbled.

The boulder dropped into the water with an enormous splash, a hundred yards short of the left-hand,

As it grew, he coul[d] [see that]
but blue smoke. [...]
*so much* bigger. [...]

"Down!" he sh[outed] [...]
repaired back-an[d] breast [...]
on the paving st[ones] [...]

He reached ou[t] [...]
clad ankles of the [...]
level. Then the [...]

"There's a blo[ody] hold [...]
big iron barrel [...]
enthusiastically.

**a crater,** Cen[...]
of Adrian's min[d] [...]
spirit-machine [...]
minded instructo[r] [...]
Grove.

The Gellerts [...]
wall's parapet, [...]
olives, fish, ham [...]
into the food w[...]
the shore and [...]

"Yes, as long [...]
batter it to pi[eces]
Adrian said.

Esmond nod[ded] [...]
their camp tha[t] [...]
the trebuchets [...]
take out the m[en] [...]

"Accuracy w[...]
surprised and i[...]
in terms of th[e] [...]

**Weapons te[ch]**
**else,** Raj said [...]
amused at the [...]
***of growing c***[...]

southern tower side of the causeway. The water was shallow enough there that the tip of it remained sticking up above the water. Men began pelting back, their mouths open Os of fright—conscripted local workers, he noted with somber pride, not Confed soldiers.

"First Spear, evacuate the causeway," he said heavily. "Everything but enough men in the towers to stand off a fast attempt at a landing."

Wouldn't it look lovely on his record if he pulled everyone out, and a commando set the towers on fire *again*? But he wasn't going to waste more troops, not if this got as nasty as it might.

The evacuation was orderly enough; five minutes later men were filing past him in columns, profanely shepherded along by his troops, and they were taking their baskets and hammers with them, their carts and beasts and timbers. One of the surveyors was jittering around the edge of the circle of Demansk's personal guards, probably come to complain about the interruption to his work.

"Heads up!"

Another quarter-ton boulder. This one grew with remorseless speed, dropping down from the sky like an anvil thrown by the gods from heaven, like the dim legends of the end of the Golden Age before history. Demansk traced its curve with his eye and sighed.

*CRACK.* It hit the forward left corner of the southernmost of the pair of towers. Iron plates sprayed out as the bolts and spikes that held them to the wooden frame sheered off. Fragments of rock and iron and wood sprayed across the forward end of the causeway, knocking down a few men not yet withdrawn; he could see the sudden red gush of arterial blood, imagine it running pink into the sea, and the sudden frenzy of sea life there—scavengers had gathered from all over, and swimming had become much less popular.

"Get the men o
"Sir—"
"They're going
there's not a fucki
Luckily, whateve
to take a long tin
need to get the ul
but at least five t
archers and artille
in disciplined but
when the third r
length. The who
backward, and th
Demansk wince
through the surf
glancing angle as
*a god,* he though

In fifteen minu
southern one was
could see dayligh
more shots, and
*thousand arnkets*
alone; metals we
mention the mar

More waitin
skimmed the nc
deadly splinters
one fell with mal
he could hear th
down the center
served to send i
groaning, rendin
world. When th
prone, the hole t
an eye in the s
timbers that ma

Another pause

*nonsense, but come up with a better way of cracking skulls and they'll fall all over themselves to get their hands on it.*

"But pretty soon," Adrian said, "it's going to occur to the Confeds that nothing we've shown them is much good against moving targets—like ships, for instance."

Esmond's smile turned to a scowl. "King Casull will support us with the royal fleet," he said.

The brothers' eyes met. *We hope,* went unspoken between them.

" . . . save the arm," someone was saying.

Justiciar Demansk's eyes blinked open. There were two physicians hovering over him, and Helga. He looked down; his left arm was immobilized with bandages and splints, and just beginning to deliver a ferocious ache. For the rest he felt the usual sick headache-nausea you got from being knocked out, and bruises, wrenches and sprains. *About like a bad riding accident,* he decided, and pushed the body's complaints away with a trained effort of will. The scents of canvas and the sharp smell of medicine made him want to vomit, but that passed as well.

A few curt questions settled that he wasn't badly damaged—his First Spear had taken a bad head wound, been trepanned, and they were unsure whether he would live; now, *that* hurt.

When the doctors were gone at last, Demansk let his daughter raise his head and bring a cup to his lips. A distant sound like thunder made him jerk a little and spill the water on the thin sheet.

"More?" he said.

Helga nodded; the tent was dim, and it made her eyes seem to glow green at him. "More. The causeway is in ruins."

"Not to mention the reputation of everyone concerned with this fiasco," he said, laying his hand down on the pillow. "You know, this young man of yours—"

"Scarcely mine, Father!"

"—this Adrian Gellert, he threatens the whole course of things as they are. Starting with the Confederacy."

She snorted. "Oh, come now, Father. We'll take Preble, eventually."

"We may, but it's going to be very expensive. Why do you think the world is the Confederacy and some outlying regions now, instead of a tangle of little cities and valley kingdoms, the way it used to be?"

"Because we've got a better army, of course. And the gods favor us, supposedly."

"The two often go together," Demansk said dryly, not returning her smile. For one thing, it hurt too much. "But one reason is that cities don't hold out for years, the way they did back during the League Wars, or even the wars of the Alliance. The Confederacy can take most towns in a month or less. Your . . . this Freeman Gellert has made sieges a lot more expensive again, all of a sudden. If these *innovations*—" the word had sinister connotations of decay and evil, in Emerald and the Confederation's tongue as well "—spread."

Helga laid a cold cloth on his forehead, and he held back a groan of relief. "Always thinking of the welfare of the State, eh, Father?"

"If a Demansk doesn't, who will?"

She nodded. "But Father, what's to prevent *us* from using these . . . new devices?" He noted that she avoided the word he'd used. "A city's a big concentrated stationary target. From what I've seen and heard, hellpowder would be hell on fortifications."

He blinked, startled. "You know," he said, "there may be something to that . . . I've been sort of focused on getting into Preble *against* the Emerald's toys." He thought for a moment. "That bears considering, girl. It certainly does."

# TEN

"All hail to the King! O King, live forever! All abase themselves before King Casull IV, King of the Isles, Overlord of the Western Seas!"

The leather-lunged herald cried out the call as the flagship of the Royal fleet dropped anchor. The vermillion-painted oars of the quinquereme pulled in all together, the crew trained to the precision of dancers. Behind it the hundred and twenty hulls of the Isles' war fleet—not counting a score or more of transports and storeships—closed in, not quite as precisely, but with a heartening display of fine seamanship.

*Especially heartening when you compare it to the Confed fleet's,* Adrian thought, as he went to his knees along with all the other thousands of onlookers. Watching the Confed quinqueremes wallowing into their temporary harbor down the coast had been reassuring, especially when a couple fouled each other in the entranceway, breaking oars and killing rowers. Reassuring, until one saw how many there were.

Standing near Prince Tenny with the high command he had the luxury of kneeling and pressing his forehead to a soft carpet instead of hard slimy cobbles, at least. He still came upright as quickly as he could, looking hungrily at the low turtle-backed shape with the covered wheels on either side that followed along behind a quinquereme, the tow rope coming free of the blue-green water now and then in a shower of spray. That was *his* particular baby. The warships made a formidable bulk, even in the magnificent circular harbor at the northern edge of Preble, and even with all the merchant shipping that had crowded in to take advantage of wartime prices when it became obvious the city wasn't going to fall quickly. The docks were black with people, or gray and red depending on the color of turbans and veils. So were the flat roofs of the houses that rose in a three-quarter circle above the water.

Casull came ashore glittering like a serpent in armor washed with silver and gold; the nobles and household troops around him were only a little less gorgeous. The trident banner of the Isles floated above him, and over the gaudy, metal-shining mass of ships and troops behind him. The citizens of Preble cheered themselves hoarse, throwing dried rose petals before Casull's feet. Priests in white robes and spotted leoger-hide cloaks sprayed scented water and intoned prayers; as the King set foot on land, the knives of sacrificers flashed and greatbeasts and woolbeasts died on altars.

"So," the King said at last, when the processions and sacrifices and speeches were over. He took off the tall spired helmet with its scarlet and green plumes. "I hate that polluted thing—even heavier and hotter than a war helm, when the sun's out."

Adrian smiled politely. The meeting was small: he, Esmond, Sharlz Thicelt, Enry Sharbonow, the admiral of the Royal fleet, a few aides and Prince Tenny, sitting on cushions amid blue tendrils of incense smoke from fretted gold censers.

Casull went on, looking around the round chamber

walled in rose marble where the Syndics of Preble had once met: "They do themselves well here—I'm surprised some enterprising Confed didn't have it shipped to Vanbert!" The smile hardened. "I've heard good things of how the defense has gone here, under my son."

Tenny bowed, smirking.

Esmond bowed and spoke. "Lord King, live forever. Under the Prince's inspired leadership, we've smashed their attempt to build a causeway out to Preble, and we've inflicted heavy casualties—several thousand men, as opposed to a few score on our side. Even Justiciar Demansk, second-in-command of the Confed forces opposite us, was badly injured. However, the Confed fleet is now nearly ready to take to sea. The city can't hold if the Confeds command the seas around it."

Casull nodded, leaning forward on his cushions. "The map," he snapped.

"My lord." The admiral in turn snapped his fingers, and a young aide who looked like his son, and probably was, brought it forward. "Speaker Jeschonyk has built an artificial harbor here, about a mile up the coast— out of trebuchet range. He sank two rows of merchantmen laden with rocks out into the sea, built wooden forts at the outer edges, and is basing his ships there. A hundred and thirty fighting keels, about the same number as ours."

"Hmmm," the King said. His finger traced down the map. "This town, Speyer, it's got a good harbor, I think—why not there?"

Thicelt bowed his head; he had an aigrette of diamonds and feathers at the clasp of his turban now.

"O lord King, the currents and waves are unfavorable—it's a bad row for a warship, the crews would be exhausted by the time they reached here."

"While ours would be rested." Casull nodded; that was the sort of calculation that any sea commander had to make. You couldn't keep the masts up on a ship that expected to see action anytime soon. "Besides which . . . wasn't Speyer ruled from here?"

"Yes, O King," Sharbonow said. *His* turban clasp was even more ornate than Thicelt's, and his cloth-of-gold jacket and red silk cummerbund were sewn with small black and steel-gray pearls. "And many families here have kin there. Marcomann's troops stormed Speyer, and they were not gentle. I have many spies active there, men zealous in your interest and full of hatred for the Confeds."

"So." Casull's finger returned to the improvised Confed harbor. "As many ships as ours, but many more quinqueremes—we're better sailors, but they can overmatch us in a boarding action. If they can drive off my Royal fleet, then they can isolate Preble and, in the end, retake it. If we can eliminate their fleet as a consideration, then Preble is ours and we can drive them to distraction by raiding along the coast, and cost them heavily by interdicting their commerce."

The shrewd dark eyes raked the brothers. "You, sons of Gellert. I am staking a great deal on your innovations." He used the Emerald word, with its connotations of the unnatural and perverse.

"Lord King," Adrian said softly. "We have advantages they do not suspect. A great victory here will surely render the Kingdom of the Isles safe from Confed aggression for many years."

"And a great *defeat* here could see the Confeds in Chalice within *this* year," Casull said, and then forced himself to relax. "We must trust to our seamanship, and to your weapons."

"I said, it's working well!" the new-minted engineer bawled in Adrian Gellert's ear.

The steam galley *Wodep's Fist*—the crew called it *Wodep's Prick*, from the shape of the ram at the bows—

lay quivering with life in the great harbor of Preble. Adrian was quivering with shock at the heat, experienced before but forgotten; he understood why the crew mostly worked stripped to their loincloths, despite the risk of being pitched against rough timber or red-hot metal. Decorum required him to wear at least a linen tunic, and it was already a sopping rag plastered to his skin. The great arched interior of the revolutionary craft was dim, red-lit by reflected flames from the boilers, full of sweat-gleaming near-naked figures, like something from the fate of wicked shades. Most of the interior was taken up by the riveted iron tube of the boiler, hissing and leaking steam now from half a dozen places.

That floated in muggy clouds around the rest of the machinery. At either side stood a cylinder of cast bronze, as thick through as a small woman's waist, fixed at the bottom to thick timbers and joined to the boiler by pipes wrapped in crude linen lagging. From the top of each cylinder protruded an iron rod, joined to one end of a beam; the beam pivoted on an axle fixed to the hull, and the other end had still another rod that worked a crank running out through the hull. Like melancholy monsters run mad, the grasshopper beams worked up and down, up and down, with a smooth mechanical regularity like nothing Adrian had ever seen before.

He coughed. The air was thick with moisture, with the lard used as lubricant on the working surfaces, with the odors of sweat and scorched metal and wafts of soot where the twin stacks leaked smoke. Behind the boiler men were working in a frenzy, passing lengths of log to throw into the firebrick-lined pit beneath it; behind them others stood ready at the ropes and tackle that controlled the tiller, hitched to the world's first sternpost rudder.

"I say it's a wonder it's working at all," Adrian bawled back cheerfully.

He set hands to the ladder that ran up between the smokestacks, and gasped with relief as he came up into the square blockhouse that protruded four feet up through the turtleback deck of the *Wodep's Fist*. Narrow slits lined it on all four sides, and looking through them he could see Preble spread out around him—as black and gray and blue with heads and faces as it had been for King Casull's arrival yesterday. Now people flocked to see the latest wonder of the wonder-worker Adrian Gellert, their savior. . . .

*And I do wish they wouldn't* call *me that*, he thought. He could see King Casull's eyes narrow every time some fool yelled it out in the street, and Prince Tenny's reaction was even worse.

He took a cork out of one of the speaking tubes, whistled sharply through it, and shouted into the funnel: "Left full rudder!"

An answering whistle came, and he grabbed for handholds as the *Wodep* heeled sharply. One of the paddles came nearly out of the water, and Adrian winced as the piston rod on that side danced wildly up and down for a moment, then again at the crunch as the paddle bit solid water once again. The fabric of the ship groaned, and he could hear water sloshing around in the boiler. A thought struck him, and he bent to peer down and check on the safety valve. *Good*. Back in Chalice some enthusiastic soul had fastened it down once, to make the engine go faster.

"Pass the word!" he called, and shouted into the three speaking tubes. "We're going on a ramming run!"

More cheers, which made him shake his head in bemused wonder. Just sailing this thing on the straight and level was bad enough. . . .

"Do you see her?" he asked the Islander skipper.

"Yes, lord. That's the *Icebird's Claw*. Sun God, but my father served in her!"

The skipper was a young man; that might even be

true. The galley lay drifting in the slow harbor eddy, its scarlet and blue paint chipped and faded, a low slender shape on the water a thousand yards away. Nobody was aboard but a crew of hastily trained criminals to man the catapults, promised their freedom if they put on a good show and impalement if they didn't.

"Helm forward," Adrian commanded. "All ahead full, but wait for my command on the reversing levers. *Go!*"

The paddles beat faster, throwing foam up higher than the command blockhouse. Occasional droplets came through the vision slits, welcome coolness even when they stung the eyes. Water broke aside from the ram, and washed up the deck as far as the triangular-board wave breaker he'd rigged to keep the bow from digging in too deeply; he didn't want to think what might happen to this wallowing tub in any sort of sea. The forward motion built, like nothing he'd ever felt at sea before, even under oars—there was a blind purposeful waddle to it, a *mechanical* feeling. The galley grew, larger and larger. It was vastly lighter than the *Wodep*, but longer and higher at the gunwales. A dart arched out from the catapult, and another; distance made them seem to start slow and accelerate as they neared. They glanced harmlessly from the octagonal iron plates, with nothing but banging and sparks to show for it. Adrian ducked as one seemed to be coming straight for his eyes, but it caromed off the blockhouse as well. Closer, and he could see the empty oar ports of the trireme, the white faces of the men winching the catapults back.

*Bang! Bang!* More bolts skittering off the armor. They were aimed forward of the galley's midships, at a thirty-degree angle.

"Brace for impact!" Adrian shouted into the speaking tube. A man began pounding on a bell with an iron bar, loud enough to be heard even over the monstrous *CHUFFF . . . CHUFFF . . .* of the cylinders.

"Reverse engines!" he cried again, and wrapped his arm through a cloth-padded iron loop bolted to the timbers of the blockhouse interior.

Closer and closer, the sudden lurch as the paddles reversed, but far too late to do more than begin to slow the ram. Then . . .

*BOOOMM.* The hull of the galley thundered like a giant drum, then cried out in a shrieking of snapping planks and timbers. Adrian was wrenched forward with a violence that almost pulled his arm out of its socket, and banged his head hard enough to bring blinding tears to his eyes, despite the padded leather helmet he wore. Somewhere there were screams of agony; men with broken bones, or those thrown against scalding metal and losing skin and flesh. When Adrian blinked his eyes clear and looked out the vision slit, he whooped nonetheless.

The galley was sinking, and fast. The *Wodep* hadn't just punched a hole in its side; the glancing blow had ripped ten yards of planking free of the slender strakes, and cracked most of those. Galleys *had* to be built lightly, if they were to be rowed at all; the *Wodep* was a massive lump of oak and iron by comparison, and when the two came together at high speed it was like a crockery pot striking pavement. As he watched, the other ship heeled over, raised its bow high and went straight down like a stylus punched into a watermelon.

"Left ten, paddles ahead one quarter—and well done, well done!" he shouted into the speaking tube.

The skipper yelled delight also, and pounded him on the shoulder. "With this ship, and you in command, sir, we'll sweep the Confeds back to the peasant pigstyes where they belong."

Adrian's grin left his face. "Rejoice," he said. "You're to have the honor of serving under the direct command of Prince Tenny, son to our overlord King Casull."

"Oh, shit," the man mumbled, staring at Adrian with dismay and then clapping a hand over his mouth.

"You really don't want to say that," Adrian murmured.

"Ah—thank you, sir. Yes," he went on, in a louder tone. "The Prince will lead us to glory!"

*Well, he can't go far wrong, with a good crew and this ship,* Adrian thought.

**Don't count on it, lad,** Raj thought grimly. **You haven't seen as many high-ranking nitwits pull defeat from the jaws of victory as I have.**

**probability—**

"Don't tell me," Adrian muttered. "There isn't a damned thing I can do about it anyway."

He looked eastward. There the Confederacy fleet was making ready for battle; according to intelligence, Justiciar Demansk was leading one squadron. Helga was still with him . . . and maybe *he* could make her keep to shore. Adrian was painfully conscious of the fact that he couldn't imagine stopping her from doing something she wanted to do, whether as husband, father, or god incarnate with a thunderbolt in his hand.

# ELEVEN

"Well, thank the *gods*, sir," the coastland skipper of the galley blurted, his nasal singsong accent strong under fairly fluent Confed.

"Yes?" Justiciar Demansk replied, raising an eyebrow. "I merely said you should adjust the rowing pace as you saw fit."

"I was thanking the gods I'd gotten one who understands a ship isn't commanded from the same end as a velipod. Sir. *Thank* you, sir. I don't mind the risk of getting killed, it goes with this trade, but I'd rather not lose my ship because some damnfool landsman won't *listen*. Thank you again, sir."

Demansk nodded frostily and turned his attention elsewhere. The Confederacy's Grand Fleet of the West was making as good time as he could expect . . . when everyone was supposed to keep station so close their oars were almost touching. Speaker Emeritus Jeschonyk thought that that would reduce the risk of the fleet being disordered; as long as they kept to the holy line, the faster, lighter Islander vessels wouldn't be able to nip in with ram-and-run attacks.

*It's won naval battles for us before,* Demansk thought sourly, shifting his injured left arm to test it. A little pain, not too bad—not nearly as disagreeable as making Helga stay on shore had been; in the end he'd had to point out that coming might mean watching her precious Emerald die.

*I just don't like the implications of this formation. We're conceding that the enemy are better than we are.* That was true, on salt water; he still didn't like admitting it. The Confed fleet was fighting the way Emerald phalanxes had, in the old days; shield to shield, all spears out. It had a lot of punch—one of Demansk's ancestors had written in his memoirs that seeing four thousand men come over the brow of a hill in perfect alignment was the most frightening thing he'd ever seen in his life—but it lacked flexibility. That was how the Confed armies had *beaten* the Emeralds, using small units under independent command to work around flanks and into gaps, coming to close quarters with the stabbing assegai.

"At least it's calm," he muttered, and the sailing master nodded again. A calm sea was like fighting on a flat, even field—everything in plain sight, no surprises, no broken ground to disorder the formations. If he *had* to fight in a phalanx, that was the best place to do it.

*Thing is, I just don't like fighting a battle this way, relying on brute strength and massive ignorance,* he thought. It was . . . uncraftsmanlike.

He had to admit that the fleet made an imposing sight. The working parties that had gotten them ready for sea hadn't stinted on paint and gilding, either. The hulls and upperworks were almost as bright as the helmet plumes and armor of the officers, lacking only the fierce glint that the sun broke off edged steel. Each craft had a figurehead in the form of a snarling direbeast; there was a remote mythological connection, to the legendary pair who'd supposedly been raised by one and founded

Vanbert. He was surprised that the Confederation made so much of that myth, sometimes—the rest of it wasn't at all creditable, involving fratricide, kidnapping, woman-stealing and general mayhem. But then, Vanbert had been founded by a bunch of bandit fleecebeast herders, if you read between the lines.

"We've come a long way," he said to himself, watching the vermillion-painted oars flashing in unison, churning the wine-purple sea to foam, the bronze beaks lunging forward and splitting V's of white to either side. The oarsmen knew their business, hired men mostly, with some conscripted fishermen from the coastal villages. They were used to the shattering labor, but not really to working in teams; there had only been a month or so to train them.

Ahead, the Islander fleet was matching them stroke for stroke—backward, southwest, away from the shore, on a course that would take them out past Preble if it went on long enough; he could see the walls and stubby towers in the ocean beyond them. Demansk's squadron was second in from the left, landward flank of the fleet, and that section had come a little forward; it gave him a good view down to the massive quinqueremes of the center, where Jeschonyk's personal banner flew. The ability of the Islander fleet to back water as fast as the Confeds were advancing was dauntingly impressive, in its way—they weren't charging, but the pace wasn't leisurely, by any manner of means.

He stared ahead and to his right. *King Casull's banner there—standard formation, like ours, quinqueremes in the center, triremes on the flanks.* The great ships rode the ocean like floating wooden walls, each with two banks of huge five-man oars swinging with ponderous force. Casull's capital ships looked a little different, with low wooden forts on their forward decks, spanning the gangways along either flank. *Hmmmm. That must make them a little more sluggish,* he thought. *I wonder why they're doing that? Usually they stay as nimble as they can. And what's that column of black smoke from behind the flagship?*

He sincerely hoped it wasn't some sort of incendiary trick. He was getting thoroughly sick of those. He also hoped Jeschonyk wasn't just going to mirror their movement until the Confederacy fleet had been drawn well out to sea. Right now, the left flank at least was secure, anchored on the land. Out in deep water, the Islanders might get up to any amount of devilment.

A messenger galley came racing down the line of ships, flying Jeschonyk's banner and pulling just under their sterns; orders from the command, then. It was a light shell, undecked, with no ram—and a mast still stepped, although it hadn't set any sail. A galley always unstepped and stowed its mast before action, of course; the shock of ramming would send it overboard, otherwise. Demansk took the sailing master's speaking trumpet and stepped to the rail.

"This is Justiciar Demansk!" he shouted as the light craft came within hailing distance. His voice was a hoarse bull roar, roughened by a lifetime of cutting through the clamor of battle. "What orders?"

In theory, the officer commanding the racing shell shouldn't have told him anything. In reality, a Justiciar was hard to refuse.

"The left-flank squadron is to move forward and cover the causeway, while we resume construction," he shouted. "All other ships to maintain station."

"Carry on!" Demansk said aloud. *Oh, shit.*

"What in the Shades are they doing?" Esmond muttered from the quarterdeck of the ship he'd named *Nanya's Revenge.*

"Not what they should," Adrian said. "But then, neither are we."

**correct,** Center said. Center and Raj had agreed—

they didn't, always—that Casull should put his gun-equipped ships out to the left, seaward, and use them to crumple the Confed line inward. That would throw them into disorder, and then the more agile Islander vessels could strike at the flanks of maneuvering quinqueremes. Instead, Casull was playing it safe, keeping all the heavy ships, the ones with the cannon, and the steam ram with him in the center.

*Usually a mistake, when you're the weaker party but have better quality troops,* Raj noted clinically. *That's when you have to throw double or nothing, and hope to win big. If you fight a battle of attrition, it usually ends up with the last battalion making the difference.*

"We've been here most of the day," Esmond fretted. "And done damn-all but back up. They're not going to follow us out to sea, and even with summer it's going to get dark in five, six hours. We should—wait a minute, they're not just getting out of line, they're moving."

Ten triremes of the Confed fleet's landward wing *were* moving, their oarsmen stretching out in a stroke . . . stroke . . . stroke . . . pace that they could keep up for an hour or so, but that wouldn't exhaust them the way ramming speed did. Their smaller line was ragged as it drew away from the main body, but not impossibly so.

*They're heading for the causeway,* Raj thought. *Probably the Confed commander got nervous and decided he had to do something. A mistake. Anything that opens this battle up is to our advantage.*

"They're heading along the coast, south to the causeway," Adrian said. "Esmond, they're going to cover the causeway—start getting it repaired. We can't let them do that."

"We certainly can't," Esmond said; he'd put too much work and risk and blood into turning that into a disaster for the Confeds. "I'll send a dispatch to the King."

Adrian caught his arm. "No *time*," he said. "We're in the perfect position to intercept them, here on the right flank. If we wait, they'll be past us and we'll have a stern chase."

Esmond hesitated, looking around. He was in command of the right, the landward anchor of the Islander line, six triremes manned entirely by Emeralds—most of their people had some seagoing experience, after all. Adrian's arquebusiers were on board too, and the Strikers were working in their flexible light-infantry armor. It made the ships a bit heavier, but it would give any Confed that tried boarding a nasty surprise, and they were still faster and more agile than any but the very best of the enemy vessels.

"Six to ten . . ." he mused. Then, decisively: "We'll do it. Signal *follow me* and *prepare to engage*." To the helmsmen at the steering oars: "Come about. Oarmaster, take us up to cruising speed."

Esmond's *Revenge* heeled, turning in almost its own length, then came level on a course that would intercept the ten Confed vessels, bouncing forward with a surge that made most on the quarterdeck grab for rail or rigging. "Half a mile," he mused. "Flank speed!"

"All-father Greatest and Best," Justiciar Demansk said. "They're going to be massacred."

The Confed triremes were strung out almost in a line, as close to the shore as they could and not be in the surf. Demansk was no seaman, but he could see the mistake *there*—the commanders were landsmen like him, and they thought of the shore as safety. Instead it was a trap waiting to kill them on their left hand, while the Islander squadrons' rams—

*No, not Islanders, by the gods!* he thought. A banner was flying from the quarterdeck of the leading enemy ship, and it had the silver owl of Solinga on it! *Not royal ships. Mercenaries.* That must be

Esmond Gellert, the man who'd vowed to see Vanbert burn.

Justiciar Demansk lowered his head a little, unconscious of the movement, like an old battered greatbeast, lord of the herd, snuffling the air and shaking his battered horns. *We'll see about that, bucko,* he thought.

A quick glance showed him that his squadron overlapped the landward end of the Islander fleet now; the ships there were opening out their spacing to compensate for the squadron that had peeled off, moving with dancer's grace. Still, they'd be thinner—probably wouldn't try anything, not for a while.

*And while Esmond-burn-the-Confeds Gellert takes the detached squadron in their flank, I can take him in his,* he mused.

"Signal," he said. "Squadron will form on me, and advance to the attack. Flank speed!"

"They're coming after us," Esmond said, pounding one fist lightly on the rail. "Damn! That's more initiative than I'd have expected from a Confed commander, and as tight a formation as they've been keeping."

"They're certainly making a hash of it, though," Adrian said, watching two of the Confed triremes fall afoul of each other, oars clashing. Confusion followed, until enough oars could be remanned to push the vessels apart. "They'll be late to the party."

Esmond shook his head, looking right to the Confed squadron that was his prey, and left to the other arrowing in to the rescue. "Or waddling to the rescue," he said. "They might as well be barges, but we can't let ourselves get trapped between them." He swore again, vicious disappointment in his tone.

"No, wait!" Adrian said, pointing seaward. "Look!"

There where the massive quinqueremes faced each other, something was happening. A snarling cheer ran down the Islander line, and a drumbeat signal from ship to ship. Signalers with flags relayed it.

"*General Attack*, by the Gray-Eyed Lady of Solinga," Esmond swore, but happily this time. His head whipped back towards the Confed line. The squadron that had lunged out to protect its comrades had halted. No, they were backing water! Probably recalled by their high command, to meet the Islander charge.

"Steady as she goes!" he shouted exultantly, looking ahead to the ten Confed ships. "Their arses are *ours*!"

"Ram, sir?" the helmsman said.

"By no means," Esmond laughed. "Bring us parallel, just out of dart-caster range."

He grinned like a direbeast, and Adrian nodded agreement. The enemy ships grew nearer with the always-surprising speed of meetings at sea, where you could be alongside one minute and hull-down when you looked back. Suddenly the ant-tiny figures along the enemy rail were men, and human limbs could be seen through the oar ports of the outriggers as their rowers strained and heaved to a quickening beat of the hortator's mallets.

Adrian winced mentally, imagining being down there . . . never knowing when a dart, or fire, or the bone-crushing blow of an enemy's ram was going to come through. Solinga had been a democracy for a long time after the League Wars—a democracy as far as freeborn male citizens were concerned, at least—and the main claim of the lower classes to equality with the farmers who provided their own armor was that it was the poor freemen who rowed the City's ships to battle. The Scholars of the Grove had always held that a specious argument, a sign of the City's decline. Now he was inclined to agree with the rowers.

His voice was steady as he spoke: "Aim for their catapults. The catapults only until further orders."

"Sor, yessor," Simun said, looking up from the port rail. The long weapons were leveled now, men kneeling with a hand over the lock to keep spray out of the priming powder, their barrels out over the uniform centipede motion of the oars. "Catapults it is, sor."

"Signaler, pass it along!"

Turning southward, the Emerald-manned ships were a line parallel to the coast, coming up on the Confed ships from the rear, with Esmond's in the lead. Four minutes of straining effort brought it level with the foremost Confed. Water was creaming up along the ram, curling down the side, and the ship had a slight rocking-horse motion as it clove the low swell.

"Open fire!"

*Baaammmm.*

Twenty arquebuses fired as one. The Confed ship had three catapults a side, two dart-casters and a stone-thrower, on pivot mounts. The stone-thrower fired, as the man standing behind it yanked the release-cord—not voluntarily, but as he was thrown backwards by a four-ounce lead ball smashing through his body and out the other side, to kill the man behind him as well. The rock fell halfway between the ships, a moment's unnoticed fleck of foam against the green-blue of the shallows.

*Baamm. Baaam. Baaam.* Over and over again, the long jet of dirt-colored smoke. The smell swept aft, sulfur and rotten eggs and the flint-on-steel scent underneath it. Less than half the shots struck the enemy ship, and less than half of those landed around the catapults, but enough did. He saw splinters flying from the machines and the deck they were mounted on; a throwing arm snapped forward as a holding line was cut; another pinwheeled up as a ball sliced through the twisted greatbeast sinew that powered it.

"They're out of action," Adrian said.

Esmond nodded, still smiling that disquieting smile. "Steersman, close us in—long arrow-shot."

Adrian turned to Simun. "Take out their archers and slingers."

Those had been crowding to the rail as the Emerald-manned ships approached, with the twenty or so Confed regulars standing behind them—as much to keep them to their tasks as to back them up; the missile troops were hirelings or noncitizen allied levies. A flight of arrows winged out, and fell a little beyond the foam lashed up by the galley's port oars.

"Fire!"

*Baaammmm.*

This time the target was bigger. Four men flew backwards, dead or dying—the heavy balls of the three-man arquebus would rip a limb completely off or turn a torso into a draining sack of ruptured flesh and shattered bone.

*Baaam. Baaam. Baaam.*

One of the arquebusiers whooped exultantly. "This is like gaffing fish out of a garden pond!" he shouted, and fired again.

Esmond nodded; he was looking back along the line. The other ships of his squadron were keeping pace and repeating his tactics; a little slower, perhaps, without Adrian to keep their arquebusiers on-target, but getting the job done.

When he turned back to look at the closest ship, the slingers and archers had vanished. He saw one take a running leap over the landward side of his vessel, and come up again swimming overarm—no Confed landsman *there*. Another tried the same, to fall overside with a Confed regular's assegai through his back. More were leaping down the hatchways, and the steady pace of the enemy vessel's oars went ragged as the missile troops threw themselves down on the lower gangway between the benches, anywhere to get away from the crushing, invisible death of the lead balls.

"Steersman! Close in!" he shouted exultantly.

The Confed marines threw their futile darts and

waited behind raised shields—all but the last; he threw his down and ran, howling, until he splashed overside. *He* wasn't going anywhere but to the bottom, not with fifty pounds of armor on him. Esmond's ship was barely beyond oar's length from its opponent now.

"Adrian!"

His brother nodded. "Gunmen!" he called. "Targets of opportunity—grenadiers, prepare to throw." There was the slightest trace of a sigh in his voice. "Throw!"

His own grenade arched out with four others. Three struck; one straight down a hatchway, as if guided by Wodep's hand. The explosions were quieter than arquebus fire over this distance, but they scythed the trireme's decks free; the remaining sailors were over the side and swimming like eels, those not lying silent or thrashing and screaming. The arquebusiers were firing straight into the oarbanks now, through the ports or through the light planking of the deck; the massed shrilling of the oarsmen was deafeningly loud. And . . .

"Sor!" Simun shouted from the gangway. "She's afire, my lords! Burnin'!"

Another look back along the line of ships showed two more in flames; one was grappled alongside a galley of his, and taken; another two were adrift, their oars limp as their entire crews swam for it. That left four unengaged, and *they'd* turned for the shore, hoping to beach their ships—at a guess, the Confed marines aboard had "insisted" on that with their assegais pressed to the helmsmens' kidneys, and others guarding the hatchways to keep the oarsmen at their tasks.

"Well enough," he laughed. "We can tow them off when they're beached. Bit of a present for the King!" He turned, shading his eyes with a hand. "I wonder how that's going?"

"Speaker Jeschonyk!"

The Speaker Emeritus of the Council of Vanbert was

in a small boat, with an aide and two men rowing. He looked up at Demansk.

"My flagship is gone," he said. "There."

Demansk looked up as hands pulled the commander onto the trireme's quarterdeck. The Speaker's great quinquereme was wallowing, its starboard oars broken. From beyond it came a shape like nothing Demansk had ever seen by land or by sea, like a great turtle with two tubes belching smoke from the uppermost part of its . . . deck, he supposed it should be called . . . and a small square structure just before them. Wheels thrashed the water on either side, churning up more foam than a quinquereme's oars, and driving it forward as fast as a trireme at ramming speed. It gleamed like wet iron . . . it *was* iron.

"But iron can't float!" he heard himself say.

"It is iron," Jeschonyk said bitterly from beside him; he started slightly. "Arrows bounce off it, catapult bolts do no damage—it sheared off the starboard oars of my ship *and* the one next to it in line, and—"

The iron ship was turning, a wide circle, much wider than a galley. After a moment it lay a hundred yards off, pointing at the command quinquereme's stern; the ram that split the water ahead of it as it gathered speed was *entirely* comprehensible, unlike the rest of it. Demansk could hear a mysterious *chuff . . . chuff* . . . from it as it made its run, like the panting of some monstrous beast.

"A monstreme?" he said, bewildered. "A galley propelled by monsters?"

The wheels reversed and whipped froth mast-high as the ram slid into the quinquereme's stern with a smashing crunch of timbers. The weird vessel backed off smoothly, and the quinquereme settled by the stern as water rushed into the huge rift. Its deck boiled with men as the hundreds of oarsmen ran screaming on deck, brushing aside the marines posted at the hatchway and throwing themselves into the water like fleas from a dying dog, heads turning the water black.

"What makes it *move*?" Jeschonyk cried, bewildered.

"At a guess, sir, it has something to do with fire— look at the smoke coming out of those two tubes."

Demansk thought that that was the most likely *logical* explanation. He sympathized with the half-dozen vessels he saw beating a hasty retreat northwards, although he'd see their commanders poled and their crews decimated if he survived this. His gut was showing him pictures of monstrous clawed feet pounding a treadmill inside that iron weirdness, and huge fanged mouths gasping out *chuff . . . chuff . . .* Jeschonyk was flinching in time with it, nerve shattered.

A thunder-loud noise rippled across the water, over- riding the clash of timbers and the screams of thousands of men in pain and fear of death. A billow of smoke rose from the odd square structure on the forecastle of an Islander quinquereme. Less than a second later, a fountain of splinters and body parts rose from a Confed vessel. More jets of smoke, and the prow of the Confed vessel dissolved in a shower of smoke and wreckage; when it cleared water was already running over the decking. Square fins rose out of the water and swam closer, waiting. Demansk could feel the blank black eyes and hungry mouths beneath them. That was normal, at least. They always got scavengers around a battlefield, land or sea.

Then the *Islander* vessel's forepeak vanished in an explosion even louder, and left a huge bite out of the structure—enough to shatter the upper part of its hull as well.

"Whatever that thunder-weapon is, it isn't always reliable," Demansk said aloud. "They smote themselves, by the gods!"

He looked around. "You! Escort the Speaker below!"

There was a cubbyhole of a captain's cabin on a trireme. "Sailing master!"

"Sir?"

"Take a look at that . . . thing. Doesn't it look to you as if those wheels are *pushing* it through the water?"

"Sir . . . I've never seen anything like it in all my life, and I've been at sea since I was six. Yes, that's as likely as anything."

The iron ship had just rammed another Confed quinquereme. This time it hung up for a moment, ram caught by a pinch of its victim's shattered timbers. Brave men leapt down from the quinquereme to its deck . . . and over into the sea, as their hobnailed sandals slipped and slid helplessly down the sloping iron. Demansk could see one man striking sparks as he windmilled for an instant and then went over with a splash.

"Lay me a course to ram it right in the center of the port wheel. Hundred-commander!"

The underofficer in command of the ship's Confed marines came up at a run. His face might have been carved from granite, but it was wet with sweat and rigid with tension under the transverse-crested helmet.

"Sir!"

"Have your men take off their marching sandals—I want 'em barefoot."

"Sir?" The man had been obviously, prayerfully thankful for orders; now he looked as if he feared the Justiciar might have joined the day's madness.

"Look at that thing. No, don't stare, just *look*. It's obviously timber, plated over with iron like a scale cuirass. Hobnails won't grip. Feet will! There are men inside, and I intend to kill those men."

"Yes, *sir!*"

The man strode off, bawling at his command. Demansk caught a strong whiff of the smoke boiling out of the iron ship as his trireme heeled and turned; honest wood-smoke, right enough.

*If there* are *men inside, and not monsters*—he thrust an image of claws on treadmills aside—*then they have to be steering from that little boxlike thing in front of the tubes. So they can't have a very good view, looking through slits like a close-helmet, and with all that smoke.*

He gave a quick, unaccustomed prayer to Wodep and Allfather Greatest and Best that he was right. His life and the Confederacy's western provinces both depended on it.

"Ramming speed!" he ordered. The iron ship was swelling with frightful suddenness.

"That's discouraging them," Esmond said.

Another Confed trooper on the beach staggered three steps backward and dropped, arms flung wide and shield spinning away. An arquebusier beside one of the *Revenge's* steering oars chuckled and stepped back, letting his assistant and loader work. They moved in a coordinated dance, automatic now, grinning past the powder smuts that turned their faces into the masks of pantomime devils. Esmond's galley rose and fell with the surf, but the gunmen on it and the rest of his squadron were keeping the hundred-odd Confed troopers on shore from interfering.

"Line's hitched!" a sailor said, climbing over the stern naked and glistening wet.

Esmond nodded. "Take her out."

The oars had been poised, waiting. Now they dipped, driving deep; there was a unanimous heaving grunt from below, and again, and again . . .

"She floats!" the steersman said, letting his oar pivot down into water deep enough for it. "We've got her off!"

Esmond looked about with pride; five of his six ships were towing captives, the enemy ships coming after them oarless and sternfirst, the traditional sign of victory at sea. The other five triremes of the Confed squadron

were burning hulks, or sunk. One was sticking out of
the waves, its bronze beak planted firmly in the sandy
mud of the shallow coastal waters. Wreckage floated
past with the tide . . .

. . . an awful *lot* of wreckage. Esmond looked
seaward, losing the diamond focus of commanding his
own small section of the battle, and shaped a soundless
whistle.

"Wodep!" he blurted.

The neat lines had vanished—he looked up at the sun
and blinked astonishment—in only an hour. Instead there
was a melee that stretched from here to the edge of sight,
and almost to within catapult range of Preble's walls.
Galleys were burning and sinking everywhere he looked;
as he watched, a Confed quinquereme went nosedown
and slid under the waves, shedding what looked like a
coating of black fur at this distance, and that he knew
was men clinging desperately to a life that sank beneath
them. A little further off an Islander capital ship fired
its four cannon directly into the deck of a Confed trireme,
shattering the marines clumped to board into an abat-
toir mass of blood and torn meat, and punching through
the deck into the crowded oar benches beneath. Even
as it did a Confed quinquereme ranged up along its other
side, and the boarding ramps slung up by ropes crashed
down to link the ships, driving their iron beaks into the
lower deck of the Islander vessel. Marines launched a
volley of their weighted darts, and then swarmed across
like implacable warrior ants. Here, there, a confusion no
eye could take in. . . .

"Where's the ram?" Adrian was half-shouting, his eyes
wild. "What has that donkey-fucking idiot done with
my *ship*?"

"Allfather!" Demansk snapped.

The shock of impact threw him to his hands and
knees on the deck, driving bits of armor into his flesh.

ocean. "I do not abide by a plan that has failed," he grated. "We'll retreat." He looked at the *Revenge*'s steersman. "Set course for the nearest ship still in our hands. We'll have to arrange a rearguard, if we're to get to Preble in one piece."

He looked at Esmond then. "Where is my son?"

Esmond met his eyes. "Lord King, the enemy holds the *Wodep's Fist*. Beyond that, I do not know."

Casull sighed, his eyes dull. "If he lives, we'll hear before sunset; demands for ransom, enough to leave the kingdom poor. If not . . . if not, we'll drink his spirit home to the Sun."

# TWELVE

The King's eyes were alive and bitter by the time the sun had been down two hours; they were bloodshot and a little inclined to wander, as he lay on the cushions downing cup after cup of unwatered wine, but his voice was only slightly slurred. The air of the chamber was thick with incense, with attar of roses and patchouli oil from the courtesans who danced and sang and drank with men on their cushions, with the smells of wine and sweat and ointment on bandaged wounds. Light flickered from the lamps on the gilded plaster of the ceiling, worked in sea monsters and figures from legend, and on the pale stone of the walls and their lapis inlay of flowers and trees.

"A toast!" the King of the Isles said, glaring at the Emeralds where they sat halfway down the great municipal banqueting hall of Preble. The dull roar of conversation died, except for snatches of drunken song from those too far gone to care. "A toast to my son, the shining warrior, Prince Tenny!"

"*Prince Tenny!*" the hall roared back.

Casull threw the cup to one side, and the priceless

Vanbert glassware shattered. A servant shoved another into his hand.

"And another toast! To the bastard son of a whore, Esmond Gellert, who lost the battle by running amok without orders!"

Esmond stood, graceful and tall in a plain tunic and swordbelt. His hand fell unconsciously to the place where a hilt would have been, if men could feast armed before the King. The guardsmen leaning on their great scimitars tensed slightly; a fighting man like the Emerald was never entirely disarmed. Before he could speak, Adrian rose beside him, bowing:

"O King, your kingdom's heart bleeds with you in your honorable grief for Prince Tenny, fallen like so many others on this day of sorrow!" he said, the trained rhetor's voice filling the chamber without straining. "Yet even in grief, a King remembers justice!"

The red-veined eyes turned on him. "You speak of justice, bumboy?" he grated.

"Indeed, Lord King," Adrian cut in, smoothly enough that it did not seem to be an interruption—one art both the Grove's school of rhetoric and the lawcourts of Vanbert taught. "It would not be just to punish the only squadron commander in your fleet who today sank his own numbers in Confed vessels, and brought as many more behind him, towing them in victory to lay at your feet."

That brought Casull to a halt for a second, his mouth open. Adrian swallowed, his own so dry that he was insanely tempted to stop for a drink; his temples pounded, and his body dragged with the weariness of the day's fighting. He flogged his brain into functioning, as merciless to himself as he'd been throwing grenades into the oar decks of Confed galleys.

"And indeed, he did so on my urging," he went on. Casull's eyes narrowed. "Not that I, a mere artificer, would have dared to put my word against the King's!

May the King live forever! We are as dust beneath his feet. No, my own wisdom is only wise enough to know that I should never interfere in such matters. Yet before the word of the shining Prince Tenny, the hero and heir, what could I do but obey?"

"What is this?" Casull said, visibly trying to gather his wits. He didn't need to be sober for the sort of temper-fit he'd had in mind, or to give the necessary orders afterwards. He hadn't expected to be engaging in the *elenchos* of the Grove.

"In this very harbor, while I showed him the ship *Wodep's Fist*, Prince Tenny commanded me on pain of his utmost wrath that any Confed movement towards Preble must be stopped—since the Royal garrison would be on shipboard for the great battle. Thus I saw Confed ships break away towards Preble, and thus I laid the commands of the Prince upon my brother. What could he do but obey, my lord King? What could I do? We were as dust beneath his feet. And see the wisdom of the Prince's commands; the walls of Preble stand, a strong base for our next attack!"

"Next?" Casull roared, shaking a fist. "You want me to lose my *whole* fleet, and see the Confeds sacking Chalice? Are you in their pay?"

"Ah, my lord pleases to jest! See how I laugh, taken by his wit! My lord will have noticed today, that our triremes—those that carried, as I advised, many arquebusiers, rather than spreading them about in small numbers—could devastate the slower Confed ships from a range that neither catapult nor bow could match. Thus were five sunk, and five captured, with hardly any loss. Next time—"

"Get out! I've had my belly full of your lies, and my son is dead, and I must beg the Confed commander for his body. Get out, before I kill you!"

"The King commands," Adrian said, bowing again.

✧     ✧     ✧

"What *are* these things?" Helga asked, fascinated, touching one gingerly but trying to make it seem as if it was to steady herself against the gentle rocking of the anchored ship.

Demansk frowned at his daughter, but it wasn't really a formal occasion where it was grossly improper for a woman to speak. Most of the Confed force's commanders were asleep in their tents, and so were most of the surviving men. Only a few aides and some troopers to hold torches were with him on the deck of the captured Islander quinquereme.

He peered at the bronze shape that lay on a carriage of oak with four small wheels, amid a cat's-cradle of ropes and pulleys. A smell hung about it, of hot metal and sulfur. *Death farts from the Lord of the Shades,* he thought sardonically.

"It's like those arquebuses, only much bigger," he said. "Look, there are the stone balls it threw—or those sacks of lead ones. Hellpowder down the muzzle, the ball or bag on top, set fire to it, and out it goes—smashing ships and men." He shook his head. "This changes the whole face of war, forever, do you understand?" His anger was distant, muffled. "We can't keep it secret, now—not with the Islanders still having more. If they use these things, we must too, and . . ." His voice stopped with an enormous yawn.

"And you can curse Adrian more tomorrow, Father," she said. "I still think you weren't recovered enough for a battle—even if you *did* destroy the iron ram all by yourself."

Pride glowed through the sarcasm of her words, and Demansk felt himself swelling a little. Well, it *was* something of a feat . . . perhaps enough for a triumph in Vanbert? Perhaps even the Speaker's chair; there was so much that cried out to be done, to make safe the State.

*And I'm out on my feet and getting delirious,* he told himself severely. "Back to camp."

The captured quinqueremes were with the surviving
capital ships of the Confed fleet, tied up to bollards
at their bows, sterns out into the artificial harbor. They
couldn't be drawn up like the dozens of triremes
beached on either side, but they were secure enough
here. *More than secure,* Demansk thought. The rock-
filled merchantmen that made up the breakwaters
reached well out into the ocean, defining a rectangle
five hundred feet by a thousand; out at the entrance,
two wooden forts rested on two large cargo carriers
each. Flaming baskets of wood reached out on poles,
to show the boom of chain-linked logs that sealed the
entrance against raiders. The forts had archers and
slingers and catapults, and they were well within range
of each other. Shoreward were the dockyards and the
whole Confed camp, still sixteen thousand regulars and
as many auxiliaries—they'd even had time to run up
timber barracks and housing, while the fleet was being
made ready.

He glared out towards the dim lights of Preble, just
visible on the southwestern horizon. The battle had
been about even, which made it a Confed victory—and
next time they'd have had time to study the new
weapons, come up with countertactics of their own, *and*
they'd still have the weight of men and metal on their
side. Next time . . .

"The King was angry," Adrian said judiciously.

Esmond drank and wiped his mouth. "The King was
ripshit," he said. "The King may have us all impaled
before morning, if he doesn't pass out first—he may
regret it when he sobers up, but that won't help *us.*"

**probability of execution in the next 6 hours is
67%, ±7,** Center said helpfully.

*To be fair,* Raj said judiciously, *Casull really
doesn't understand the new weapons. He's a fair
to good commander with what he does understand.*

Adrian looked around the small rooftop platform; he and Esmond, and their seconds-in-command, plus a scattering of Striker officers . . . Nobody was looking too cheerful. *Frankly, I doubt anyone here is in the mood to be particularly fair,* he thought.

"We're the only ones who kick Confed ass, and we're in line to be buggered by the Oakman," Donnuld Grayn said. "Ain't no justice in this world, not if you're a hired soldier. Fuck all Islanders, anyway. If *Lord Gellert*'d been in command today, we'd be drinking Jeschonyk's wine." He grinned with a friendly malice. "And Lord Adrian here would be back diddling Demansk's daughter."

Adrian flushed. How *that* news had gotten out, the Gray-Eyed alone knew. Although letting it do so was more in Gellerix's line, if you listened to the old stories.

"Esmond would have done better," he agreed neutrally.

*Because he'd listen to you,* Raj said. *I think that left to himself, he'd make a battle plan and then use the new weapons in it, not build the plan around their capacities. Of course, he doesn't have Center to lean on. He's a better than middling commander, with the weapons mix you have here— very good indeed.*

There were times when the sheer *objectivity* of his invisible companions could get a little wearing, even to a Scholar of the Grove who'd striven for detachment all his days. All things in moderation, even moderation.

*And we want the new weapons to make a difference,* he observed.

**correct,** Center said. **to break this planet from its stasis, the innovations must be shown to be decisively superior. it must be shown that the future is qualitatively different from, and superior to, the past—an essential shift in overall paradigm.**

"The question before us now," Adrian said aloud, reverting automatically to the *elenchos* of the Grove, "is what course of action can *save* us from being . . . ah, buggered by the Oakman."

"Well, we could bring the whole Confed fleet back for the King to roast prawns over," Esmond said morosely. "*And* all the captured ships, and all their cannon and hellpowder."

"Gunpowder," Adrian corrected automatically, and then froze. He was conscious of the others looking at him, but within his skull there was a blinding light; it was not unlike the near-orgasmic ecstasy of having an insight, but multiplied by three and with the resonances of three separate personalities added in.

"Wait, wait!" he said, holding up a hand. "Look, it's a longshot, but it beats being impaled. Here's what we'll do—"

When the words stopped tumbling forth, the other four men were staring at him with the stars reflecting in their wide eyes.

"Suicide," Esmond whispered.

"Oh, no," Adrian said. The thought of what he proposed to do stopped him for a moment, and his smile was a trifle ghastly. *All men are initiates of the mysteries of death,* he reminded himself sternly. "Waiting here for the King to decide we're to blame for his son getting killed, *that's* suicidal. This is just risky."

Grayn rubbed his chin. "Couldn't we just run off and take up piracy?" he said.

"That's slow suicide, with all the people we'd have pissed off at us," Adrian snapped back. "Confeds *and* the King of the Isles after our asses? I don't think so."

The mercenary nodded. Adrian looked at Simun. The grizzled little man shrugged. "Well, you're the lord, sir, so whatever you order's fine with us." He sighed and heaved himself erect. "Better go get the men ready, before they're too deep in the jug or dipping their wicks—makes a man grumpy if you interrupt him, and sleepy if you don't. Been a long day . . ."

His voice trailed off as he trotted down the stairs. Grayn was staring at the stars. "Getting out of the harbor, that might be a bitch," he said thoughtfully. "Got the chain boom up."

It was Esmond's turn to smile. "And we've got squads with the militia in the towers either side of the harbor mouth," he said. "Prince Tenny, bless him, didn't rearrange that—and I suppose the King hasn't had time to look into details."

"So, all we've got to worry about is the Confeds," Grayn said, rising and gathering up sword and helmet, and fastening the clasps of his armor. "All twenty-fucking-thousand of them, and a couple of hundred of us. Wodep, I should have stayed home and farmed olives with my brothers."

"Wish I was going with you," Esmond whispered as Adrian put his foot on the rope ladder over the side of the *Revenge*.

Whispering was unnecessary; they were well beyond hearing distance from the Confed harbor, far enough away that its watchfires were simply a dim glow in the distance, a glimmer that might have been phantom lights chasing each other across a man's closed eyelids.

"I'm glad you're not," Adrian said. "There has to be *somebody* out there to haul my ass out of the crack, big brother." Seriously: "May the Gray-Eyed Lady of Wisdom hold Her shield above you tonight, brother."

"And over you—you're her favorite." Then he snorted laughter.

"What's funny?"

"King Casull. He'll *just* be getting the news we've deserted!"

Adrian grinned back at him and dropped the last foot into the launch. There was a glimmer of white, a slow chopping *shssshhhh* as the trireme and its companions pulled away northward and west, looping out from the coast.

"Let's get going, then," Adrian said, when the ships had vanished in the moonless dark. He turned his head, and a glowing arrow painted itself across his vision.

"Yessor," Simun agreed; he and a nephew were acting as Adrian's loaders and rowers tonight, at his gentle insistence—he *was* a fisherman's son, as he pointed out, and as at home in small boats as any.

"All right," the older man went on to his relative. "Now lay out—row dry, ye dickhead, and row soft, or this oar'll cob you. Show no white on yor blade when it cuts the water, now. Row soft."

The soft glow grew ahead of them as they angled in to the northeast. A half-hour, and Simun and his nephew were breathing soft and deep; he could smell their sweat in the warm summer night. A touch of mist lay on the water, low curls of it; that was helpful. It was quiet enough that the occasional *plop* of a jumping fish was distinct and sharp through the darkness. Now square shapes cut the night, blotted outlines against the frosting of stars on the eastern horizon.

Adrian's vision brightened with Center's passionless certainty. Now he could see the fire-baskets out on poles from the wooden forts at each end of the artificial harbor, and diffuse fire glow from the vast Confed camp beyond. And smell it, the rank odor of so many men crammed together. The fires above the water had died down to dull glows.

*Careless,* he thought. They should be kept bright with pine knots the night through.

**They've had a hard day too, lad,** Raj said. **It's hard keeping men up to the mark when they're that exhausted. Although you're right; I'd have the rank-tabs off any officer I caught letting this happen.**

"We're coming up on the boom," Adrian said softly

from where he knelt in the bows of the small boat. "About a thousand yards. It's just barely awash. Big logs."

"Eyes like a cat, sor," Simun grunted, looking over his shoulder as he rowed. "Suppose it comes of bein' favored of the gods, like."

"Rest easy," Adrian said, clambering between them into the stern of the boat and carrying the big net of clay jars with him; that tilted its prow up, nearly out of the water. "All right—fast as you can!"

"Row!" Simun called softly to his nephew. "Fast now, boy, stretch out—*rapppiipai! Rapppippipai!*"

The two men leaned into their oars, rising and falling with breathy grunts of effort. Adrian waited, poised, while the towers loomed on either side like the gates of the land of the Shades—only the giant three-headed hound was lacking, and there were watchdogs enough in the towers, and in the camp behind. *I* am *insane*, went through him. *This has all been a delusion, and I'm completely fucking insane*—

Center's vision showed him the floating barrier of logs ahead. He waited; then the boat's keel ground on the rough wood with an ugly crackling, crunching sound.

"Forward!" he called, and leapt into the bows, using the shock of impact to power his jump.

The two at the oars followed him, and the stern came out of the water. The boat teetered, wavered . . . and then slid forward with a splash that sounded to Adrian's ears like the launching of a quinquereme down a slipway, with a flute and drum corps in accompaniment. Even his own breathing was like a bellows, and he slowed it with an effort of will, hissing the others to silence. The boat drifted, the oars loose on the thongs that secured them to the muffled oarlocks. Simun scrambled back on his hands and knees, swearing softly and checking the bottom of the boat with his fingers for the welling leaks that might show a cracked strake.

Nothing; no shouts, no blazing lights. The towers were looking for bigger fish . . . if they were looking at all, and not just dozing. Adrian sat for a moment controlling his breathing, feeling the slowing of a heart whose pounding shook his chest.

"All *right*," Simun said, his voice low and fierce. "We *did* it, sor!"

"'Well begun, half done; half done, not begun,'" Adrian said, quoting an old Emerald folk saying. The founder of the Grove had been fond of it, too; it was *whispered* that he'd been a stonecutter and the son of a peasant himself. "This way."

The artificial harbor was as rectangular as men could make it, in the Confed style. They hadn't straightened the beach at the inner end, though; that was a half-moon, turning the whole affair into a U-shape. The low irregular line of the rock-filled ships loomed on either side, five hundred feet apart, with waves breaking on the outer sides and throwing a little white foam over the bulwarks. This arrangement would never survive a series of winter gales, but it only needed to last as long as the siege of Preble . . . and there at the base of the U were the ships.

Center's lightening of the darkness intensified; Adrian felt as if an invisible line were being wound tighter and tighter around his forehead. Then it eased, and a strobing arrow marked their course.

**the four captured quinqueremes,** Center pointed out.

Adrian looked up. "It's after midnight," he said. "Nobody'll be around."

"Deck watches, sor," Simun pointed out, nodding towards a dim lantern on the stern of one of the Confed vessels.

"But nobody on the captured ships, not yet. Take us in, but keep as near the middle as you can; beach her right next to the left-hand quinquereme of those four.

When these"—he tapped the clay jugs—"start going off, things are likely to get a bit hairy, so be ready to push off when I get back."

"Bit hairy, sor." Simun chuckled softly. "Take yor time, but by Gellerix' cunt, don't linger, eh?"

The oars bit, and Adrian—slowly, cautiously—loaded one of the jugs into his staff-sling. The jugs held a mixture of fish oil, sulfur, naphtha oil that oozed out of rocks, and quicklime. Experiment had shown they'd burn like the heart of a forge fire and couldn't be put out. They were also fairly fragile.

"Coming up on the shore," he said. The darkness grew more absolute, as they ghosted into the shade of the captured quinquereme; it had the faint sewer stench a rowing vessel always did, even if the bilges were pumped regularly. "Lay on your oars."

The two men did, and Adrian hopped over the side. His sandals grated on pebbles and sand, and he reached back in for the sack of what Center, for some reason, called *molotovs*.

"Back in a minute," he said casually, and walked up the beach.

The rams of the quinqueremes almost glowed with Center's unearthly vision, serrated bronze catching faint starlight. Off somewhere a man's voice raised in song, then ended in a squall—probably a wakened sleeper hitting him, Adrian thought distantly. He walked casually: if you looked as if you belonged, you'd shed a casual glance—people saw what they expected to see. Turning, he took his stance and aimed. *Left to right,* he thought.

Swing, swing, *throw.*

The jug arched out, wobbling a little as the liquid within shifted. It struck the first quinquereme right on the forecastle, on the timber square added to bear the weight of the guns. *Crash.* Not very loud, but distinct amid the wave lap and insect buzz of the night. A flicker of light, as the air found the quicklime. *Crash*. One more, to make sure. *Crash. Crash. Crash. Crash. Crash. Crash* . . .

Fire on every one of the four captured ships. Enough to brighten this stretch of beach quite perceptibly; paint and rope and dry pinewood caught easily. Now all he could do was pray.

**probability of optimal outcome 51% ±3,** Center supplied hopefully. **in this instance, "optimal" requires the survival of adrian gellert.**

*I'll still pray,* Adrian thought, jogging back to the boat.

"*Good* to see ye, sor," Simun panted.

They shoved off and began rowing, not so quickly as to attract attention . . . he hoped.

"Uh-oh."

A horn winded through the night, and then an alarm drum. With the gathering light from the burning ships, the harbor looked much smaller than it had in darkness. Much smaller, and the fire baskets on the entrance forts suddenly blazed, as they were swung in and then out again with a fresh load of pine knots. The huts nearest the beach held the deck crews of the Confed warships; men were swarming down to the shore, wading out and climbing up the sides of their vessels. Already officers were beginning to warp them away from the burning ships—excess caution, really. They were close, but not that close, and without rigging or sails aloft it would take more than heat and sparks to set them alight. Confeds *might* have been able to extinguish the fires on the captured ships if they'd gone straight there, Adrian mused—anything to distract his mind from what might happen, and what he couldn't do a thing about. They had no chance at all once they'd finished seeing to their own ships, but trained reflex was stronger than thought in an emergency. It had to be.

Flames licked higher from the prows of the ex-Islander warships. Adrian suddenly felt like a bug on a plate, his head whipping to and fro as he tried to see in all directions at once. Simun and his nephew were cursing in antiphonal harmony as they dug their oars in madly, like the chorus at a Goat Song festival play. Men were crowding onto the parapets of the wooden forts—archers. A six-oared launch put out from one of them, and the officer in the bows was pointing at *him*. More and more men ran down to the shore, and the growing buzz from the Confed camp was like some great beast awakening, grumpy and angry from its winter sleep . . . and growling.

*Sisst.* A flight of arrows came slanting down out of the dark, into the water off the skiff's bow. *Sissst.* Closer now, and the raiders' own efforts were driving them further into range. The light grew ever brighter, as well. He could see quite plainly now, for several hundred yards; see the crew manhandling a catapult around on the tower top, a dart-thrower that could skewer a man at a thousand feet, much less the four hundred that separated his own tinglingly vulnerable body from it.

His head whipped back to shore. There were other small craft there; men were shouting and pointing at Adrian's skiff, and launching the boats. *All men are initiates of the mysteries of death,* he repeated to himself. And: *Helga. Damn it . . .*

The world ended.


"What's *that*?" Donnuld Grayn gasped.

"That is my brother," Esmond said, throwing up a hand and shouting.

He needed to do both. The Strikers had been creeping up toward the Confed encampment in the dark, their ships lightly beached behind them to the north. For a moment the night turned bright as day, a huge globe of fire rising to silhouette the rear of the camp's wall where the magazines of the captured Islander quinquerimes had exploded. Streaks and ribbons of fire shot up from it, and huge burning timbers pinwheeled through the sky. When they fell, whatever they landed on burned as well; the other ships in the harbor, the long sheds above the shoreline crammed full of pitch and tar, turpentine and rope and boards and sails, the warehouses of olive oil and grain, the rough pine barracks the Confeds had raised . . .

One of the wooden towers along the landward wall was blazing, too; a twenty-foot baulk of pine flaming like a torch had dropped out of the sky on it. Men swarmed along the parapet, frantically tearing at the burning wood and dashing futile buckets on it.

"Fire!" Esmond called, startled out of his wonderment. "Fire, and save your lord!"

The arquebuses of Adrian's men began to bark with a methodical eagerness. And on the wall of the Confed fortress, men began to die.

*Oh, shit,* Adrian thought, as he pullled himself up.

His ears hurt, and his head when he shook it to clear his vision of the spots strobing across it. When it did clear, a grin spread over his mouth despite the pain. Half the harbor was burning, and half the camp beyond—and most of the men there were *far* too occupied to be concerned with the small boat they'd spotted a moment before. *Make that three-quarters,* he thought, as another Confed vessel began to blaze out of control, and its deck crew scrambled ashore or over the side.

*Sisssht.* More arrows plowed into the water around the boat; this time two stuck in the thwarts, humming like bees.

"I'd be afraid if I had the time," Adrian said quietly. Louder: "Row for the north bank of the harbor—that ship there!"

He pointed to one of the sunken merchantmen, just within sling range of the north tower. Then he stood, trying to compensate for the pitch and roll of the little skiff with his knees, sling dangling from his hand. The enemy launch was quite close now, close enough to see the firelight glitter ruddily on the spears of the men between the rowers.

Swing. Swing. *Throw*.

His hand moved in blank obedience to Center's direction, fingers releasing the thong when the red dot blinked. The firebomb—*molotov*—arched out with a steady, inevitable trajectory. He could hear it shatter against the breastplate of the officer in the launch, and hear the man's scream as the flames took him even more clearly. Luck—Adrian's, not the man's in the launch—pitched him forward into the arms of his men, to spatter fire among them, lighting hair and tunics and the wood of the craft with impartial ferocity.

"Row, gods condemn you!" Adrian roared to Simun and his nephew.

The towers had seen what was happening, and worse, where he was going. He felt at the burlap sack; three more *molotovs*. Arrows fell around them, and more stuck quivering in the wood of the skiff. One passed by his ear, close enough for the feathers to sting; two inches left, and the last sound he ever would have heard would have been that one crunching into his brain.

Shock of impact; the prow of the boat was level with the railing of the sunken rock-filled merchant ship. The wood was splintery under his hands as he vaulted aboard, the deck wet and unstable underneath his feet. Two ships down, a party from the tower was clambering towards him, shields up and assegais out. Their faces were red with the light of the burning camp; he must be a black outline to them, a figure out of darkness and night.

"Behind you!" he screamed at them. "Your tower's burning too, you velipad fuckers!"

Swing. Swing. *Throw*.

The *molotov* whipped out, not at the soldiers but at the wooden fortress behind them. Heads followed it, and saw where it left a streak of red fire on the wood.

Swing. Swing. *Throw*. A sharp pain in his leg, above the knee, and the limb threatened to buckle. The pain was distant, and he ignored it. Ignored the weakness, forcing the muscle rigid. Swing. Swing. *Throw*. A last crackle against the wood of the tower.

One of the troopers clambering towards him bawled in panic and threw away his shield, leaping into the sea; not *quite* total madness, since he hadn't had time to don his mail shirt. He struck out for the other side of the harbor with a clumsy threshing stroke. As if that had been the first rock of an avalanche, men began to throw themselves out of the tower into the water.

Adrian felt a great tension drain, and his strength along with it. The leg gave under him, and he found himself somehow seated on the deck, staring without belief at the black-fletched arrow through the fleshy part of his thigh. Then the pain struck, and he bit his lip to hold back a moan.

Simun was bending over him. "Not serious, sir. Head's right through, clean. Here, I'll break it off and pull this out—"

"*Nnnghg!*"

"There we go, m'lord, right as rain when I tie it up—"

"Uncle."

Simun looked up, and saw the last two Confed troopers clambering onto the prow of the merchantman. "Well, fuck me, some people don't know when they're not welcome," he said, scooping up Adrian's staff-sling. He scrabbled in his own belt pouch, came out with a lead bullet the size of a small plum, and dropped it into the cup.

*Crack*. The first Confed pitched backward, with an oval hole in his forehead and his eyes bulging with hydrostatic shock from the blow that had homogenized his brain.

Simun dropped the sling and drew his sword, unhooking the small buckler from his belt. "Spread out, Davad," he told his nephew.

The two Emeralds did, and the Confed began backing up—he had shield, helmet and assegai, but not his mail shirt.

"And hurry up," Simun said, moving forward, light on his feet. "We've got to get the boat over this whore of a hulk and out to where Lord Esmond's waiting for us. The commander ought to get to the surgeon, too."

# THIRTEEN

"Why do I feel as if this is a noose?" Esmond muttered under his breath as he backed away from King Casull with the chain of gold and emeralds bouncing on his chest.

The mutter might have gone unheard in the screaming roar of the crowd, if Center had not been filtering Adrian's perceptions. *I wish you could make the leg hurt less,* he thought. To his brother: "It well might be, if we're not careful."

The King of the Isles was all benevolence as he waved from the dais on the harborfront to the crowds, spreading an arm to indicate the Gellerts. Adrian didn't miss the slight narrowing of eyes as the cheers mounted into hysterical abandon. The Gellerts were far *too* popular now, with the Confed fleet in ashes and all but a precautionary garrison retreating eastward. Far too popular, and far too likely to be candidates to rule Preble themselves. The populace certainly wouldn't object; the problem would be to keep them from deifying Esmond and Adrian both, and sacrificing to them. After months with the horrors

of a Confed sack hanging over the city, it wasn't
surprising.

*Nor safe, from Casull's point of view,* Adrian thought,
as the sons of the Syndics of Preble—who'd vied for
the honor—picked up the poles of the carrying chair,
to take him to the state banquet. *And I don't think he's
the type to forget Tenny, either.*

"In a week," he said to his brother—they were close
in the sedan chair, "he'll have convinced himself we
deliberately set Tenny up, so we could seize Preble
ourselves and set up as kings."

Esmond's eyes narrowed. "It's what he'd have done
himself," he pointed out. Adrian nodded; King Casull
IV was no son of Casull III, after all—he'd started out
as an ambitious general. "In fact," Esmond went on, "it's
not a half-bad idea. We could cause the Confederacy no
*end* of grief here, running things."

Adrian looked around in alarm, fast enough to draw
a fresh throb of pain from his bandaged leg. It was
healing so quickly as to be near miraculous in this hot
climate—Center had had some hints about spirits of
wine—but it was a serious wound.

"No, don't worry, little brother," Esmond said. "We
couldn't get away with it—not between Casull and the
Confeds. The Confeds might take us on as client-kings,
but that's out of the question, of course." His smile
became a little strange. "Their camp burned, but
Vanbert still stands . . . and Nanya's not avenged yet."

Adrian swallowed and looked away. "Well, there's an
idea I've had," he said. *I and my friends.* "It would get
us away from Chalice, which Casull would like; it'll cause
the Confeds a lot of grief, which we'll both like—"
*though you more than me, brother,* he thought sadly.
Center's merciless visions left a man little of the loyal-
ties he'd been brought up with. "—and I think it might
*really* change things."

"As long as it's a change the Confeds hate, I'm for

it," Esmond said, waving to a bevy of hareem beauties leaning out of a window and throwing dried flower petals. The sons of the Syndics were making heavy weather of the crowds on the way to the Town Hall, even with a squad of Esmond's Strikers going before them with active spear butts. "Tell me more."

"O King, live forever, your favor has been lavished on us like the Sun's light on the fields," Adrian said, gagging slightly on his own fulsomeness. It didn't sound quite so bad in Islander, but he could see why his ancestors had fought so hard in the League Wars to keep the Islanders out of the Emerald cities. "We wrack our brains for a means whereby we may repay a tenth, a thousandth of the kindness you have shown our unworthy, outland selves."

*When you're dealing with an autarch, lay it on with a trowel, lad,* Raj's voice said. *At least, when he's got the jump on you. Part of the cost of doing business.*

Despite the riches and titles King Casull had showered on the Gellerts—he had little choice, with the greatest Islander victory over the Confeds in five generations dropped in his lap—it was notable that the Gellerts were no longer invited to small informal audiences. This one was in the Syndic's Hall of Preble; besides the guards who lined the wall behind the throne there were a brace before the dais as well, and a quartet of hard-faced Islander admirals—or pirate chiefs, if you looked at it from another angle—flanking the King.

"I'm sure you'll find a way," Casull said, leaning his bearded chin on a fist and the elbow on an arm of the throne. The aigrette of peacock feathers and diamonds nodded over a face more lined and gray than it had been when the Gellerts first saw him. "Do go on."

"O King, the Isles are strong at sea. The Confederation is strong on land; not least because of the endless number of their fighting men. This is the Isle's most insoluable problem, because while the Confed's numbers may learn skill, the Isles cannot bring forth a half a million peasants to draft into an army."

"Yes, yes." An impatient gesture of the hand.

"Would it not then follow—" Adrian caught himself falling back into the cadence of a Grove lecture, and gave himself a mental shake "—be sensible, I mean, to make alliance with the only other power which commands manpower on the same scale?"

Casull's brows rose. "Now you really *do* interest me! What power is left in the civilized world, beyond the Isles and a few little scraps, and Confed client kingdoms and puppets?"

"No *civilized* kingdom, lord King."

Adrian waited, sweating, while the lights went on behind the King's dark eyes. Inwardly, he asked once more: *Are we really going to serve civilization by arming* barbarians? *We call the Islanders that, but the South-rons—they're fucking savages, no mincing words.*

**given a continuation of present trends, civilization on the northern continent will fall; the probability is as close to unity as stochastic analysis allows,** Center thought remorselessly. A vision unrolled before Adrian's eyes, one he had seen before—the gap-toothed grin of a Southron horseman as he pursued a silk-clad woman down a street in burning Vanbert. Adrian blinked it away with a shudder; his own mind had painted Helga's face on her.

One of the admirals snorted laughter. "The South-rons? They'd have trouble organizing an orgy in a whorehouse. They're fierce and numerous, yes, but the Confeds slaughter them like pigs in a pen, when it comes to open battle."

Adrian inclined his head. "My lord is acute," he said. "Yet the ignorant may learn . . . and I have some things to teach them, I think."

"Ah," King Casull said, sitting up. "You wish me to send you to Marange." The great, sprawling anarchic freeport that was the closest thing to a capital the southern continent had, and its only city. "Much might be done in Marange. The Southron lands are rich in men . . . and timber."

"But not in seamen," Adrian said. *Well, I knew Casull wasn't any kind of fool*, he thought. "As Your Majesty knows, the Gray-Eyed Lady herself couldn't teach the Southrons to sail a piece of soap across a bathtub."

An unwilling smile bent the monarch's lips; Adrian could hear a muffled snort from Esmond, where he stood at parade rest behind his brother with his helmet tucked under one arm.

"But fighting on land, that's another matter. Yes, most of them are brainless yokels, and a century of defeats wouldn't teach them not to run at the nearest foe like a greatbeast bull in musth running at a gate," he went on. "Yet have not emissaries from some of their chiefs come here to the Isles, speaking of alliance?"

"Yes, from Chief of Chiefs Norrys," Casull said absently; most of his attention was turned inward, to his own thoughts. "Or rather, from his kinsman, Chief Prelotta. Prelotta spent five years in Vanbert as hostage for a treaty, if I recall correctly."

Adrian nodded enthusiastically. Exposing a barbarian to civilization might convert him . . . or it could just teach him technique, sharpen his appetite, and show him where the really *good* loot was. In either case, it usually made him more dangerous.

"Yes," Casull said. "I will speak the truth; despite your services to me, the thought of my son comes between me and happiness when I see your faces. But this . . . yes, we must think upon it." He rose. "You may go."

Adrian and his brother knelt, rose, and backed out of the presence; Casull was already deep in conversation with his advisors.

"Phew!" Esmond said, in the corridor outside. "I'm getting nervous at these audiences—as Grayn would put it, my arse feels the shadow of the Oakman every time the King looks our way. I suppose that's why you came up with this crazy stunt."

"I haven't gotten us killed," Adrian pointed out. His brother's hand clapped down on his shoulder.

"Yet," he said. A cruel smile lit the handsome face. "But together we've gotten an entire *shitload* of Confeds killed—and this scheme sounds as if it'll be even better. The Confederacy can be wounded at sea, but to kill it you have to go ashore."

Adrian shivered slightly as he followed his brother's tall form out into the brightness of the courtyard.

"Men," the elder Gellert said to the waiting officers and noncoms. "Looks like we're going on a trip."

# EPILOGUE

Helga Demansk turned in the saddle to look back at the wreckage of the Confed camp. Anger warred with pride as she looked at the ribs of the burned ships, stranded like the blackened remains of dead sea dragons on the shore. A brisk autumn wind brought the smell of the sea and soot to the rear of the Confederation column where the Justiciar and his daughter rode. She dabbed at her mouth with the back of one hand; she'd been ill, a little, lately. It was a cool brisk day, and waves were breaking high over the lines of rock-laden ships; in a month of storms they'd be driftwood and scattered stones on the beach. In two years, only mounds beneath the grass would show that men had ever come to make war here. For now there was a forlorn look to the empty barracks and the neat gridwork of roads, the lines of raw dirt where the earth walls had been spaded back into the ditches.

"Quite a mess," she said. Spies from Preble had brought word of who was responsible; and that the Gellerts had left, none knew where. "But Adrian won't be bothering us here anymore."

Her father worked his wounded arm, testing the healing. "My dear, I'm afraid we haven't heard the end of either of the Gellerts," he said. "If not here, then elsewhere." He raised the arm in salute, as one should to a capable enemy. It cost nothing to be polite, even when duty required that one kill a man; he went on:

"Still, it was a first-rate job of work. Maybe the gods *are* whispering in that young Emerald's ear." Another snort of laughter. "Maybe he's a god in disguise, as the old stories tell of—and this *was* like the War of the Thousand Ships.

His daughter's grin grew wider, and she ducked her head towards her saddlebow. *In that case, Father dear, I suspect you're going to be grandfather to a demigod.* It was better to laugh than cry.

She looked out to sea. And she suspected her father was right; sooner rather than later, they *would* be hearing from Adrian again.

Helga Demansk decided she was rather looking forward to that.

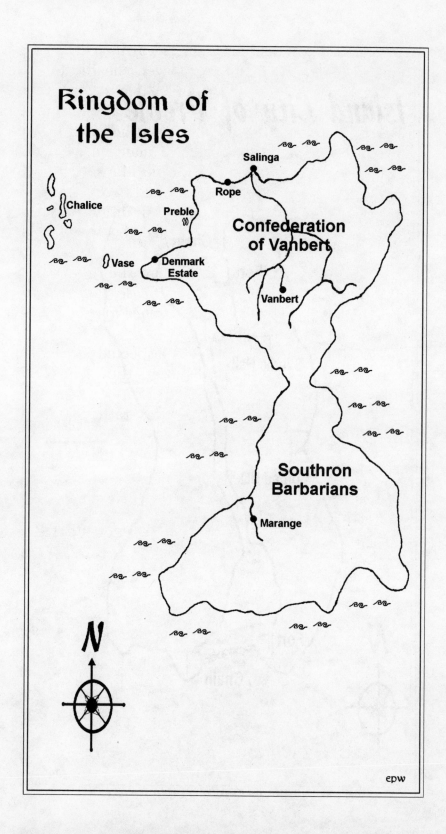

# Island City of Preble

Chain

Fort

Syndic Hall

Mainland

Confed HQ

N

Fort

Chain

EPW

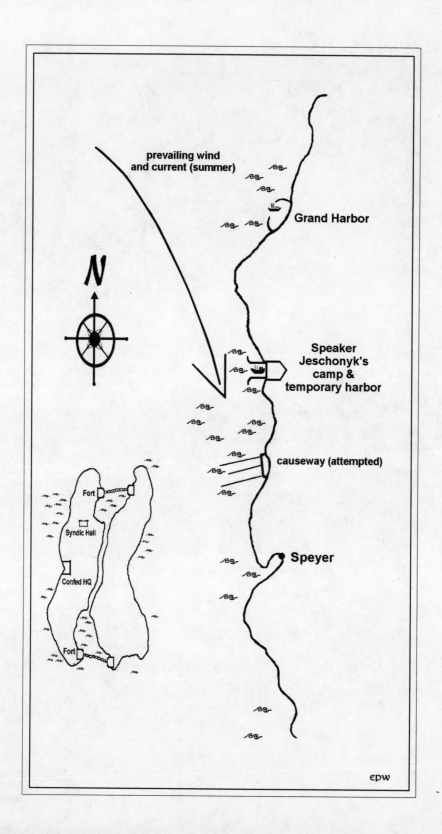

prevailing wind
and current (summer)

N

Grand Harbor

Speaker
Jeschonyk's
camp &
temporary harbor

causeway (attempted)

Fort

Syndic Hall

Confed HQ

Fort

Speyer

epw